RICK PARTLOW

DROP TROOPER BOOK FOUR

DIRECT FIRE

www.aethonbooks.com

DIRECT FIRE

©2020 RICK PARTLOW

CONTACT FRONT
KINETIC STRIKE
DANGER CLOSE
DIRECT FIRE
HOME FRONT

Why do I do this to myself?

I should have been going over battle maps, reviewing the operations order, hell, just staring at the inside of my helmet. Anything would have been better than tying my suit optics into the visual feed from the dropship. I couldn't do a damned thing to affect the battle, could barely tell who was winning it. All I could see were flashes of light in the darkness at the extreme range of the dropship's optical cameras, the visible remnants of invisible struggles, missiles being intercepted by other missiles or lasers, our assault shuttles and missile cutters or their dual-environment fighters and corvettes dying unspectacular deaths in the dreadful silence.

Just one stray missile, one well-aimed laser or coil gun round and we'd be dead. The dropships were armored as well as they could be, enough to save us from the fragments of a surface-to-air missile, maybe enough to take a shot or two from a ground-defense laser without coming apart, but the main gun of a Tahni corvette would obliterate us like we'd never existed.

The planet swelled in a false promise of safety at the left edge of my view; blue, white and green, and welcoming, but it was all a disguise. Port Harcourt was a hornet's nest and we were about to stick our dicks in it.

Of course, the battalion briefing had tried to dress the operation up with smiles and unicorns and rainbows...

———

The battalion leadership was jammed into the main dining room of the best and biggest restaurant in the capital city of Dolabella, and by inference, the biggest and best on the whole Silvanus colony. It was a nice place, decorated in what I was told was mid-Twentieth-Century European style, with lots of hand-polished wood and brass. I felt out of place, and not just because of the décor. Everyone was staring at me, or at least that was what it seemed like. I was the guy who'd gotten six of his own Marines killed, who'd let his platoon sergeant make the sacrifice play to save everyone because I'd been too badly wounded to do it myself. I was the only Officers Candidate School platoon leader in my company while the other four were Academy grads. I was the street kid, the petty criminal, the guy who *had* to join the Marines or go to jail. The loner.

But not alone. Not anymore.

Vicky Sandoval shot me a smile from the table beside us, at the outer edge of Alpha Company as I was at the outer edge of Delta. It was a comfort having her back from OCS, even if we were in different companies now. I'd even gotten used to her hair being shorter. She didn't have it cut clear of her interface jacks the way a lot of Drop-Troopers did, letting brown strands drift over the implant receptacles instead. She'd had a buzz cut when I'd first met her, when we were both PFCs, but she'd let it grow out until OCS, then chopped it down to just above her collar. Her face had leaned out, the pain and the stress adding lines beside her eyes and at the edges of her mouth, but the smile was the same, the intelligence and determination in her eyes.

I'd expected her to be there. I hadn't expected the man beside her, the new platoon leader for Fourth Platoon of Alpha Company. He was tall and lanky, almost gangly, his grin boyish and enthusiastic. I'd met Freddy Kodjoe at OCS and never expected him to be assigned to my battalion, but the war was changing and units were being shuffled to meet needs.

"I like this planet," he said, projecting his voice to be heard over the gabble of the collected officers of Fourth Battalion, 187th Marine Expeditionary Force (Armored). "It reminds me a lot of Nigeria. What about you, Cam?"

I assumed he meant it was the city of Dolabella that reminded him of Nigeria and not the restaurant and tried to answer in kind.

"It definitely doesn't remind me of Trans-Angeles," I told him, shrugging. "And it's nothing at all like Tijuana, at least not since they cleaned up the battle damage from the Tahni occupation. So, it has that going for it. I guess it's nice, except I already have three Marines in my platoon who've been busted for drunk and disorderly." I ran a hand across the back of my neck, feeling a weariness that was more spiritual than physical. "Not to mention the four that want to get married to locals. It's enough to make a guy miss Hachiman. I mean, your pee would freeze before it hit the ground in the winter, but at least there were no civilians for the Marines to assault, batter, or impregnate."

I'd laughed at the stories my barracks-mates had told when I was an enlisted man, rolled my eyes at them as a squad leader, and somehow had never expected just how much less funny they would be, how much trouble they would cause me as a platoon leader. The Marine Corps might cut an officer some slack for breaking regs to win a battle, but God forbid if I was late filing a report on military dependents.

"God, you've become a cynical bastard." Freddy nudged my arm. "What happened to that idealistic officer trainee who risked it all to improve our OCS training class?"

"That trainee became an actual platoon leader," I shot back. "You know the drill, man. I've spent twice as much time filling out and filing personnel forms and incident reports as I have organizing tactical training."

"These are the easy days, my friend," Freddy said, nodding as if he had suddenly become the aged, sage philosopher of the group. "You'll miss this place when we're gone. Enjoy it while you can."

"Well, don't get too attached to it," Vicky warned us, nodding toward the front entrance to the dining room, "because I think we're about to get our marching orders."

The door was as old-fashioned and anachronistic as anything else in the restaurant, and its brass hinges squeaked as it opened. The first Marine through was the Skipper, Captain Covington, my company commander. He was lean and rangy, not particularly imposing physically, and you could almost overlook the man until you caught a glimpse in those eyes. They were killer's eyes; the eyes of a man who knew death on a first-name basis.

I was primed to push myself up from the table, waiting for the call to attention, but it didn't come for the Skipper, because there were other captains in the room. Technically, I suppose he had them on time in grade—he'd been in the Fleet Marine Corps since the Pirate Wars over twenty years ago—but that wasn't going to bring a room full of officers to their feet.

The woman following behind him did. She was tall and commanding, with an arch to her eyebrow that always made me wonder if I was in the middle of fucking up and she was the only one who could see it.

"Attention!" Captain Cronje, Vicky's company commander,

did the honors. His voice was a little on the high-pitched side and he always seemed a little manic for my tastes, but she insisted he was well-respected and not a bad guy to work for.

"At ease," Colonel Voss told us, striding purposefully across the room, the soles of her boots clomping on the hard wood floor as she claimed her table at the front of the cluster of Marine officers.

Her XO, Major Lundy, followed behind, clutching a tablet in his right hand as if it contained the secrets of the universe. I was sinking back into my seat when Covington slid into the chair beside me, nodding a greeting.

"Show's about to start," he said. I wasn't sure if he meant the briefing or the next phase of the war. Or both.

"Sir," I asked the question softly enough not even Vicky could hear it, "just how come you're not up there?" At his narrowed eyes, I went on. "I mean, how come you're not a battalion commander? Or a general for that matter? I mean, you've been in longer than anyone I know except for Top."

The Skipper didn't smile much, but he did now.

"The hardest battle I have ever fought," he confided to me, just as quietly, "was to avoid getting oak leaves pinned on my shoulders, Alvarez. I joined the Marines to fight, not to manage. If I'd wanted to be a manager, I'd have gone to business school and got a job in the Corporate Council." He nodded toward the battalion commander. "Listen up, this is going to be...interesting."

Colonel Voss had the pinched face and perpetual look of disapproval of one of the primary school teachers I'd been foisted upon when I'd first arrived in Trans-Angeles. I'd never liked her and had no reason to respect her because I'd never seen her do anything more substantial than brown-nosing the brigade commander, but I was curious about what she had to say. She touched a control on her 'link and the image of a planet snapped to life near the ceiling, projected from the holotank installed there. It was a living world, a temperate one from the look of it, not a steaming hell-hole like Inferno or an iceball like Hachiman.

"This is Port Harcourt," Voss said, her tone dramatic, perhaps intentionally so. "That isn't what the Tahni call it, obviously, but their name is pretty much unpronounceable, so we're going with Port Harcourt."

A low roll of chuckles at that, though not from me.

"Port Harcourt is the outermost of the Tahni core worlds, their oldest and most heavily populated colonies. It's our first steppingstone in the campaign to take down the Tahni Imperium."

"Ooh-rah!" The exclamation came from several of the officers, but the closest was Cronje, and he added a postscript. "Time to kick their asses, ma'am!"

"Ooh-rah!" she agreed, and somehow made the battle-cry sound pretentious and academic. "This is a key objective in our campaign. It's vital that we gain control of its resources to stage supplies for the push toward Tahn-Skyyiah, their home system. And more than that, we need to make sure we close off avenues of attack to prevent the Tahni from making an end-run assault on the Solar System to try to draw our forces away."

She traced a line on her 'link and bits of space lit up in red.

"The Tahni are quite aware of this, and the system is heavily defended in the area around Port Harcourt." A baleful glare scanned over us. "This is going to be the most heavily fortified system we've hit so far, be forewarned. However, the Fleet is fully committed to this mission and will be bringing along three cruisers and every available carrier for the assault." She spread her hands. "They'll clear the way for us as best as they can, but the approach is still going to be a nightmare. Even after we drop, there's going to be significant enemy air assets to get through. All five battalions of the 187th Expeditionary Force will be involved in the operation. There is no other military target, we are all in on this one, ladies and gentlemen."

"Question, ma'am." Captain Geiger, Bravo Company commander. I didn't know her other than her name, but she had a steady, thoughtful demeanor. "I understand we need control of the system, but have you been given any guidance as to why we're not bypassing the planet altogether? As you said, it's a huge commitment of troops and once the Fleet has taken out their space assets, what's the strategic importance of controlling the population?"

I forced myself not to cringe, but I wanted to, not because it was a bad question but because it was a *good* one, which usually made it a forbidden one. It was an old debate I'd heard over many a burn barrel and after-hours round of beers. Ground troops had been needed to retake our occupied colonies because we had to think about the lives of the captive colonists. But ever since we'd taken the last of them back, the world we were standing on, the talk had begun again.

"We should just wipe all of them out," Cronje declared, not quite loud enough to reach Voss.

"The decision has been made," Voss said, resorting to that old passive voice officers used when they didn't want to blame stupid decisions on the high command or, worse yet, the President, "that it's crucial to the prosecution of this phase of the war for the Tahni populace to truly accept their defeat. The last thing we want is to fight this war again in another twenty or thirty years. If we leave their population with their ground defenses and their pride intact, with humans never setting foot in their cities, they'll never believe they've been beaten." She shrugged. "Of course, the alternative would be to simply devastate their cities from orbit, and there have been calls to do exactly that, but so far, anyway, the President has resisted any such suggestions because it would be against the rules of war to kill noncombatants."

"No Tahni is a noncombatant," Cronje muttered, apparently unconcerned whether his subordinates heard him doubting higher command. "They're all a bunch of fucking fanatics."

And I couldn't really disagree. But...

"If we bombard their planets," I said softly aside to Vicky, "they could do the same thing to ours, and then there'd be nothing left for either of us." I shrugged. "And I don't know if I could live with myself being part of slaughtering a bunch of civilians."

She regarded me with an expression flatly cool, not as if she were angry with me but more that she considered what I'd said to be irrelevant to her.

"I'm more worried," she declared, "about my Marines than I am their civilians."

I couldn't really disagree with that either. It seemed even more reasonable burning in hot at six gravities of boost, with hellfire burning all around me.

———

"Two minutes until orbital insertion," the dropship's crew chief contributed, always trying to be helpful.

Not drop, just orbital insertion. At least then, we could stop worrying about possibly catching a round from the space defense satellites and start thinking about the fighters flying to intercept us, and air defense turrets shooting at us from the ground. That would be *so* much better.

I switched to the platoon net and said something just to hear myself talk. Well, and also because it didn't hurt to remind them all of the objective just in case their leadership got themselves killed and one of them had to step up. I was living proof that wasn't impossible.

"Remember," I told them, "our target is the deflector dishes at the spaceport. We take them down and the assault shuttles have a clear shot at their defense turrets and can provide us with air support. Our job is to clear the way for the company Boomers to come in and blow the shit out of them. Fourth Platoon is securing our left flank and Alpha Company is on our right. We got no reserves unless and until we take out those deflectors, so the objective comes first."

"In other words," Bang-Bang said, breaking in on my monologue, "don't be looking for someone to hold your fuckin' hand if the going gets rough. This is our fuckin' job and we're gonna do it."

I snorted a quiet laugh. Gunnery Sgt. Bernie 'Bang-Bang' Morrel had stepped into the platoon sergeant's spot in my unit after Scotty Hayes died and it hadn't been easy to get used to someone other than Scotty helping me run the platoon. But Bang-Bang hadn't tried to be Scotty. He'd just been himself and the difference was enough to make it easier to deal with Scotty not being there.

"Hold on," the crew chief warned us. "We got incoming fighters. The assault shuttles are engaging, but we might have to do some evasive maneuvering."

"Oh, great," I murmured, making sure my mic was off. "Evasive maneuvering is my favorite thing."

I must be a glutton for punishment because I tied back into the external cameras. The curve of the planet took up the whole screen, only the slightest tinge of black indicating we were coming in from orbit. Blue atmosphere wrapped us in it embrace, the primary star an early morning warmth just passing the terminator. The Tahni reception wasn't quite so warm.

Usually in space, the enemy is too far away to see except on sensors, but in the atmosphere, it's a different thing. Electromagnetic jamming rendered missiles nearly useless, so everything was a knife fight at beam weapon range. The Tahni dual-environment fighters were daggers cutting through the sky, aimed right at our hearts, but our assault shuttle escort moved to intercept and we got the hell out of the way.

It's hard to imagine a ship over a hundred meters long and nearly as wide going into a barrel roll, and it felt nearly as unimaginable as it sounded. There was a reason I was in the Marines and not a Fleet pilot, and it wasn't just because I hadn't had a chance at the Academy. My stomach rebelled after about ten seconds of pitching, yawing, and rolling, and abandoned me somewhere around ten thousand meters up, and I had to clench my jaws shut to keep down breakfast.

It would have been nice to shut my eyes, but that would probably have made the airsickness worse, so I was forced to deal with the chaos of the air battle, with the actinic lightning-bolt flares of proton cannons, and the scintillating plasma sheaths of lasers, and all of it seeming way too damned close to us. I don't even know if I was scared of dying in a fight anymore, not after working so much instinct into my movements, but I was petrified of dying in the dropship. I'd had one shot out from around me on Brigantia and it was every nightmare I'd ever had squeezed into a neutron-star mass and dropped into the bottom of my gut.

I'd talked to a psych counselor about it, but she'd just told me it was the most common fear of all Marines and I'd have to deal with it. Which seemed awfully easy for her to say, since she'd never once set foot on a dropship, much less left one involuntarily.

Something exploded off to our left, a starburst of white light hundreds of meters across and I wondered if it was one of theirs or one of ours. There were so many aerospacecraft packed into the sky that I couldn't have kept them straight if I'd been tied into the sensor readouts, and no one would bother to tell me unless it was something that affected our mission, like another Delta Company platoon burning in, or maybe one of our supporting companies. That was something of a relief, since I was fairly sure it wasn't Vicky or Freddy.

Another explosion and we were rolling again, banking left away from it, seeking temporary safety in some unoccupied portion of the sky, if such a thing existed. Everywhere I looked was an enemy aircraft or the dazzling signature of an energy weapon, and I felt a dread certainty deep in the pit of my stomach that this was the drop where my luck would run out.

Sometimes, when I was feeling philosophical, usually after a few shots of tequila, I would consider the concept I'd read about in one of the Continuing Education courses they forced OCS-commissioned officers to take in order to maintain their rank. This course had been on quantum physics, and the concept had involved the Many Worlds Interpretation, the idea that every event from the quantum level on up both occurred and didn't occur, and that both those realities existed, separate and parallel. The virtual instructor had suggested, only half-seriously, that maybe each one of us is living in the reality where we didn't die in all those opportunities we had to die, that maybe each of us was immortal in our own separate timeline.

I wished I could believe that, particularly in times like these.

And maybe it was true. I hadn't died yet. But the day was still young.

"Ten seconds to drop," the crew chief announced, and I blinked. He had to have called it at two minutes and then again at thirty seconds, and I'd been so wrapped up in the gut-wrenching maneuvering that I hadn't noticed.

"Ten seconds," I echoed to my Marines. "Follow your squad leaders, stay in formation once we're down."

"Ooh-rah, sir!" Bang-Bang enthused, and the others echoed it. I wondered if any of the rest of them twigged to the fact that he was being ironic.

"Drop!" the crew chief said, a warning light in my HUD mirroring the command.

"Drop!" I ordered. "Drop! Drop!"

The drop control for the suit gantry was manual. To this day, I still don't know the real reason it's not an automatic function controlled by the pilot or the crew chief. I've had instructors tell me it's because last-second faults can develop before the system has a chance to detect them and we didn't want to drop a malfunctioning suit into the shit. I've had officers insist it's for morale reasons, that the high command wanted Marines who went into battle to have to make a conscious decision to go, that it helped to keep them focused, which sounded as good as any other reason.

I yanked the lever and light flooded the drop gantry and I was falling. Below, a whole world wanted to kill me.

[2]

It was madness. There was no other word to describe dropping out of a spaceship at four hundred meters above an enemy city in broad daylight.

Sure, there were reasons for it. Day was no different than night when everyone has enhanced optics, and there wasn't any hope of catching anyone asleep when the space battle had already been raging for hours before we hit atmosphere. And we were coming in from the east, backlit by the primary star, which might throw off their targeting.

I knew all that, and yet there I was, my ass hanging in the wind, the broad, fusion-form pavement of a spaceport landing field stretched out beneath me, two gigantic deflector dishes facing opposite directions like inverted mushrooms, with a forest of anti-aircraft turrets in their shadow, bristling with coil guns and electron beamers, ripping apart the morning air with static discharge and shock diamonds. They weren't particularly aiming at us—their targets were the assault shuttles screaming from one side of the sky to the other, probing the deflector shields with one proton blast after another, the actinic bolts of man-made lightning coruscating into glowing halos of static electricity when they met the electromagnetic fields.

The knowledge that a single stray tantalum slug, a single off-target electron beam could have ended my life with the snap of a finger should have been terrifying, should have dropped my heart into my stomach. But it didn't. Instead, my thoughts churned with the details of the operations order, the timing of the assault, the spacing of my platoon. It was too much to think about to be afraid of dying, too much to worry about to allow any concern for my life to intrude.

My platoon was spread out in a chaotic, scattershot pattern, constantly bobbing and weaving as we dropped to make it harder for anyone on the ground to discern a pattern of motion or a formation which they could use to target us. Back when I'd first enlisted, I'd heard stories about company commanders and platoon leaders who tried to get their people into formation during the actual drop, like flocks of geese in neat V's across the sky. And the enemy had picked them off just like those geese and that had been the end of that.

The drop consumed the space of a few seconds, yet it seemed to drag on forever, as if my suit was filled with helium, lighter than air, floating with the wind currents. And then the ground was rushing up with incredible speed and I gritted my teeth, some part of my animal hind brain sure I was going to hit too hard and break my legs or damage the suit and wind up stranded there, waiting for the medics or the enemy, whichever came first, while my platoon fought without me. Neither happened, of course, as I knew it wouldn't from dozens of drops in combat and training, and the landing was a solid thump up from the soles of my boots into the core of my gut.

Data flooded my HUD, the positions of my Marines, the positions of the other platoons in our company, the positions of the companies flanking us, the sensors readings of possible enemy positions ahead of us, a wash of information that no one person could possibly pull together into a whole. But there was an art to it, to letting the non-essential bits flow past me like a wave on the beach and just catching what I needed, building a sandcastle that reflected everything I needed to know.

It coalesced into a whole before my eyes, the data shaping itself into an image of the reality around me. First squad was up front with Sgt. Medina, the new squad leader who'd come in to replace Joanna Carson. She'd been a good person and a passable Marine, but not the best squad leader in the Corps by any means, and Medina was already doing a better job. Second was behind me, already setting up the rear guard of our perimeter under Sgt. Sung, a competent enough leader. Third and Fourth were on the flanks and everyone was set like a runner at the starting blocks, just waiting for the gun to go off and send us in the right direction. Waiting for me.

Off to the left, Second Platoon was just touching ground, their jump jets kicking up dust devils across the flat expanse of the landing field, nearly empty of ships, all of the enemy vessels put out to sky or space to oppose us. First and Fourth were still in the air, with Headquarters coming up last with the Skipper and Lt. Xander, his XO, and Top. And the Boomers. They were the key to this operation and no one was taking any chances with them.

Alpha Company was already down, beginning to form up on our right, heading inward toward an industrial park at the edge of the spaceport where we suspected there might be a concentration of enemy troops.

And two kilometers ahead of us, coming out from beneath the cover of the deflector dishes, was wave after wave of High Guard battlesuits, Tahni front line troops, the best they had to offer. I'd asked the Skipper once why they were called the High Guard since they were just about the same thing as us Drop-

Troopers and spent most of their time on the ground, and he had said it was a direct translation from Tahni. It wasn't a reference to their ability to deploy quickly from landers via jumpjets, it was a statement of their place in the military hierarchy. The Commonwealth Marines tended to put their best troops into Force Recon, but the Tahni took the opposite approach. Battlesuits were expensive and complicated to produce and they put the absolute best soldiers they had into them. Which was why they'd kicked our asses for so long before we managed to get our shit together.

I felt exposed out there, a bug on a plate, waiting for the giant hand to slap me down, and I wanted to move, wanted to get the platoon into the fight, but I knew I had to wait for the Skipper's order. That big picture I'd gotten used to seeing was still a smaller one than his, and he might see things differently.

"Third Platoon," Captain Covington's voice buzzed in my ear, "engage the enemy. Keep them off us until we're down."

Or he might see things exactly the way I did.

"Target enemy suits and launch missiles," I ordered. "Free volley, empty your racks and advance by squads while they deal with the incoming."

I took my own advice and fired my missile load as well, one after another, the weapons kicking free of the launch tube on puffs of inert coldgas before the main rocket engines ignited and they streaked away, the first still in the air as the last came out of the tube. We followed our missiles into battle, tromping forward with First squad in the lead and I fell in just behind them and in front of Second, while Gunny Morrel brought Third and Fourth along beside us and slightly behind, each squad forming into a wedge.

The enemy hadn't launched first because they were still trying to figure out who they should be firing at, with our battlesuits spread out over about three kilometers, but once we sent our barrage their way, the choice must have become clear. Their missiles crossed ours in mid-air, the crisscrossing vapor trails spider-web filaments a hundred meters overhead, and there was suddenly no other choice.

"Jump!"

Someone should, I thought, try to come up with jump-jets that wouldn't overheat so damned easy. It was probably harder than it sounded and I was sure there was a military R&D lab somewhere working on it and they'd likely announce a fix right about the time the war ended, but it would have been so much more convenient. The main reason we couldn't just fly the suits around like miniature spaceships was that the jets built up heat way too damn quick and all sorts of bad things could happen when you superheated turbines spinning at thousands of revolutions per second.

But the jets were plenty to get us across the kilometer and a half that separated us from the enemy, and to do it fast enough to get us out from under their flight of missiles before they could adjust the targeting. Missiles corkscrewed out of the air, some self-destructing as they lost their target lock, others simply plowing into the pavement. Of course, that left the Tahni with exactly the same choice, and there were a *lot* more of them than there were of us.

"One volley by squads and then hit the ground," I instructed. "Remember the drill."

I didn't have to tell my platoon to open fire because none of them were idiots. I led by example and fired my own plasma gun because this battle was way too big to try to live by the old axiom about how an officer shouldn't have to fire their weapon if they're doing their job right. Whoever had said that had never had hundreds of Tahni battlesuits flying at them, shooting electron beamers.

Our plasma guns packed a heavier punch than their electron accelerators, enough to take one of them out with a single shot, but the downside was, our capacitors took longer to recharge between shots and hanging in the air waiting to take a second shot was a particularly stupid form of suicide. The drill I'd mentioned was one we practiced in live fires and simulations constantly, though it hadn't come up all that many times in actual combat because we'd never been stupid enough to try to invade a Tahni core colony before. We fired together, each squad targeting a rank of the incoming enemy, then cutting their jets and hitting the ground running.

Ten steps, maybe twelve before the capacitors recharged and each squad took to the air again, flying a slightly different angle of approach and firing a second time before touching down. It put us a half-second ahead of the electron beams trying to seek us out, white-hot probes of energy, surgical scalpels looking to excise the cancer of us human invaders from their sacred territory.

We still would have wound up dead in moments, taking on that many enemy suits alone, but thank God and Captain Covington, we weren't alone. The rest of the company had launched missiles as well, and there were just too many incoming warheads for the Tahni countermeasures to take them all out. They tried, though, and the distraction cost them their lives. Star-bright bundles of plasma crossed the hundreds of meters between us in a fraction of a second and metal burned.

It was times like these I really came to appreciate the armor, not just for the protection it offered or the massive weaponry it could carry, but for the separation it provided from too much reality. Outside, I knew the air was crackling with static discharge, sparking off the skin of my Vigilante battlesuit like I was some ancient thunder god brought to life, and filled with toxic fumes and heat that would have been fatal for an unarmored human. Artificial lightning tore rents in reality all around us and fireballs of hyper-ionized hydrogen burst in gouts of hell-fire. Even inside the Vigilante, I was pouring sweat, rivulets streaming down my scalp and the small of my back beneath my skinsuit, the stench acrid in the close confines, almost enough to pull me out of the immersion into the suit interface and remind me I was sitting inside a metal coffin.

If I had been just staring out at the nightmare hellscape of the battle through a clear visor, I would have been overwhelmed by the sensory input, lost, unable to fight an instinct to find the nearest cover and curl into a ball behind it. But the helmet of the Vigilante was a faceless sheet of armor, and the Heads-Up Display projected inside it was more a computer construct than it was a visual image, one or two steps back from reality. Every-thing made sense, everything was in its place.

A Tahni battlesuit turned to retreat and I shot him in the back, targeting him by unthinking instinct while still concen-trating on the fact that the enemy was pulling back in the face of one platoon after another of Marine Vigilantes dropping out of the sky. They weren't running, because Tahni didn't run and especially not on one of their own worlds, but even these fanatics knew they had to regroup.

We couldn't give them time for that.

"Delta," Captain Covington ordered, "press the attack, put their backs against those deflector dishes. First and Second, circle around to their right flank and try to force them away from the industrial park and out into the open landing field. Fourth, stay a kilometer back in reserve. Third, you're the tip of the spear. Drive it into their hearts."

I chuckled in the privacy of my helmet. Here we were in the most advanced pieces of technological hardware in the history of human warfare, yet the commands we gave wouldn't have seemed alien to Alexander's troops marching across Eurasia nearly three thousand years ago.

"Third Platoon." I passed the command down the line, "pursue and maintain volley fire. First squad, you're on point."

Which meant Private Delp was on point. An image of his pale, thin, death's-head of a face floated through my vision, agitated, annoyed, sweating, the way I'd seen him that last day on Silvanus.

———

"Close it behind you, Delp," I said, some of the impatience I felt leaching into the abrupt flick of my finger toward the ancient, oak door in its hand-worked frame.

We were in what had been the offices of some shipping firm before the invasion. If the owners were still alive, they hadn't objected to us taking over their old business. There wouldn't be any commercial shipping until after the war, most likely, and I hoped the residents were turning all their energy to construction. Or reconstruction, rather.

Delp pushed the door shut a bit too hard and it closed with an echoing bang. I speared the younger man with a glare I'd learned from the best, Captain Covington, and his already-pale face lightened a shade.

"Sorry, sir," he said, and it sounded as if he meant it.

I considered bracing him, making him stand at attention while I yelled at him, the NCO instinct I hadn't yet shaken off despite OCS and a few months in rank, but decided against it. He seemed stressed and annoyed, but not at me, I thought.

"Sit down, Delp."

I fell into my chair behind the desk, a larger and more opulent one than I would ever have back on Inferno. Hell, back on Inferno, my office would have been a closet. But I'd never seen it, since I'd gone directly from OCS into the field. And I likely never would. This one would do. Though I'd had to take the former occupant's photos off the wall and put them respect-fully in the desk drawer, because I hadn't felt comfortable with her husband and kids staring down at me.

Delp folded his skinny frame into the mismatched, plastic folding chair across from the desk and let his hands hang at his sides, finger fidgeting with his existential discomfort at being here.

"What the hell is bothering you lately, Vince?" I asked him. Using his first name was, I admit, a tactic. I was trying to disarm him, bring down his barriers and get the truth out of him. "You're a hell of a Marine...in the field. Then we get to Vistula and you got into a dust-up with that local...."

"He was asking for trouble, sir!" Delp insisted, leaning forward in his seat like he was about to jump up and argue his case. "He thought he was hot shit because he'd taken a potshot at the Tahni during the occupation, like he could have kicked them out without our help."

"Those people were living in a nightmare for months," I reminded him. "Think how pissed off and humiliated you'd be if that happened to you." He squirmed in his seat as if really considering the notion for the first time.

"Yes, sir. I guess you're right. But I was pretty drunk at the time and so was he."

"And you were drunk last night, too." I sat back, folding my hands over my chest ,and regarded him down my nose, another tactical trick I'd learned, not in OCS but from Top. "You were drunk when you started dancing with that girl—that *seventeen-year-old* girl, by the way."

He winced.

"I didn't know they'd let girls that young into that kind of place, sir."

"You're not that much older yourself," I observed. "You're

from Earth, Greater Boston. I know you'd be too young to drink if you were back home."

Not that it had stopped *me*. In the Underground, you could always find someone willing to sell you liquor...or whatever. But I'd read Delp's file and he'd been something of a straight-arrow, at least as far as his juvenile record knew. No apparent gang affiliation, no detentions, no reformatory sentences. Just a kid who wanted out of the rat maze.

"I never drank before Vistula," he confessed. He'd been meeting my eyes, but now his gaze went to something far away, a ghost of a memory.

"Yeah." I didn't elaborate. It wasn't something I could talk about.

We'd caught the last of the Tahni element on the colony right after they'd executed their hostages. They'd tried to surrender, and Delp and Joanna Carson had burned them down where they stood. I hadn't taken part, but I'd done nothing to stop it. I hadn't told anyone what had happened, and I wasn't going to talk about it now. I'd *thought* it was done and over.

"Do you need to talk to a therapist, Vince?"

He glanced up sharply, seeming as shocked as if I'd suggested he marry his sister.

"I went to see one, after," I confessed, and I think he may have been even more shocked at that. "She helped. It could help you, too."

"I don't know if I could talk to someone who wasn't a Drop-Trooper, sir." He shook his head. "They wouldn't understand."

"Private Delp," I said, putting an edge to my voice, "I would rather not make it an order." I tilted my head to the side and regarded him. "You broke that guy's arm and busted up the bar in the process. You've been arrested by the MP's on both of the last two colony worlds we've liberated. You can either seek behavioral counselling or I will have no choice but to give you an Article 15." Which was non-judicial punishment, not a court-martial, but still...

"I'll take the Article 15, sir," he insisted, the set of his mouth mulish.

"It'll delay your promotion to corporal," I told him. "Do you want to be a squad leader? A platoon sergeant? Because this could hurt your chances of either."

"I'm best at running point, anyway, sir."

"So was I, Delp." I cocked an eyebrow. "I still am. I'm not bragging when I tell you that I'm better in a suit than anyone else in this platoon. Hell, anyone else in the company besides the Skipper." And maybe Top, but I wasn't sure. She was too busy riding herd on everyone else to do much fighting. "But the Marines need leaders, or at least that's what they told me. They need people who are the best to teach others to be good enough. I thought maybe you could do that, eventually. But not if you keep this up, the drinking, the fighting."

"I won't, sir," he insisted. "I swear, no more drinking. I won't even go out."

"Not any time soon," I agreed. "You're restricted to base for the next thirty days." I jabbed a finger at him in warning. "And if I hear you've been drinking on base, you're heading to the brig, and *then* to a therapist, whether you like it or not."

I stood and he leapt to beat me to it, coming to attention.

"Dismissed," I barked at him.

When he'd closed the door behind him, I sank heavily into a chair that should have been comfortable, but wasn't. And I wasn't sure if it ever would be.

———

Delp had been as good as his word, and I thought that being away from human colonies might be good for him. He'd used the confinement to put in more time in the simulators, and I could see that he'd gotten better, smoother, though still not as much of a natural in the Vigilante as me, or Henckel.

Volley fire was a tricky thing, involving intricate timing to make sure a third of the platoon was firing constantly while the rest let their capacitors recharge. It was hard to do even in training and ten times as difficult when we were under fire, which was why I'd made sure the whole platoon worked on it every opportunity we got during the train-up for the invasion. In practice, if done right, it was devastating.

They did it right.

If a single discharge from a plasma gun was like taking a slice of the sun and shoving it into the enemy's face, volley fire was a firehose stream of unrelenting hellfire with no respite, turning everything that it touched into molten, smoldering wreckage. The Tahni ranks in front of us had no chance to organize a counterattack, no response beyond sporadic, barely-aimed burst from electron beamers. First squad took some hits and I could see flashes of red in the damage-control reports beside their names on the IFF transponder displays, but no one was out of the fight.

We'd pushed the enemy back into the support columns for the deflector dishes, massive stanchions three meters around, sunk deep into the ground. They huddled there, using the supports for cover, leaving dozens of their number lying helpless on the pavement, some obviously dead, others with huge chunks blown off their armor, the ends melted, hiding the physical devastation inside. I tried not to think about how they must feel, crawling away from impending death, fear warring with agony, their legs burned away and the rest of their body scorched by the heat that had made its way into their suits. I'd been there and I wouldn't even wish it on a Tahni.

"Boomers firing in five," Lt. Xander, the XO announced. He

was technically the platoon leader for the Headquarters Platoon, though the Skipper commanded it in practice, but Covington must have decided to let the man have his chance at running the Fire Support Team.

Boomers wasn't their official nomenclature of course, the military lacking in flair and imagination as usual, but sometimes the unofficial nicknames were the ones that stuck. And so, the Vigilante XB Fire Support Suit become the Boomer. If the Vigilante could be described as a metal gorilla, the Boomer was a gorilla playing a pipe organ. The regular suit had a single missile launcher, built flush into the side of the suit's backpack, but the Boomers had twin launchers, one at each side, protruding nearly a meter above the head of the suit. Flanking the launchers were another set of paired weapons, fat and cylindrical, extending back a meter behind the Boomers' shoulders and forward another meter. They were coil-guns, slow-firing and too cumbersome for general use and they made for a big-ass target, but devastating and handy for the special weapons team.

And especially handy for blowing up big, tasty targets like deflector dishes.

There were eight Boomers in the Fire Support squad and sixteen coil guns fired as one, the concussion from tungsten slugs the size of my hand being expelled at hypersonic velocities enough to throw my Vigilante sideways a step. Debris and smoke rose from the pavement as if in appreciation of the show of power, braiding into twisted funnels in the wake of the projectiles, but the reaction of the support columns was even more impressive.

The initial punctures weren't much to look at; ragged holes about the size of the projectiles, four in each of the columns facing the spaceport, but the mass of the deflector dish did the rest, shredding the metal at its weak points. Hundreds of tons of metal collapsed in on itself, the electrostatic field discharging as the power feeds were ripped away, making the hair on my arms stand up even through the insulation of my suit.

The Tahni were buried where they stood, and not even centimeters of armor could save the ones caught under the weight of that much metal. Clouds of dust rolled away from the wreckage, enveloping us hundreds of meters away, and everything in my helmet display turned plasticky and unreal as the computer was forced to simulate the picture from thermal sensors alone.

"Shift fire!" Xander snapped, sounding very proud of himself, like he'd personally invented the Boomer and pulled every trigger himself. "Target second dish and fire!"

I don't know how the hell they could see it. They were farther back than we were, so maybe the dust cloud hadn't obscured their field of view as much as it had ours, but all I heard was the chest-deep thump of the coil guns discharging again, then the agonized shriek of rending metal. I'm sure the second dish coming down was just as impressive as the first, but you couldn't have proven it by me.

"Both targets serviced, sir," Xander reported, making the announcement over the company band rather than a private one with Captain Covington, which I thought was pushing things a bit too far.

"We're not Fleet pilots, Lieutenant," Covington chided him, his tone so dry two of the words could have started a fire if rubbed together. "We don't 'service targets.' We're Marines and we blow shit up. And I will allow you blowed that shit up real good."

I barked a laugh, making sure my mic wasn't hot.

"First and Second," Covington went on, his tone turning businesslike. "Proceed to secondary objectives and secure the spaceport facilities. Lt. Kovacs, you're in command."

"Yes, sir," Kovacs said. "Come on, Marines, let's move out!"

He was a good officer, but I didn't like him. He reminded me too much of the popular kids at the group homes in Trans-Angeles, the ones who thought being the big fish in that small of a pond meant something.

"Fourth Platoon," the Skipper went on, including all of us in all of his orders as a matter of course, because, as he liked to remind us, any one of us might have to take command at any time, "you're with me and Headquarters. We're heading east to support the Force Recon units landing at the military barracks. Third," he said to me, "hook up with Alpha and act as a reserve for them at the industrial park. Once they've secured the area and Captain Cronje turns you loose, report back to me at the military barracks."

"Yes, sir."

And thank God. At least that would get us out of the dust cloud.

Overhead, turbojets were screaming and proton beams were raining fire onto air defense turrets and troops strongholds throughout the city. I let myself draw in a deep breath. We had aerospace superiority. The Tahni didn't know it, but they'd already lost the battle. Maybe Port Harcourt wasn't going to be as bad as I'd thought.

Famous last words.

[3]

Things hadn't gone quite as well for Alpha, that much was obvious the second we jetted in behind their lines. Two of the smaller buildings in the industrial park, what might have been business offices if this were a human world, though God only knew what the Tahni did in them, were already burning fiercely, and most of the company had taken cover behind a series of storage tanks. The tanks probably held raw materials for fabricators, since I didn't think even Cronje would be stupid enough to hide behind something volatile while electron beams and coil guns took shots at him through it.

At the center of the ring of warehouses and fabrication plants was a bunker at least fifty meters across, its roof curved and covered with soil, bristling with gun turrets on all sides. They were firing nonstop at the Marine positions, smoke and steam billowing away from the massive, globular storage tanks with every shot.

"Bang-Bang," I said to my platoon sergeant as we touched down half a kilometer behind the ring of buildings, "take Third and Fourth squad and go around the other side of the perimeter. Let's see if we can get that thing in a crossfire."

"Yes, sir," he growled, sounding dubious about the order. "Though I don't think we got anything that'll touch that bunker."

"Medina, Kreis, you're with me."

We approached the storage tanks at a cautious trot, darting between the buildings to avoid attracting fire until we reached an Alpha Company platoon huddled in the lee of what looked like a fabrication center. The IFF transponder told me it was Vicky's platoon and I lumbered up to her Vigilante. It wasn't until I could see around her and the suits beside her that I noticed four troopers sprawled out on the ground beside the wall of the building. One was clearly dead, most of the armor's chest plastron melted away by an electron beam, and if the others were alive, it was only barely.

"You guys got a problem here?" I asked her, the question not as light and bantering as it would have been a few seconds ago.

A coil gun round bit off a corner of the fabrication center, spraying us with fragments of concrete and a shower of dust, and I ducked out of instinct.

"Gosh, you think?" she snapped. "Those turrets were concealed under thermal masking panels. They caught us right in the open and took down half of Third squad before we could get to cover. There are more casualties over behind the storage tanks."

"Shit," I muttered, spotting the downed suits hidden in the shadows of the globular tanks as Vigilante battlesuits shuffled back and forth, searching for imagined safety. "Hold on a second."

I switched to Cronje's frequency, struck by the realization that he'd been pinned down here while we were taking out the deflector dishes.

"Captain Cronje," I said, stepping over his argument with a platoon leader that I pretended not to hear. "This is Lt. Alvarez from Delta. I've been sent over by Captain Covington to provide support for your objective. We took down the deflectors and the assault shuttles are already hitting the air-defense installations. You might be able to call in an air strike on this bunker by now."

"Already tried it." Cronje's response was terse and hard-edged. "They haven't taken the down the jammers yet. I can't get a signal through to the satellite relays and trying to get out into the open for a chance at laser line-of-sight is suicide with those turrets shooting at anything that moves."

I scanned my long-range sensors and picked up aircraft on thermal but he was right, there was no direct line-of-sight opening to contact them, and that was even assuming the communications laser from a battlesuit would reach them with the particulate scatter in the humid, smoke-filled atmosphere. I turned my scan downward and leaned out far enough around the corner to see the bunker. A heavy KE gun swung toward me and I pulled back just ahead of a burst of tantalum darts. *Shit.*

"There's gotta be some other way into that thing," I reasoned, still on the frequency with Cronje. "They didn't climb in through the gun turrets. There's an underground entrance to the bunker." I leaned out again, tempting fate but needing to see. A quick scan of the buildings surrounding the bunker, then back. This time, the burst came closer, coating the shoulder of my Vigilante with dust from the pulverized concrete.

"Are you *trying* to get yourself killed?" Vicky demanded on a private line between us.

I didn't answer, reading the scans from my impromptu recon. There were no thermal signatures in the buildings on either side of the bunker, at least none that looked like Tahni. The warehouse at the far end had a massive jumble of Tahni-size thermal readings on the bottom floor, all clumped together.

"There are Tahni civilians in the warehouse down there," I said, motioning straight down the concourse from the storage tanks, past the bunker.

"Yeah, we know," Cronje said, sounding even more impatient now than he had been before. "We checked in there first but we didn't see any armed troops."

"Why?" I shot back. "Why would they put dozens or hundreds of civilians in a warehouse? It's not particularly safe and it's not like they don't have underground shelters for their civilians. Did they look like workers who maybe got trapped here?"

"How the fuck should I know?" Cronje demanded, but Vicky cut him off.

"My platoon checked the building. They were older males. Too old to be soldiers."

"But not too old to be *retired* soldiers," I said. "The Tahni don't have anti-aging treatments. They don't believe in them, remember? So, once a male gets too old to be a soldier, they retire him. And if they needed some civilians to put in a building to conceal the entrance to a bunker..."

"...they'd probably use retired soldiers," Vicky finished for me.

"It's your idea, Alvarez," Cronje declared. "You and your people can check it out." It sounded more like a punishment than a compliment. "Kodjoe, your platoon will go back them up," he added, apparently deciding they had nothing better to do.

"Kreis," I told the Fourth squad leader, "you take point. Cross open spaces in groups of two and vary your spacing by ten seconds between you. Every third group hit the jets and take it high. Majid, I'm between Fourth and Third. I want you to bring up the rear and if anyone gets hit, take them back behind cover."

"Yes, sir." The two men spoke so close together that they might have rehearsed it.

I held my breath as Fourth squad crossed from the fabrication center to the storage tanks, each group chased by a burst of KE gunfire. After the second team crossed, the bunker turrets began hosing the gap with a firehose stream of tantalum darts, just like I thought they would, and the next group jetted across about ten meters off the ground. If we'd done it too many times, they would have figured out the pattern, but we managed to cross without anyone taking a hit.

"If nothing else," Cronje said, turning in his Vigilante to wave a left-handed salute at me as I passed, "you're gonna wipe out their ammo supply. We'll lay down some covering fire once you've diverted their attention."

Freddy's platoon was moving away from the storage tanks, stepping carefully to avoid gaps in the cover, and I could tell from the transponder when he led them up behind my Third squad.

"We got your back, Cam," he assured me.

Which was fine and everything, but it wasn't my back I was worried about.

Crossing from the storage tanks to the building beside it was the hardest part, but thankfully by that point, Alpha Company was splashing plasma flares against the armored facing of the gun turrets, drawing their fire for the few seconds it took us to get through the gap.

"What's the plan, sir?" Bang-Bang asked me, not even bothering with the NCO's gentle chewing out for a junior officer taking too many chances. Maybe he'd already heard too much about me to bother.

"I believe the entrance to that bunker is in the warehouse at the end of the park," I told him. "Captain Cronje has voluntold us to go investigate. Fall in behind us with First and Second squads."

"Remind me to send the captain a thank-you card."

We swung out wide of the last structure on the right. I couldn't tell what it was from the appearance, not yet an expert on Tahni industrial architecture despite how much of it I'd blown up in the last four years. If I'd had to guess, I would have said a chemical production plant, from the cylindrical tanks lined up across the back of the building and the arsenic level warning from the external sensors. Whatever it was, I didn't want to be too close to it when an energy weapon hit those storage cylinders.

And maybe the Tahni would think we were bugging out, just trying to get away or go for help. But who the hell knew what the Tahni thought about anything? I'd tried to put myself inside their heads more than once, but they weren't human. Would humans still be sitting in that damned bunker after the deflectors fell, after they lost aerospace superiority and the end was all but inevitable? Would we sit there, trying to kill every enemy we could until they found a way to root us out?

I remembered Brigantia and decided maybe the Tahni weren't that different from us after all. This was their world, and in their eyes, we were worse than invaders, we were blasphemers. It was hard for me to think that way, probably hard for anyone raised on Earth. No one on Earth *believed* in anything as much as the Tahni did. Not enough to die for it. Even the gangs didn't believe that hard. But I'd learned a lot of history during my time in the Marines, and gained a perspective not just on how people used to live in the past but how they still lived out in the colonies, where belief still counted for something.

And I believed it had worked. They'd stopped shooting at us, whether because they thought we were bugging out or because they couldn't see us anymore. I was sure they had spy cameras out here, but this place had been pounded by EMP when the deflector dishes went down and I doubted if any electronics not shielded by military-grade insulation could have survived it.

At least I didn't have to worry about mines or booby traps. That was one area where the Tahni believing so hard hurt them. Their religion didn't allow automated weapons. Life and death were the purview of their version of God, and God worked through them, his chosen people, to give life and to take it. We were far enough ahead of them in computer engineering that I think we could have disabled or hacked anything they could set up for us even if they didn't have the screwy belief system, but it would have taken time we didn't have. And again, was it really so screwy? After all, we didn't go for automated weapons either, and if we justified it by bad experiences in the past, was that any more logical than saying "God doesn't like it?"

The lookouts at the warehouse weren't automated, though. They were civilians, old males, dressed in the strange arrangement of braided and woven strips of cloth Tahni of both sexes wore. There was a certain look about them, a sturdiness across the shoulders and a straightness to their backs that told me I was right, that they were old soldiers. They disappeared back into the rear doors of the warehouse at the sight of us and I knew we were running out of time.

"Hit the jets!" I said, then threw myself forward, not waiting to see how quickly the rest of the platoon obeyed.

We were two hundred meters away from the side door to the warehouse, oval and segmented and big enough for three of us to pass abreast if we wanted, and it took a good three seconds of flight to reach it. Kries was a good leader and a good follower too, and his squad hit the doors first, but I was right behind them, probably too close, but I had to see. The civilians retreated before us, skittering back across the open causeways through the stacks of cargo containers spaced about four meters apart and rising up twenty meters high to the curved ceiling overhead. I had been worried they might have weapons, might try something stupid, but they were playing it just right if their aim was to convince us they were harmless refugees, just trying to sit out the battle. Their eyes, though, were sharp and watchful, and not nearly scared enough.

"No females," Kries commented, entering the building with a slow, healthy caution, his rounded footpads scraping against the concrete.

"Not unusual," I told him, scanning the cargo containers before I followed Fourth squad inside. "The females live apart from the males once they reach sexual maturity. Apparently, and no, I'm not making this up, the Tahni males go into heat and can't control themselves around females."

"Yeah, I remember being a teenager, too." He paused about ten meters into the building. "I ain't seein' no enemy troops in here, boss."

"And you won't," I assured him. "That's the point. Watch my back."

I advanced and kept one eye on the civilians as I scanned the floor. Solid concrete as near as my thermal and sonic sensors could tell, all the way through the first sixty or seventy meters of stacked containers. Nothing in the containers, either, no heat sources, no chemical signatures, no sound. The males moved back as we moved forward, but only to a point. They clustered around a dull-grey dome of poured concrete near the center of the warehouse.

I'd seen them before, had been told by people who claimed to know that they were intended to store valuable goods, things that were easy to steal. I wasn't sure if I believed that. The Tahni were so fanatical, so devoted to their belief system, it was hard for me to grasp the concept of one of them stealing, but maybe I was idealizing the enemy. Captain Covington had warned me that was a problem some militaries had faced in the past when fighting someone outside their own culture, the temptation to either write them off as subhuman animals or to put them on a pedestal as some sort of warrior ideal.

But I didn't think the dozens of retired Tahni soldiers huddled around the five-meter-tall concrete dome were there to take advantage of the attack to loot it. I levelled my plasma gun and aimed it at the center of them.

"Move," I ordered, and my public address speakers translated it into Tahni, a consonant-heavy trip-hammer of a language. "Move now or I fire."

They still looked reluctant, but they slid aside as if they'd rehearsed the motion and I grabbed the handle for the heavy, metal door with my armor's articulated left hand and yanked it open. The interior was empty of cargo, empty of any goods the Tahni or anyone else might want to steal. It was full of children.

Juveniles, to be precise. Tahni males who had hit puberty and gone to live with their fathers and uncles and grandfathers and great uncles and etc... Thirty or forty of them, all crouched like animals ready for fight or flight, their faces just a bit more human than the adults, with their brow ridges less pronounced, their jaws narrower, not like the steam-shovels of the adults, their eyes slightly less sunken into their sockets. It was easy to mistake them for human teenagers at first glance.

"What the fuck?" Kries wondered.

Yeah, what the fuck? Them being in here didn't make any more sense than the other civilians. Except...behind them, nearly flush with the floor of the storage dome, was a hatch. I missed it at first with the young Tahni males shifting around over it, trying to hide it with their bodies.

"Get out!" I told them, yelling it this time, the translation echoing off the interior walls. "All of you, get out!"

They didn't move, so I did. The kids were brave, insanely brave if they'd been humans, but when a three-meter-tall metal giant stomps into a closed room with any kid, human or Tahni, they're going to run. They were chickens fleeing the henhouse at the entry of a thieving dog, flapping around the edges of my Vigilante with a fluttering of stripped cloth. I wondered how hot the metal skin of my suit was after all the fighting and flying I'd done in the last few minutes since drop. God, had it only been a few minutes? It felt like hours.

"Kries," I said, "get in here and bring a fire team."

I didn't wait for him. The Tahni would know we were coming and I didn't want to give them any more time to get ready. The hatch was locked, but the hinges and the lock were visible and I didn't even hesitate, blasting the lock with my plasma gun. Heat flooded the suit, making my skin crackle like I'd been lying out in the sun at mid-day in an Inferno summer, and it was a damned good thing the kids had run away because they would have died in an instant from flash burns. The lock was manual, old-fashioned and clunky, and it had melted away from the blast, letting the hatch fall inward.

Inside it was a ramp sloping gently downward, a broad tunnel heading under the courtyard, out to the bunker. And swarming up at me were row upon row of Tahni Shock-Troopers, clunky and broad-shouldered in their powered exoskeletons but still a meter shorter than my Vigilante and hundreds of kilos lighter. Tantalum darts ricocheted off my chest armor, leaving cracks and craters but not quite powerful enough to penetrate, even at this range.

There was no room for the grenades from my suit's launcher to arm down here, and I wasn't one hundred percent certain they would be enough against the Shock-Troopers' armor, so I gritted my teeth and fired my plasma gun again. It was as if the entire tunnel had ignited, and my breath caught in my throat from the wash of searing heat.

It was worse for the Tahni. A blast that could burn right through the chest-plate of a High Guard battlesuit melted the outdated Shock-Trooper armor to slag, cutting down a full rank of the onrushing soldiers and sending the others rocking back on their heels. I didn't wait for the gun to recharge, instead wading into the next rank standing and swinging my left arm like a giant war club. I was a medieval knight fighting children who were playing at war in suits of cardboard armor. My first blow smashed one of them into the side of the tunnel, crushing armor and flesh and bone and cracking the concrete, and when I swung away, he sank to the floor, his chest caved in.

A helmet crunched under my fist and wobbled off to the side at an unnatural angle, an arm bent backwards and then my capacitors were recharged and I fired again. More heat, more sweat pouring off me, and when I grasped at the nipple of my helmet's water bladder and tried to force moisture into my cotton-packed throat, the water was scalding hot. I drank it anyway and as the smoke and haze cleared ahead of me, I could see the Tahni running.

It made no sense. There was nowhere for them to go, but panic had taken hold and whether they were human or not, every animal behaves the same when the panic sets in.

Kries was beside me now and he fired less than a second after I did, adding to the inferno, leaving another handful of armored Tahni bodies lying on the floor, burning fiercely. Crates of ammo were stacked by the walls of the bunker, narrowing our path even as the walls broadened out. The gunners had abandoned their turrets, unarmored and unable to stand the stultifying heat, trying to cram against the far walls alongside the last of the Shock-Troopers.

"You can surrender," I told them. "You don't have to die down here. If you surrender, you'll be treated well…"

A burst of KE gunfire greeted my offer and Kries and his Alpha team leader Corporal Chelimo shot simultaneously, a half-second before me. It was enough. When the haze had cleared, none of the enemy troops were left alive and the remote controls for the turrets were melted and sparking wildly.

"You know better than that, Lieutenant," Kries told me. "Tahni don't fucking surrender."

"Well, they're going to have to," I told him, "unless we want to kill every single one of them."

[4]

"Sir," Bang-Bang told me, waiting just outside the entrance to the concrete storage hut, left fist braced against his armor's hip like a disapproving teacher watching a misbehaving student return from recess, "you gotta let someone else do that shit. You know that, right?"

"I know, Sergeant," I assured him. "Next time. I promise. Did someone tell Captain Cronje we're clear down here?"

"Yeah, that Lt. Kodjoe sent the relay from outside." Bang-Bang waved a hand at the civilians, who had retreated to the other end of the warehouse, huddled around the huge wheels and flat cargo beds of three freight trucks parked beside the broad, open doors at that end. "Whaddya wanna do about these jokers?"

"Hey, we're just the support, right?" I pointed out. "Let Captain Cronje worry about them. Get all our people outside and into a defensive perimeter and I'll go ask him if he needs us for anything else."

"Now that we did his fucking job for him," Bang-Bang added, and I chuckled...right after I checked to make sure he was using our private net.

Freddy Kodjoe was outside the warehouse door when I emerged, and I stopped beside him while Kries led Third and Fourth squad out behind me.

"Nice job in there," Freddy told me. "You saved us a lot of heartburn."

"You still got heartburn to go," I warned him. "There's a shitload of civilians inside the building, older males mostly with a few dozen juveniles, too."

"Yeah, your Platoon Sergeant told me. Captain Cronje wants my platoon to go find some place to secure them until the Fleet lands more troops."

"Who the hell is going to be responsible for occupying this place?" I wondered. "Not us, I assume. And there just ain't enough Force Recon to do that kind of work."

"Jesus, man, you don't read the monthly briefs from Commonwealth Command?"

"Not lately," I admitted. "I'm still getting used to the whole officer thing."

"You and me both," he reminded me. "We graduated the same class. But there's a whole brigade of troops coming in behind us, right out of training. Guys who couldn't cut it in Force Recon and didn't have the simulator test scores for Drop-Troopers. They're like glorified janitors if you ask me, but their official name is the Security Command. They'll be pulling in as we pull out."

I gazed out at the city, smoke rising high above it, buildings on fire, assault shuttles pounding enemy positions with lightning raining out of their proton emitters.

"Good luck to the poor bastards."

Kodjoe's Marines were filing into the entrance as ours exited and I noticed a commotion even before I switched to his platoon's net and heard the shouting voices.

"They've started up one of the trucks!" someone was yelling. "They're trying to drive out the other side."

"Shit!" Freddy hissed, hitting the jets and heading over to the opposite end of the warehouse.

"Kries!" I said, rocketing away into a jump right behind him. "On my six, and bring Alpha team with you!"

The situation at the freight entrance on the other side of the building was, in the language of the Marine Corps, a clusterfuck. Civilians were streaming out on foot, the older males holding the hands of the younger, and at the head of them was one of the massive cargo haulers, its two-meter-tall, knobbed tires crunching pavement beneath it. Several of the older males were crammed into the cab of the vehicle, visible through its transparent windscreen, while a score of others had climbed onto the flatbed. There was something else on the bed with them, a cargo cylinder identical to the others stacked inside the warehouse, but this one secured with straps.

A fire team from one of Freddy's squads was already moving into the path of the truck, yelling warnings at the driver in amplified Tahni, but I knew as I arced downward toward them that they couldn't see the civilians in the back of the truck, pulling open a small hatch in the side of the cargo cylinder, doing something in there.

A warning flash popped into my HUD, telling me it had detected the Tahni version of HiPex...chemical hyper-explosives.

"Get out of there!" I bellowed on the open net. "It's a bomb!"

I was too late.

Something swatted me out of the air and I was tumbling for all of about five meters before my shoulder smacked into the pavement and my teeth clicked together. I tasted blood and saw stars, and didn't see much of anything else.

———

I couldn't have been out for more than a few seconds because the buzzing of damage warnings and the flashing of IFF transponders brought me back to alertness almost immediately. I squeezed my eyes shut for a moment against a dull pain in my head, the remnants of the concussion I'd received even through my armor from a combination of the shockwave from the explosion and the five-meter fall. When I opened them, I was in hell.

Or close enough.

Where the cargo truck had been was a crater, billowing smoke and still raining debris. Where Freddy's fire team had been was nothing. Something wet and biological smacked down on the pavement beside me, and I tried not to look at it.

The Tahni civilians...where were they?

The ones who'd been near the truck were gone, of course, blown to pieces no larger than the ones that had just rained down near me, but there'd been dozens, hundreds more inside that warehouse. My eyes began to focus and I saw the Tahni hundreds of meters away from the truck, picking themselves off the pavement and standing there in a daze, the juveniles clinging to their fathers.

"What the fuck is going on?" Cronje bellowed in my ear. I was still on the Alpha Company net, which was overflowing with one transmission after another stepping on each other until Cronje used his command override. "Kodjoe, what the hell is happening over there?"

I rolled my suit onto its side and clambered to my feet, ignoring a bunch of damage warnings telling me I shouldn't do that. Freddy was just a couple dozen meters away from me, sprawled on his belly, his articulated hand clawing at the ground to gain purchase.

"Jericho!" he yelled, his voice breaking at the end. "Corporal Jericho, report!"

I wasn't certain, but I intuited that Corporal Jericho must have been the team leader. I wanted to tell him they were gone, but it wasn't my place.

"Kodjoe, you'd better fucking report!" Cronje again. He wasn't that far away. Why didn't he just come over here himself and figure it out?

I turned to face the direction we'd come from, just about ready to tell Cronje what had happened myself, but Freddy finally got his shit together.

"Sir, it was a VBIED," he said, his voice still shaky. "A bomb on a cargo truck driven by civilians. I think...." I could hear his swallow. "Sir, I've lost four Marines, Alpha team from First squad. What...what are your orders?"

There was nothing for a moment, and I wondered if Cronje was out of line-of-sight range, if the jamming was silencing him. But when he spoke again, his tone was deliberate enough that I was sure he'd been considering his words.

"Take the rest of your platoon," he told Freddy, "and clean them out. All of them."

"Clean them out, sir?" The question could have been disbelieving, could have been from a man looking for clarification because he didn't like the sound of an order and wanted to make sure he'd heard it right. But it wasn't. It was the question of a man who was *hoping* the order was the way it had sounded.

"They're insurgents, Lieutenant," Cronje growled, his voice causing distortion in the microphone. "Kill them."

Hackles rose on the back of my neck, a haze of disbelief that I might have blamed on the concussion but was more just a wanting it not to be true.

"There are children in that group!" I said. I tried to take a step forward, but my right hip actuator gave out and I collapsed to a knee. "You can't!"

But Freddy's platoon was flying in, touching down beside him, fanning out to pin the civilians between them and the explosion crater and the fierce heat still emanating from it. I couldn't hear his commands to them because he was using their platoon net and I wasn't authorized to listen in on it, but their left forearms rose high, elevating the grenade launchers built into the suit there, our auxiliary weapons for use against infantry.

I still didn't believe they'd do it, or perhaps I'd convinced myself they wouldn't so I wouldn't have to do anything about it.

They fired as one, the grenades arcing up into the air twenty or thirty meters and coming down at the clusters of civilians out in the open. The waves of heat streaming off the bomb crater saved some of them, altering the flight of the grenades just enough to keep them out of the center of the group, hitting near the edges instead.

The explosions were tiny, audible only as soft crumps, their ignition a supernova flare of HiPex turning sintered metal into plasma spears that sliced through the front rank of the Tahni, sending a score of them crumpling to the ground like marionettes with their strings cut.

"No, Goddammit!" I yelled.

Since I couldn't walk, I hit the jets and came down beside Freddy, slamming my shoulder into his and nearly knocking him over.

"Stop this!" I yelled at him. "There are fucking *children* in there, man!"

"Get away from me!" he snapped back, punctuating the demand with a shove that sent my crippled armor sprawling. "What the hell is wrong with you, Cam? Those are the enemy!"

"Kreis!" I said, praying the man was close enough to get the laser line-of-sight transmission. "Get your squad in front of those Goddamned civilians right now! Block those grenades! That's a fucking order!"

A second barrage of grenades fell, these course-corrected by the shooters or perhaps the targeting computers in their suits, and thirty or forty more Tahni fell as they ran back toward the warehouse. Some of the bodies were small, a head shorter than the others.

I snarled and jumped, the boosters kicking me in the pants, jarring muscles already sore from the shockwave of the explosion. I landed on one leg and tried to balance, standing a hundred meters ahead of Freddy's platoon, staring out at them, putting myself between them and the Tahni civilians.

"You have to stop this shit!" I yelled on the general net since I didn't have their platoon frequency. "This is a fucking illegal order! You can't do this!"

"Get out of the way, Cam," Freddy insisted.

Another flight of grenades launched, but I'd set my suit to target them as hostile fire and my own grenade launcher popped rounds to intercept. I fired my plasma gun into the path of the barrage and the rush of superheated air set most of them off, a firework show at mid-morning. And that would have been it, as much as I could have done. Another fusillade would have gone past me and the civilians were still in range, half still trying to head back to the warehouse, half just running hell-bent for leather *away*.

What came out over the open stretch of pavement wasn't another flight of grenades, though. It was Kries and Fourth squad, answering my call. They landed beside me and faced back towards Freddy's platoon; plasma guns levelled. I blew out a breath, frankly amazed they'd done it.

"What the fuck are you doing?" Freddy was screaming now. "Those motherfuckers killed my Marines! You're letting them get away!"

"The one who killed your fire team died with the bomb, Freddy." I was pissed off, not at Freddy but at Cronje, and I knew I couldn't let it through in my voice, not if I wanted to reach him. I kept my tone as steady as I could, firm but not strident. "And if there are more insurgents with that group, we should have arrested them and let Fleet Intelligence take care of it. Killing unarmed civilians is against the UCMJ." The Uniform Code of Military Justice dated back to before the Commonwealth, and it had changed quite a bit through the centuries, but some things had been illegal from day one right through to the end of the 23rd Century.

Things were quiet for a few, long seconds, and I thought maybe I had gotten through to Freddy, but when a group of Vigilante battlesuits came trotting up behind him, I realized he'd merely been on comms. The IFF transponder showed the identity of the Marines inside the suits, but I would have recognized them by the insignia on the chests. It was Alpha's Headquarters Platoon, led by Captain Cronje, and he wasn't happy.

"Lt. Alvarez!" he exploded, advancing until he was nearly chest to chest with me, as if that somehow increased the clarity of our suit comms, since neither of us could see the other's face. "You are disobeying a direct order!"

"In fact, I was not, sir," I told him, unable to keep the loathing out of my voice as hard as I tried. "I received no orders. I merely tried to keep another platoon leader of the exact same rank and date in grade as me from carrying out an *illegal* order."

He raised the left hand of his suit, and for a second, I thought he was going to hit me. I noticed Kries' plasma gun track just slightly to his right, covering Cronje. I think Cronje must have seen it, too, since he lowered his hand.

"It's not your fucking job to interpret orders, Lieutenant!"

"Sir, I was taught from Basic all the way through OCS that it is *every* Marine's responsibility to refuse to obey illegal orders.

The order to kill unarmed civilians is illegal. The order to kill unarmed *children* isn't just illegal, it's morally reprehensible."

While we spoke, the rest of my platoon arrived, led by Bang-Bang. The platoon sergeant didn't take the time to question me as to what was going on and why we were facing down other Marines, he just formed them up beside me, arrayed in a semi-circle. Other drop-troopers were flying or walking in as well, the rest of Alpha Company, all watching us. Did they know what was going on? Were they uncommitted or just confused?

I could identify with their confusion. I didn't know what the hell I was doing or why. But I'd made the decision and it was too late to go back on it now.

Cronje's helmet scanned back and forth, an instinctive motion since he didn't actually need to move his helmet or his head to see what was going on around him. His left hand rose again, the claw-like fingers clenched into a fist, but then he lowered it.

"Kodjoe," he said over his company net. "Pull out of here. Go search for remains of your fire team."

"But sir...," Freddy began to protest, but Cronje cut him off.

"Do as you're fucking told, Lieutenant."

"Yes, sir."

Freddy turned back to his platoon and began directing them away from the warehouse, out toward the crater. But Captain Cronje still faced me, still less than a meter away from me, his rage seething like the heat pouring off the blast site.

"Don't think this is over, Alvarez," Cronje hissed at me, and I could see on the HUD that he was speaking on a private channel between us. "Don't think I'll forget you took their side and betrayed your fellow Marines. You're going to regret the day you were promoted from PFC."

"Believe me, sir," I assured him, my voice steadier than my stomach, "I already do."

[5]

The pulse carbine dragged at my shoulder by its webbed sling, awkward and out of place. I felt like an idiot carrying it, like a child playing soldier. And yet simultaneously, I felt incredibly exposed on the streets of Port Harcourt, the carbine completely inadequate to deal with a city, a *world* filled with enemies who wanted me dead.

I was being imprecise, calling the city Port Harcourt rather than the world, but since we weren't staying here long, I hadn't bothered to learn the Tahni name for the place, and the official Fleet reports just called it "the Capital," which was a commentary on lack of imagination in the military structure. There were two dozen other cities on the world, which seemed simultaneously far too many for us to take and far too few for a whole planet. But the Tahni didn't tend to spread out, preferring to live in clusters, so there were no small towns or outposts here.

Not too different from Earth, but a departure from human colony worlds. Even on the core colonies, we liked our elbow room, liked have some space between us and our neighbors. It was a commentary, I thought, on the type of people willing to leave Earth in the first place. Anyone happy crammed into a mega-city could have stayed behind.

That didn't include me anymore. I wasn't happy at all crammed into this particular city, even on the outskirts in the industrial district where the Marines had established their base after the Security Command had landed and began setting up their new structure to govern the planet. Half the industrial district had burned to the ground in the battle, and what was left was ragged and strewn with debris, but we'd made do with worse. Our company had set up a hooch city in the same empty warehouse where we had the maintenance gear for our suits, which made them easier to guard, but by some quirk of planning, the suits, our cots, hammocks, and cooking gear were almost two kilometers from the battalion headquarters.

And we sure as hell weren't going to walk around here unarmed, whether it had been required or not, so out came the pulse carbines from our suit bug-out kits and we all wandered around with them slung on our shoulders like we actually knew what we were doing with a shoulder-fired weapon. I was one of the few drop-troopers I knew who'd actually used one in combat, and even I would freely admit I was little better than a novice with the thing. But no one wanted to admit we were going to depend on the Force Recon pukes to protect us.

I passed by a Force Recon security patrol, the straight-legs looking a lot taller and more intimidating when I was out of my Vigilante, their Gauss rifles heavy and imposing and so much more professional looking than my dinky little pulse carbine. I couldn't see their faces through the visors of their helmets, but I had to imagine they were looking at me with disdain, the same way I looked at them when I was in my battlesuit and they were tiny and breakable by comparison.

I stared at them as they passed and nearly ran right into Vicky.

"Oh, um, hi," I said, trying to smile.

She didn't.

"What the fuck, Cam?" she said without preamble, arms folded, a glaze of frost across her features. "You pull this shit with Cronje and then you don't even come talk to me?"

"I didn't want to make trouble for you," I told her, spreading my hands helplessly. "It's not exactly top-secret that you and I are...you know. Cronje seemed pretty pissed off at me and I didn't want you catching any of the heat."

"You could have at least called me," she insisted, slapping my shoulder hard with her right palm. "I'm hearing all sorts of shit second-hand from Freddy and the other platoon leaders and I don't have any idea what's going on! They're saying you protected the insurgents who killed Freddy's fire team!"

"The Tahni who killed his fire team were suicide bombers," I told her, trying not to give free rein to the anger roiling in my gut. "They died in the explosion. If Cronje had ordered Freddy or me or anyone to secure the civilians inside the warehouse, I would have done it. He ordered them all killed." I bared my teeth in a snarl I couldn't hold back. "He was out of control."

"Shit." She rubbed a hand across her face and rasped a sigh. "This is bad."

I glanced around, trying to see if any other drop-troopers were watching us. We were alone, so I grabbed her hand in mine.

"You shouldn't hang around with me for a while," I told her. "Let things die down. Maybe once we're off this planet, every-one'll just forget about it."

"And you think that's what they should do?" she asked me. "Just forget about it? You want to let Cronje get away with this? It's not right."

"It's a war." I shrugged it off with a casual dismissal I didn't actually feel but wanted to convince her I did. "I've done and seen a lot of things I didn't like." I stared at the ground but saw something light-years and a lifetime away, saw my mother on the dusty ground, the life draining from the wound in her chest. "I've seen a lot of things I didn't like *before* the war, and no one ever paid for any of them."

She darted in and kissed me, her hand slipping off my arm as she passed.

"Be careful."

I felt as if everyone was staring at me as I walked under the overhang of the vehicle park where we'd set up our Battalion HQ, but I shut them out and kept my eyes straight ahead, focused on our company area. Covington was standing in the midst of a cluster of seated enlisted men and junior NCOs, their noses buried in haptic holograms.

"I don't care which colonel ordered those replacement turbines," Covington was pacing as he spoke into the audio input of his 'link, "we have three Vigilantes with deadlined jump-jets and they *need* to be up for our scheduled security patrols. If you don't get them to us, I will give your 'link address to the Battalion Sergeant Major and let him deal with you." He paused both in speech and mid-step, then nodded. "Good. I appreciate it. I will expect them to be in our maintenance area by 0900 local time tomorrow."

He looked up at my approach.

"Alvarez. Do you have your schedule set up for the patrols yet?"

"Yes, sir," I told him. "I uploaded it to the company servers before I headed over here."

"Good. Come over here and sit down."

He led me to a makeshift conference room, compartmentalized from the rest of the headquarters by soundproof panels surrounding a ring-shaped table positioned around a portable holographic projector. Folding chairs were clustered around the table and he motioned me into one of them, then sat down beside me, close enough that it made me slightly uncomfortable.

"We need to talk about what happened."

I very deliberately did *not* sigh heavily or roll my eyes, though I very much wanted to.

"Sir," I said, "I put everything that happened in my report. I'm not sure what else I can tell you."

"Don't be obtuse with me, son." The Skipper raised an eyebrow. "This isn't something you can just stick in an after-action report and forget about it. You're going to have to do one of two things: either amend your report, or contact the Judge Advocate General and file charges."

"I don't want to file charges, sir," I said immediately. "I don't need to make a big deal of this."

Covington snorted.

"Too late for that. Greg's already pitching a shit-fit." At my curious look, he amended. "Greg Cronje. He came storming into Battalion Headquarters about ten minutes after we finished setting it up and demanded I write you an Article 15 for insubordination. I told him to go fuck himself, though you didn't hear that from me."

I chuckled under my breath.

"I'm sure he was happy about that. But honestly, sir, if you think I should drop the whole thing, I'll leave it out of my report."

"That might be for the best, though God knows, he deserves to get his dick slapped for this. Not just for the illegal order but letting it happen to begin with. He knew there were civilians in the warehouse and didn't bother to detail anyone to secure them."

"Maybe I should have done it, sir," I admitted. "I was right there next to Freddy...Lt. Kodjoe. I could have sent a squad to go pin them in."

"You already saved their asses from the bunker," he pointed out. "Did he want you to hold his dick for him, too? It was his company, his responsibility." He waved the subject away. "You'll amend the report and hopefully Greg will man up and stop trying to make a big deal about this. I want to make sure we get the new squad leadership..."

There was a knock on the side of the soundproofed wall.

"Sir?"

The woman was a First Lieutenant, I could tell that from the insignia on her Fleet utilities. When she moved farther into the conference room, two NCOs followed her and all three of them wore pistols holstered at their waists. They were MPs. My gut fell out at the realization and I was suddenly, dolorously certain of their purpose here.

"Lt. Alvarez," the woman said, the heel of her hand resting on the butt of her pistol, "I'm going to need you to turn over your carbine and come with us."

Covington rose from his seat, a dark cloud passing over his face.

"You'd better have some orders to show me, Lieutenant," he warned her, "or your career is about to take an unfortunate turn."

"Yes, sir," she said, her face turning pale at the words. She raised her 'link and cast something over to his. "It's directly from the office of the Judge Advocate General. Captain Cronje is pressing charges against Lt. Alvarez for insubordination, disobeying orders, dereliction of duty and threatening a superior officer. I've been ordered to remand him for custody in the Brigade HQ until a flight can be arranged up to the cruiser *Trafalgar* for return to Inferno for a court-martial."

I didn't move, couldn't. I couldn't think, could barely breathe, and probably would have sat there immobile until the

MPs hauled me away if Covington's voice hadn't cut through my fugue with a tone of firm command.

"Give me your weapon, Alvarez," he said, then motioned impatiently when I didn't immediately respond.

I stood and unslung the carbine, not missing the hands tightening on the grips of sidearms as the MP's watched me very closely. I handed the weapon to Covington and he slung it over his shoulder, glaring at the MP's but talking to me.

"Fuck amending your report," he told me. "The minute you get to Brigade, I want you to make a formal statement to the JAG Corps and the MP's and get that moron charged with murder."

One of the MP NCO's pulled out a pair of restraints, but Covington shot him a glare that would have melted lead.

"Those won't be necessary," he said. The officer started to speak, but Covington interrupted her. "I *said*, those won't be necessary. And if you wish to stay here and argue about it, I'm morally certain I can get Colonel Voss to see things my way."

"It's okay, Sergeant," the MP officer said, waving the man off.

"Don't worry, son," Covington assured me. "Everything is going to be fine."

He seemed very convinced of it. I wasn't sure at all.

———

The woman blew into the room like an autumn wind, cool and dry and bringing portents of the killing frost to come. She wore a dress uniform, white and sharp and standing out like a sign that screamed 'please shoot me' on an occupied enemy world, but I suppose the officers in Brigade did things differently.

She closed the door behind her and fell into a seat opposite me at the interrogation room table, glancing down at the loop on the table I should have been handcuffed to if the MP's hadn't listened to Captain Covington. She raised an eyebrow but didn't mention it.

"So, you're the infamous Lt. Alvarez," she said. Her voice sounded like one of my Drill Instructors from Basic on those rare occasions when they'd been talking in a normal tone of voice, like someone who'd yelled a lot their whole life and had a hard time speaking normally.

"I didn't realize I was infamous, Commander Hofstetter," I replied, reading the info off of her name plate.

She was a Fleet Commander, which meant she was the equivalent of a Marine light colonel and I should be respectful, although she was also a JAG lawyer, which meant she'd received the rank at a more accelerated pace due to her training and was probably younger than most commanders, with less experience in the military.

"Well, let's just say you've come quite close to meeting someone like me a few times in your short career. But you also have quite the list of commendations and awards, including a Silver Star, and you've participated in at least three of the most important battles in the war." She shot me what could have been described as a smirk, but I had the intuition that it was just her way of smiling. "So, when someone with a record like that is accused of the crimes you are accused of by a company commander with a spotless record and a good reputation in the battalion, we tend to go to the source."

"You reviewed our suit recordings," I assumed.

"I did."

"Pardon me for not knowing, ma'am," I said, very cautiously, "but are you here as my prosecutor or my defense attorney?"

Now she laughed and it was a sound I didn't expect from that voice, light and airy.

"Technically," she said, "I'm your defense attorney...well, I was *going* to be your defense attorney until the Provost Marshall told me about your counter-charges. At that point, I met with him and we both reviewed the evidence." She tilted her head to the side as if she was weighing up how to put what she said next. "Now, I have to tell you, there's a lot of sentiment to just make all this go away."

"Really, ma'am?" I raised my eyebrows, unable to contain my surprise. "I'd have thought Brigade would be all over this like stink on...." I paused, reconsidering my language. "...crap," I finished. "I mean, either I'm right about this being an illegal order and Captain Cronje is guilty of murder, or he's right and I'm guilty of insubordination. Either way, someone broke the UCMJ."

"You left off the other possibility, Lieutenant," she said, leaning across the table toward me. "That you're both right and both wrong. Captain Cronje was dealing with a fluid situation where he couldn't tell civilians from non-uniformed combatants, his people were dying, and he gave an order without knowing the situation. You were on the ground and tried to tell him the details, but his communications channels were overloaded by other chatter and he ignored you. You then ordered your platoon into a situation where they were pointing their weapons at friendly troops. Does this sound like a good summation of what happened to you?"

I let out a breath I'd been unconscious of holding.

"Yes, ma'am." There was no point in denying it, she'd already seen the only evidence that mattered and drawn her own conclusions.

"In fact," she went on, "if anyone is really culpable for this, it's Lt. Kodjoe."

"Freddy?" I blurted. "Why him? Ma'am."

"Because he *did* know what was going on," she said. "He *did* see the juveniles among the civilians and knew he was following what were either intentionally or unintentionally illegal orders, yet he did it anyway. And when you pointed it out to him, he still ordered his troops to fire on the civilians."

"I didn't want to get Freddy in trouble," I said, squeezing my eyes shut and running a hand over the back of my neck. My head hurt, probably from the explosion. I wondered if I'd gotten a concussion. They hadn't taken me to the medics after the battle, but there'd been so much else going on, I hadn't thought about it.

"Neither do we, particularly," she agreed. "You're both officers because of OCS, and OCS exists because we *need* good officers with combat experience. Now more than ever. You may or may not have heard, but we lost two full companies of droptroopers on this mission before anyone touched the ground."

"Shit," I hissed. I had *not* heard that.

"And we have the Security Command siphoning even more recruits away from the Marines...." She sighed. "It's all a fucking mess, Lieutenant. So, what we'd really like to do is get everyone to drop this. Just pretend it never happened." She chuckled. "I know that sort of goes against my job description, but we have a war to win."

"I never wanted to file a report in the first place," I told her. "I only did it because of what Captain Cronje is trying to do to me."

"If I can convince Captain Cronje to drop this whole thing," she said, waving a hand demonstratively as if to show me what 'this whole thing' was, "would you be willing to do the same?"

"Of course, ma'am."

Being honest with myself if not her, I wasn't happy about it. Maybe Cronje had panicked, made a bad call without having all the information, but the fact was, he was responsible for securing those civilians and if he'd done his job, a whole fire team worth of Marines would still be alive.

But like I'd told Vicky not that long ago, this was war, and shit happened in war, and I didn't have to like it, I just had to do my job.

"All right then," Hofstetter said, pressing her palms against the table and coming to her feet. "In that case, I don't think there's any reason you should have to stick around here any longer. Come with me, and I'll have the MP's give you a ride back to your unit."

I rose to follow her, something between relief and disappointment warring inside my chest for supremacy. At least it was over.

Except of course, it wasn't. Not even close.

[6]

The MP's didn't get the chance to drive me back: Captain Covington stalked into the waiting area the second I emerged from the interrogation room, the expression on his face deadlier than the business end of the pulse carbine slung over his shoulder. The two Military Police NCO's who'd been escorting me stopped where they were, sensing now would be a good time to be somewhere else.

"How'd you know they were letting me out, sir?" I asked, trying to make sure he *did* know that and wasn't just here to start busting heads. As much as I didn't want to get thrown in the brig, I *really* didn't want the Skipper thrown into the brig on my account.

"Commander Hofstetter sent word," he said, the corner of his mouth curling into something between a smile and a snarl. "I happened to be in the area. Come on, let's get you out of here before Brigade changes its mind again."

I opened my mouth to say I didn't think that was likely, but shut it again immediately. How the hell would I know what was likely after everything that had happened in what Hofstetter had referred to as my short career. It didn't *feel* short. In fact, it felt as if it had lasted the better part of my life.

The MP's in the Provost Marshal's office stared at us as we left, as if the story had already filtered down through the ranks and become legend...or maybe it was just the Skipper who was a legend. I tried to see him as they did and found it was difficult to do it anymore. When I'd first come to the unit, he'd been unapproachable, a boogeyman both to the enemy and any Marine luckless enough to fuck up in his presence. I'd rarely spoken to him, and the few times he spoke to me, it seemed as if his words were the pronouncements of the prophets.

Now, of course, I worked with him every day, and while he still retained something of the larger-than-life nature, I'd grown accustomed to it and he felt more like the head of a family than a cartel crime boss. Sometimes, granted, the very testy and exacting head of a dysfunctional family of former criminals and misfits, but still a family.

Top was outside, leaning against the side of a lightly-armored utility rover, the pulse carbine propped on her hip daring any of the passing military cops to say anything about her parking. If Captain Covington was the father figure of our family, the First Sergeant was a real mother.

"How'd you get your hands on the rover?" I wondered. "I thought Brigade had all the ones we brought down locked up."

"Don't ask questions when you'd be better off not knowing the answers, Lieutenant," Top told me, pulling open the driver's door and sliding behind the wheel.

I got in the back and I expected the Skipper to climb up front with Top, but he clambered into the rear with me, then smacked the back of the front seat. Top didn't acknowledge it, but she hit the accelerator and peeled away from the repurposed Tahni military base in a spray of gravel.

"Hey, slow down!" an MP NCO yelled at us, his whiney

voice audible through the open windows over the hum of the motors.

Top sped up.

"That backstabbing, self-centered little prick," Covington muttered, and I was fairly sure he wasn't talking about the speed-conscious cop. "I can't believe he's pulling this shit after you pulled his balls out of the fire. He totally fucked up that operation, getting his people pinned down by the fixed defenses on that bunker. If he'd properly scouted the situation, he could have called in an airstrike before the drop-ships cleared the zone."

I didn't want to question Alpha's performance on the objective because Vicky Sandoval and Freddy Kodjoe had both been part of it, and blaming Cronje would rub off on them, so I kept my mouth shut.

"Then to try to do this to one of *my* platoon leaders...," he trailed off, jaw clenching. I don't believe I'd ever seen him this angry before. He was a man who rarely showed emotion, and I sometimes thought it was because he'd seen everything you could experience in the Marines and nothing surprised him enough to make him truly angry. Not this time, though.

We were driving out of the secure area now, through what had been designated, for some reason, Route Tampa, a road from the military base, through the edge of the Tahni government sector to the industrial district and the spaceport. I didn't understand the reference and hadn't had time to look it up. There were young Tahni males out along the road, not quite of military age but close, the ones who'd have been going through their version of basic training within a year or two. They lined the route, hands filled with bits of cement block and bricks.

Through the ridged brows and the flattened nose and ears, through the shovel-like jaws and everything that made them different than us, the universal look of adolescence shown through, the smoldering fire of kids on the verge of adulthood who thought they were so much tougher than what life had to throw at them. I saw myself in those dark and angry eyes.

Top handed me a pulse carbine back over the top of the seat.

"If any of those fuckers start throwing rocks at us, shoot at their feet," she told me.

I nestled the weapon into my shoulder and checked the safety, then propped the emitter in the open window. I hoped it didn't come to that, because I wasn't at all confident enough in my aim with the carbine to be sure I would miss them.

"They're too stupid to know when they've been beat," Top added, jerking the wheel to the left to avoid one of them who stepped partway onto the pavement. She slowed down as they crowded into the road, trying not to hit them.

"So are we, sometimes, Ellen," Covington said quietly. I was a bit shocked to hear him use Top's first name. It seemed akin to a child walking in on their parents having sex. "Maybe that's why we wound up fighting each other."

Something banged hard against the left side of the car and I twisted backwards, trying to find the one who'd thrown it, but it seemed like a signal to the others and debris began to rain down, most of the missiles bouncing off the pavement.

"Goddammit," Top bit off, "I gotta turn this thing back in."

I didn't try to aim, just jammed down the trigger pad and swept the emitter sideways in a line about three meters from the side of the rover. The carbine shuddered against my shoulder, the HiPex chemical hyperexplosive cartridges igniting in the chamber and pulsing their heat energy through the lasing rod. The pulses themselves were invisible, but the intense energy ionized the air around them into a crackling tube of plasma, like miniature forks of lightning. The light show did nothing, but the bursts of focused light blew spectacular holes in the road surface, spraying white-hot bits of debris backwards into the wayward juveniles.

They cried out, their yells sounding like someone had recorded a group of human teens shouting and then played it back at half-speed. The group scattered, rushing away from the roadside, some of them with their clothes still smoking from the splash of vaporized pavement. Top goosed the accelerator and the rover leapt like it had been shot out of a cannon, taking advantage of the opening. She stuck her head out of the open window and looked back down the side of the vehicle, swearing into the slipstream.

"Little bastards scratched the paint. Now I'm going to have to sneak this thing back into the motor pool at night and exfil tactically instead of just walking out like I signed the car out and was dropping it back off."

"You know you were going to sneak it back anyway," Covington told her. He hadn't said anything during the incident with the rock-throwing juveniles, nor had he taken a shot with his carbine. "Makes you feel like you're still a private walking point."

I blew out a breath and settled back in the seat, switching on the safety. There was a pouch full of spare magazines on the floor, and I ejected the partially-spent one and reloaded.

"Do you think I did the right thing?" I asked, still staring at the road.

"You didn't kill any of them," Top assured me. "Maybe gave a few some nasty burns to remember the day by."

"That's not what I meant, Top," I told her, and I was surprised at the impatience in my tone. I was a butterbar, and Second Lieutenants didn't get mouthy with Master Gunnery Sergeants. Not if they wanted to keep their ass intact.

"I know what you meant, boy," she said, not sounding angry. "You've been around this block. You've seen more than Cronje ever will, had to make decisions he'll never have to face. So, you tell me. Did you do the right thing?"

"I thought I did before I talked to Commander Hofstetter," I admitted. "The way she laid it out, though, it sounded a lot like I didn't. Like I was hotheaded and stupid."

"She's a lawyer," Covington spoke up, finally. "She gets paid to make reality conform to the accepted narrative. That's why everyone hates lawyers."

"Even their own lawyer," Top added.

"There's only so much we can control in combat, Cam," Covington went on, ignoring the joke. "Things are being thrown at us and we work with the information we have because hesitation can mean disaster. Maybe there was some other way you could have prevented Lt. Kodjoe's platoon from carrying out Cronje's illegal order, but what good would it have done if you'd thought of it after they'd already killed all the civilians?"

"Wouldn't that apply to Captain Cronje too?" I asked. "I mean, he made a call based on what he knew. Maybe he was just doing what he thought was right."

"I might believe that if I didn't know Greg Cronje. The man's sloppy, and I used to think it was on purpose, that he was too loose and too relaxed because he knew he wasn't that good of a leader and wanted his Marines to love him anyway. But now I know it's more than that. He's mentally lazy. He gets fixated on one tactic, one way of doing things and won't look aside to the left or right. He had it in his head that the only way to stop his people getting killed was to kill the civilians to get to the insurgents. But there was no imminent threat to his Marines. All he had to do was withdraw from the warehouse, set up a perimeter and order his people to fire on any vehicles that tried to leave." Covington shrugged. "Of course, it would have taken longer, wouldn't have looked as efficient, and he'd already fucked up the mission. He got impatient, sloppy, and when it all blew up on him, he blamed you for being the one to point out his mistake."

He speared me with a stern look.

"I'll tell you this, *Second Lieutenant* Alvarez, if I had to choose one of the two of you to take over this company in combat, I would take you over *Captain* Cronje every day of the week."

"Unfortunately," Top interjected, "we're not the only ones you have to worry about."

"What?" I blurted. "You mean the JAG lawyers? The Provost Marshal?"

"She means Alpha Company, son," Covington told me. "This war is far from over, and we're going to be working beside them the whole way. I'm sure Lt. Sandoval isn't going to hold this against you, but the rest of them...." He shook his head. "It could get ugly. Fratricide ugly."

The hackles rose on my neck and I stared at him in disbelief.

"They wouldn't actually do that, would they?"

"I've seen it happen, more than once. Sometimes it was blatantly obvious and the guilty party went in the Freezer, punitive hibernation. They're still there as far as I know. Other times, all it took was pretending not to see what was going on one sector over, and no one could ever prove beyond a shadow of a doubt it had been intentional." He smiled thinly. "It's easy to get men and women conditioned to kill the enemy. It's a bit harder to make sure they remember who the enemy is."

"So, what should I do?" I asked, trying not to sound hopeless.

"Keep your head down and your mouth shut as much as possible," Top suggested. "Leave them be and let it die down, if Cronje will allow it. That's all you can do."

"And don't gossip about it," Covington suggested. "Not even with the other platoon leaders, not even with Lt. Sandoval. If one wrong word taken out of context gets back to Cronje, it could light this whole mess on fire."

"Gossiping isn't really my thing, sir," I said, chuckling.

"If anyone asks," he went on as if I hadn't spoken, "tell them the facts, what they could read if they looked up the after-action report. No opinions, nothing about who's at fault."

"Yes, sir," I said. "And you think that'll work?"

"Probably not," he admitted. "But it has a better chance than anything else."

"If that doesn't work," Top said, "there's always wall-to-wall counseling."

"Now, Master Gunnery Sergeant," Covington chided her, "company commanders do not go around punching each other over disagreements. At least not in the open where anyone can see it."

"Yes, Captain." She grinned. "Sorry, Captain. I must be thinking of *another* captain."

"Don't worry too much about it, Alvarez," Covington told me, apparently sensing I was getting freaked out. "The Tahni will probably kill you long before Cronje gets a chance to."

"Thank you, sir," I said, closing my eyes and letting my head lean back. "That makes me feel so much better."

[7]

The biggest problem with Port Harcourt, I decided, was that it didn't have any bars.

It didn't have any human population grateful for being rescued and eager to restart their prewar lives, reopening bars and restaurants and giving away free drinks to the Marines who came to patronize them before we made our way to the next planet. Those were all gone, those battles won, and now the planets we conquered were full of enemies, even the civilians. Maybe *especially* the civilians.

We huddled in our compounds and sent out surveillance drones and patrols and shuttle overflights, warning the Tahni in their own language not to oppose us and knowing they would. The Security Command had arrived three days after we'd rooted out the last organized military resistance, and we'd been happy as hell to turn over peacekeeping duties to them and stay in our occupied safe zones.

I just wished there was somewhere I could get a drink.

The mess hall was nearly empty at this time of night, well after dinner, but I had nothing else to do and didn't want to go back to the company area right now for fear someone would want to talk. That was all I'd done from the time I got back from Brigade, tell the same story over and over, first to Captain Covington and Top, then to Bang-Bang, and finally at dinner that night with the rest of the platoon leaders from Delta, who seemed to think I was like a celebrity now because I'd been arrested. I didn't have the heart to tell them it was far from the first time.

So, I sat alone at a table meant for a platoon and picked at leftover desert. I never really liked chocolate that much, but they'd gone to so much trouble to bring it along on the ship that I thought I should give it a go. I was trying to decide if I had been hasty in my childhood judgment of the confection or if maybe I was just desperate enough for anything not made of soy and algae and the boredom was making it taste better when Freddy Kodjoe walked into the mess and interrupted my train of thought.

He stared at me for a long moment, silent, and I stared right back. I didn't know what to say to the man. We'd been best buds at OCS, and if anyone had asked me, I would have said we'd be friends for life, but now I felt like we'd become strangers in the few months since we'd left, and perhaps worse in just the last few days.

"Why'd you do it, Cam?" he asked me, stepping closer. He was tense, the muscles in his shoulders bunched like he was barely controlling himself. "Why would you do that to me?"

"I didn't do anything to you, Freddy," I said, setting the remnants of a brownie back on the plate. "I was trying to keep you from doing something you'd regret later." I shook my head and leaned back in my chair, suddenly feeling very tired. "Look, it's been like four days since it happened and I spent most of the last ten hours at the Provost Marshal's office. How the hell did you even know I was here?"

"One of the squad leaders told me. And I'd like to know

how you managed to avoid getting sent straight back to Inferno for a court-martial." His lips skinned away from his teeth. "Because God knows, you deserve it."

I felt a muscle twitch in my cheek.

"If anyone was going to get court-martialed over this, it was you."

"What the fuck are you talking about?" he demanded, getting more combative with every second.

"Freddy, the JAG Corps can access our helmet recordings. They saw you order your Marines to kill those children. Cronje can claim he didn't hear me warning him about the civilians, that he didn't know what was going on, but you can't."

"I was following orders!" he insisted, rocking back like I'd punched him.

"That's not a defense against a war crime. You were following an illegal order, and your company commander might not have known that, but you did."

"If you'd just done what you were told, no one would have gotten in trouble!"

Okay, he was doubling down on the whole following orders thing, and I didn't think I was going to be able to reason with him. Time to just bail out.

"No one *is* in trouble," I told him. "It's all over with, as long as Captain Cronje agrees to drop it."

"So, you're going to use that to try to get out of the shit?" he accused, nodding slowly, as if he'd figured me out. "Blackmail him by saying I'll be charged if he goes through with it?"

"Brigade is telling him to drop it." I stood and carried my tray to the recycler. "I'm not doing a damned thing except getting out of here and going to bed."

Freddy stopped me with a hand against my chest.

"I won't forget this," he warned me. "Neither will anyone in my company. You better hope you don't need any of us to save your ass out here, because we might just have better things to do."

I smacked his hand away and stepped past him, not even bothering to respond. He was angry, and angry people say stupid things. It probably wasn't worth the effort to let him know just making a threat like that was a court-martial offense.

I stalked out into the night. At least I didn't need a jacket here, not like Hachiman. The Tahni tended to prefer warmer, more humid planets, and Port Harcourt was no exception. It wasn't Inferno levels of humid, though, and at night, it was fairly temperate, and my field utility fatigues felt pretty comfortable.

Usually. But I was sweating, my face burning, whether from embarrassment or rage, I couldn't tell. Freddy had been my friend. One judgement call, one decision about what was wrong and what was right, and suddenly, he didn't care if I lived or died.

Was this what being an officer was all about? Why the hell had I ever agreed to go to OCS?

I was so wrapped up in my thoughts, I didn't even realize how far I'd walked. The mess hall was near Battalion Headquarters, and the route back to the barracks led through several blocks of industrial buildings destroyed in the battle. Rubble had been bulldozed into piles and marked off with bright, yellow warning tape to keep us from tripping over it, but there was no street lighting. Whatever the Tahni had used had been ripped out by the violence of the battle, and if anything replaced it, the Security Command and the Fleet Engineers would be the ones to install it long after we were gone.

I was walking through pitch darkness, the only lights the pale, yellow glow of the barracks in the distance, leakage through doors and windows sealed against the humidity and the insects, which didn't bite but buzzed about annoyingly around any light source. The hum of the portable air conditioning units was an insectoid whine of its own against the buzz of the alien bugs, lulling me into a torpor.

I hadn't, I realized, reclaimed my carbine from Captain Covington yet. He'd stuck it in his office when the MP's had taken me away and there'd been so much to talk about when I'd returned that neither of us had thought about it. I should meet with him tomorrow and get it back.

The thought had barely made a casual amble through my head when I saw the three figures step out of the shadows of a single section of wall that was all left standing from a wrecked building. They were human. I could tell that from the shape, and I let go the breath that had caught in my throat. The relief faded when I got closer and could make out their faces.

I didn't know the other two men, but the tall one in the center was Jared Butler, an E5 buck sergeant, one of Freddy's squad leaders. I'd seen him talking to the man a few days ago on the *Iwo Jima* before we launched for the operation. I assumed the other two were in his squad and they all had the look of men who had joined the Marines after being given the same choice I had: go to war or go to jail.

Butler moved out to block my way and I started to walk around him, ready to run if I had to, but the other two spread out and cut off my avenues of egress, just like we were in battle.

"Those guys who died," Butler said without so much as an attempt to conceal why he was there, "they were my friends. The ones those Tahni shitbags killed. The ones you tried to protect."

"Get out of my way, Sergeant Buter," I told him, trying to keep my tone firm and calm. "I'm tired and I want to hit the rack."

"I bet it is tiring, Lieutenant," he said, mouth curling in a sneer that turned his ugly face into something even uglier, "spending all day ratting on your fellow Marines."

I could have pointed out to him that I'd spent all day with the MP's and the JAG lawyers because Captain Cronje had tried to rat *me* out, but I knew it would have been an even bigger waste of time than it had been with Freddy. Not only was this guy not inclined to listen, he was too stupid to make the distinction. He was one of those Marines who'd topped out at squad leader and would never, ever move higher, no matter how long the war lasted or how many other people above him got killed.

I let my eyes flicker across the three men. They were unarmed, so at least there was that much. All three were bigger than me, but I didn't know how much actual fighting they'd ever had to do. Strength and size are important in a fight, but experience is the real key, all other factors not being too far unbalanced. Knowing what's it's like being hit in the face and not panicking about it is half of winning a fight.

Still, there *were* three of them...

"Butler," I said, "I want to point something out to you that you might not have thought through completely. You think I'm a snitch, an informer. And yet, you're trying to intimidate me, maybe even assault me, when I'm a superior officer and if I *did* snitch about it, you'd all wind up in the brig for the rest of the war."

"Naw, man," Butler said, laughing, cracking his knuckles in a way that only idiots thought was intimidating. Though it did make me want to crack my knuckles too, in the same way a yawn is contagious. "Ain't got no helmet cameras to show to the pigs here. It's just us, and our word against yours." He leered. "And the word of some of our officers who'll swear we were back at the barracks all night long."

Ah. So, this wasn't just an asshole and his two asshole buddies taking it on themselves to teach me a lesson. This came straight from Cronje. That made things much more complicated. I began looking the three men up and down for weak spots. I was going to get hit, probably going to get hurt, and I wanted to make sure I did as much damage to them as I could in the process.

"Where you from, Butler?" I asked him, trying to distract him from what was about to happen. The less he thought about it, the less prepared he'd be. "Not Trans-Angeles, I can tell that by your accent."

"I'm from Houston 'Plex," the big man said, sounding proud of it. "Ciudad Perdida, the 416's."

The Greater Houston Metropolitan Complex, if he'd wanted to be exact, one of three megacities in what used to be the state of Texas, along with DallasWorth and Nuevo El Paso, though that one included parts of old Mexico as well. Not that anyone in Mexico cared. Ciudad Perdida was the Underground neighborhood, 416 was the housing block, and probably his gang affiliation. I didn't know them. The gangs in Trans-Angeles didn't consider any other cities as having real gangs, just violent social clubs.

"What did you do to get yourself enlisted?" I wondered, turning slowly, the three of them moving to keep me at the center. "Must have been pretty serious. Not just holding contraband or shaking down the kiosks for protection. Guy like you would have taken the ride just for the street cred. No, I'm guessing you hurt somebody bad." I sneered at him. "Probably a woman, which was why you took the Marines instead of the ride, because no one in your 416's would respect you for hurting a woman."

There was a twitch in his face, a break in the tough-guy mask he was trying to wear, and I knew I'd scored. Unfortunately, making him lose his cool and not think also made him lose his cool and not think. He lunged at me, an awkward, wild swing, the kind of punch a man throws when he's never fought someone who knew what they were doing. He'd had unarmed combat training in Basic, but that was a long time ago and, unlike the Recon Marines, Drop Troopers didn't have to maintain proficiency in it...unless we wanted to.

I slapped the punch aside, stepping to the outside and pushing. Butler stumbled forward, trapped by his own momentum, losing his balance, and I helped him along with a side-kick to the outside of his thigh. He squawked like a toddler getting their first spanking and clutched at his leg, collapsing to the ground, cursing loud enough to wake people a kilometer away. It hurt getting kicked in the big nerve on the outside of the thigh, the common peroneal. It would hurt him for a couple days, most likely, and he wouldn't be walking on it very well for at least a few minutes.

The other two looked gobsmacked like they hadn't expected me to actually put up a fight, being nothing but a pansy butterbar second lieutenant and all, but they shook it off and began to move in.

"You two shitbags might want to consider your next move carefully."

The voice was unmistakable, though I hadn't known its owner all that long. Gunnery Sgt. Bang-Bang Morrell stepped out of the shadows, hands by his sides, arms loose like he was ready to throw down.

"There are *so* many reasons why you might want to get the hell out of here," he went on, staring the two enlisted men down. "First of all, I'm now a witness who could put you here as part of an attempted assault on a superior officer. Second, you can bet people *know* I'm here. And finally, if you think what Lt. Alvarez just did to your squad leader looks like it hurt, well, let me tell you something...it was a fucking love-tap. Butler fights like an eight-year-old and the LT could have killed him if he'd wanted. And no offense to Lt. Alvarez, but I am so much better a fighter than he'll ever be."

The two enlisted men looked at each other, then took off running the other direction.

"Maybe the first good decision either of those assholes has ever made," Bang-Bang mused.

Butler was trying to stand, keeping his weight on his good leg, eyes flickering back and forth between the two of us.

"You have a pretty clear choice here, Butler," I told him. "I am way too fucking tired to call the MP's and have you hauled away while I stay up the rest of the night filing a report, but you can either stick around and let Gunny Morrell laugh at you while I kick you around some more, or you can use whatever brains God saw fit to give you that you haven't pissed away already, and get your stupid ass out of here."

Butler didn't say a word, but the hatred on his face didn't change even as he limped back into the darkness. I watched him go, wary he might have a gun hidden somewhere back there, but he didn't come back.

"Come on, sir," Bang-Bang said, waving a hand. "I'll walk you back to the barracks so no more of the big, bad men pick on my helpless little platoon leader."

I barked a laugh and fell into step beside him. I noticed his eyes flickering back and forth as we walked, though, and I knew he'd been at least half-serious.

"How did you know?" I asked him. "How did you know where I'd be, and that they'd be coming after me?"

He snorted humorlessly.

"Sir, shit like that doesn't happen without someone talking about it. Even if Captain Cronje or his First Sergeant, Breed, pulled dipshit there...." He motioned back the way Butler had gone. "...into a back room and told him to keep his mouth shut, there's no fucking way he wouldn't brag about it to someone, or make the mistake of telling the two goons he brought with him where they were going and why. Someone heard, someone told me, and here I am." He shrugged. "I coulda brought the MP's, or I coulda brought a fire team with me, but I didn't think that was how you'd want to play it."

"You know me pretty well after just a few weeks, Gunny. Thanks for looking out for me."

"It's my job, sir."

He didn't say which of those was his job, but I wanted to think it was both.

I was making a mistake. I was sure of it. But it was just the sort of mistake I'd been making my whole life, and if you keep screwing up the same way that many years in a row, it ain't a bug, it's a feature.

It had taken a few questions, a couple days of quiet observation to get the intelligence I needed to carry out the mission, but Greg Cronje was a creature of habit, even huddled in our safe zone on an enemy-infested city. Every night at 2100 hours local time, he would walk alone from his quarters down to the latrine, however far it was in whatever base on whatever planet we were on, and take his daily dump. I was frankly surprised he only took one per day, since he was so full of shit.

I'd taken a recon run on the path from Alpha Company living quarters down to the latrines earlier in the afternoon, so I knew just the right spot to wait. It would have been convenient if there'd still been a lot of wreckage scattered between the buildings, but the Fleet Engineers had come down with their industrial exoskeletons and cleared the whole area out just to make sure there was nowhere for the enemy to hide and take potshots at us. Unfortunately, one of their exoskeletons had broken down in the middle of the newly-empty lot where three walls of an industrial workshop had been the day before. It still stood there waiting for a repair crew, a sentinel watching over the ramshackle shithouse they'd dug out and set up the first night.

I leaned against the side of the engineering suit's tree-trunk leg, hidden in the shadows by the positioning of the portable floodlights, and examined the work of the Fleet Engineers with a critical eye. As shitters went, I'd definitely seen better. Sheet metal roof propped up on lifts a few centimeters off buildfoam walls with ventilation fans in the gap, and a plastic curtain door. It might have been a good setup on Hachiman, but here, it was humid, smelly, and crawling with the local insects, and I imagined for a man like Cronje who really valued his seat time, it had to be maddening.

I'd decided to make an anonymous complaint on the Brigade Morale Net and was running through the wording when Cronje ambled past me, hands stuffed in his pockets in a way that would have got him dropped for about a million pushups at OCS. He wasn't carrying a weapon because this was just a nice, friendly trip to the shitter and we were all friends in the Marine latrine.

I stepped out from cover and matched his steps from three meters back, wondering how long it would take him to notice. I'd bet myself that it would be at least ten seconds, and I was right. He spun around just two steps before the curtain door, going into a defensive stance as if Tahni ninjas were sneaking up on him.

"Nice form, sir," I said, arms folded across my chest. "You should offer to teach unarmed combat for the battalion officer corps."

He straightened, his face going red.

"What the hell do you want, Alvarez? Are you following me?"

"Oh, no, sir," I assured him. "I just had to take a dump. That's why you're here, isn't it? It's totally a coincidence. You know, it's funny, I coincidentally ran into three NCO's from one of your platoons the other night on the way back from the mess hall. It was so strange, they just happened to be sitting behind some of that rubble the Fleet Engineers cleared out, right on the way from the barracks to the mess hall. What are the odds?"

"If you have something you want to say to me, *Lieutenant*," he growled, "then I suggest you make a fucking appointment and come see me during the day."

"You know, that's a great idea, sir," I told him, shaking a finger in agreement. "I think if someone wants to deliver a message, they should do it personally, not send someone else. Because you never can count on a subordinate delivering the message you want. They just might not be up to the job."

He wanted to come after me, I could see it in his eyes. He took a half-step forward but stopped himself, teeth clenched, face turning so red I thought he might be having a stroke.

"You believe this, you worthless piece of shit, if I want to deliver any message to you, I'll do it myself, and you won't have any trouble understanding it."

I grinned, showing him nothing but a cool exterior, but inside, my guts were churning, every fiber of my being wanting nothing more than to beat the living shit out of him. I thought I could do it. He was mouthy, way too loud and talkative for someone who actually knew how to fight. He was an Academy grad, and most of them had never set foot in the Underground, *any* Underground in any city. He probably got into a shoving match in high school and thought that and a few martial arts classes meant he knew how to fight.

"If you have any messages to deliver to me, sir," I said, "I can't think of any better time than now for you to tell me. After all, I'm right here. It's just the two of us. Who knows when you'll have the opportunity again? You don't want to waste it, do you? Sir?"

Yeah, this was stupid. I was sure Bang-Bang, the Skipper, Vicky, *anyone* who I would have asked would have told me it was stupid. They would have told me I was risking a court-martial, getting busted in rank, maybe even going to the brig. Which was probably why I hadn't asked anyone, just decided to go do it.

But he was close, so very close to taking that first swing. His right fist was clenching, his left foot shifting, ready for that big right cross that most idiots who don't know how to fight try to throw to end everything with one punch.

The curtain barrier to the latrine slid open with a clatter of the plastic rings securing it to the metal rod across the doorway and Francis Kovacs stepped out, his shower kit clutched in his hand.

"Oh, hey, Alvarez," he said, stopping in his tracks. He did a double-take when he saw Captain Cronje. "Um, sir. Good evening." He looked between the two of us. "I'm sorry, was I interrupting something?"

Cronje hissed out a sigh.

"No. I just need to take a shit."

He brushed past Kovacs and stalked into the latrine. I let the breath I'd been holding rush out, the tension going out of my shoulders.

"You taking a shit too?" Kovacs wondered, looking confused.

"No," I told him, disappointment heavy in the words as I turned away. "I suppose I'm not."

———

"I can't say I'm sorry to see the last of this place," Bang-Bang told me, arms crossed, watching the power loaders marching up the ramp of the cargo shuttle with the final pieces of our maintenance equipment in their grasp like ants carrying food to the nest.

Behind us, our platoon and the rest of Delta Company was busy packing our personal gear into pallets to be loaded after the maintenance racks. We'd take the battlesuits with us onto our drop-ships, wearing it because this wasn't a secure base where we could be sure it would be an unopposed lift-off.

"You said it, Gunny." But I wasn't watching our shuttles or our people.

Less than half a kilometer down from our position, Alpha was loading up their shit, and it seemed like all my problems were there with them. I couldn't see Cronje from here, and he might be at a battalion meeting for all I knew, since I hadn't seen Captain Covington for an hour or so, either. But Freddy was out front of his platoon, directing Marines here and there and generally trying to make himself look useful. It was a rookie move, and one I'd known was a waste of time and energy back when I'd been a squad leader, thanks to the good example of Lt. Ackley, my first platoon leader. The enlisted knew what to do and the NCO's would make sure they did it. As an officer, my job was to make sure it was getting done, not to direct every move.

Vicky was doing it the right way, observing from the edges, here and there darting in to spot-check someone's work. She was my other problem. Or rather, the lack of her. It had been a solid week since the incident with Sgt. Butler and I hadn't heard anything else from Alpha Company since, which would have been fine if it hadn't included Vicky. I hadn't pushed it, though. I understood the predicament she was in and I'd told her to lay low and stay away from me until things smoothed over.

I just didn't know when that would be.

"Lt. Alvarez."

I spun on my heel at the voice coming from where there'd been no one a moment ago and nearly had a heart attack before I realized it was Top. Delta Company First Sergeant Ellen Campbell's forehead came up to my nose and she probably weighed fifty kilos, but I would have picked her in any fight in or out of the armor. She'd been in the Marines since before the beginning of the Commonwealth, on and off, and she was probably the oldest person I'd ever met. I figured that meant she came from money, because the only people back in those days who could afford the anti-aging treatments were rich, but I'd never dared to ask her about it.

"Yes, First Sergeant?" I said, trying not to act as if I'd just about jumped out of my skin, but the quirk at the corner of her mouth told me she knew.

"Captain Covington wants to talk to you," she said, nodding back to the other side of the shot-up storage building where my platoon was packing up.

"Right."

That was odd. If the Skipper wanted to talk to me, why hadn't he just called me on my 'link? And why would he send Top? That was like sending the managing partner of a restaurant to go refill drinks. I shrugged it off and kept walking, figuring I'd find out soon enough.

Covington was waiting for me around the corner, just out of sight of the loading area...and so was Commander Hofstetter. She was still in her dress uniform, and I wondered if she even owned a set of utility fatigues.

"Commander," I said, nodding to her, hoping she understood that we didn't salute in the field.

"I'll leave you to talk," Covington said, turning on his heel.

"Sorry for the subterfuge," Hofstetter told me, "but I didn't know if you'd have time to make it to Brigade before you left, and I figured it would be better not to walk out there in front of everyone to have this conversation."

"A conversation you didn't want to have over our 'links either," I assumed. My stomach muscles tightened the way they did when I was dropping into combat in my Vigilante.

"Let's just say that Brigade would be happier if there were as little record of any of this as possible."

She motioned for me to follow her and we paced farther away from the working Marines, probably to avoid one of them walking around the side of the building to take a piss break. And they would, because Marines were only a step above the street people I'd run with as a kid when it came to personal hygiene.

"This didn't go quite as smoothly as we would have liked," she admitted. She scowled. "Captain Cronje is a stubborn, stupid son of a bitch, though you didn't hear that from me. He kept insisting that he still wanted to press charges against you and finally I had to tell him that his only alternatives were to drop the charges or wind up with a sure-fire, no-bullshit letter of reprimand in his file and a court-martial for Lt. Kodjoe, and that was if I wasn't in a bad mood and didn't decide to take my chances and include him on the court-martial, too." She snorted a laugh. "That part was a bluff, of course. You're about to ship out to the biggest battle of the war so far, and there was no way Brigade was going to lose one of their company commanders at this point." She shrugged. "But he caved, so I suppose I am not as bad of a poker player as my ex-husband used to tell me I was."

"So, it's over?" I suppose the question was hopeful, but to my ears, I sounded desperate.

"The legal part's over," she corrected me. "I have a feeling there's a personal aspect to this that won't be settled for a while."

"You don't know the half of it." I gave her a short version of what had happened on the way back from the mess hall, leaving off the names.

"That fucking moron," she spat, fists balling up as if she wanted to get into a fight herself. "Now I wish I'd actually gone ahead and given him that letter of reprimand." She blew a heavy breath out through her nose. "Well, hell, I find myself kind of envying you your job, where you can just blow your enemies away with a plasma gun."

"Not all of them," I told her. I offered her a hand. "Thanks for everything you did, Commander. I appreciate it."

She took my hand and grasped it in a tight, dry grip for a moment, but then let it slip out, as if the air was going out of her.

"I feel like I didn't do much. I certainly didn't do my job. I just swept things under the rug."

"Ma'am, our job is to win the war. And if keeping Captain Cronje as Alpha Company commander wins the war, I guess you're doing your job."

She smiled thinly, obviously not accepting the excuse but grateful for the attempt.

"Good luck, Lieutenant. I have a feeling in a few weeks, you're going to look back on this as the easy part."

I laughed long and hard at that, an honest, open laugh.

"Commander," I told her, shaking my head, "we're Marines. The only easy day was yesterday."

[9]

"You're probably wondering why," Colonel Voss said, "we're having this briefing on board ship, in this very uncomfortable place, instead of back on Port Harcourt."

I was, in fact. And it was definitely uncomfortable as shit. There was a whole battalion of us jammed into the hangar bay of the *Iwo Jima*, and it was a tight squeeze, because there were also a bunch of drop-ships, assault shuttles, loading equipment and cargo pallets competing for the space. And we were in Transition, which meant the artificial gravity was activated, so space in this case meant deck space, which cut down on the possibilities even more. But it was the largest compartment on the ship and the only one where all of us could conceivably fit.

"The answer is operational security," Voss told us. She was standing on a makeshift platform at our center, constructed by the simple expedience of stacking four cargo pallets atop one another and then lifting her up on the hydraulic forks of a loading jack. "As unlikely as it is that we would miss a signal going out of Port Harcourt, the truth is, it was possible. And our next mission is simply too sensitive to let it leak to the enemy."

"And why couldn't we just get the op order sent to us in our company area?" Francis Kovacs whined from beside me, just the slightest bit too loud to be subtle, which was exactly Kovacs's style.

"Because this is how the Marines do it, Lt. Kovacs," Captain Covington admonished, a looming presence behind us for all that Kovacs was actually taller than him. "Though if you have that strong an opinion on how battalion mission briefs should be delivered, I'm sure I'd like to see a comprehensive multimedia presentation from you on the subject by the close of business today." He smiled thinly. "On my 'link, of course, so we do it efficiently and don't waste time."

"Yes, sir," Kovacs said, gulping the words out. Poor son of a bitch couldn't take a piss without stepping on his dick.

Voss pointed her 'link at the overhead, which in the case of the ship's hangar bay was *way* overhead, and a holographic projector mounted up there lit up the space just above her position with the image of a solar system. It was generic enough that I found myself agreeing with Kovacs that this was all a huge waste of time, but I kept my mouth shut.

Intelligence, my mother had once said, was learning from your mistakes, while wisdom was learning from the mistakes of others, and I hoped I was, at least, wiser than Francis Kovacs.

"This," Voss went on, "is the last occupied system along the Transition Line between Port Harcourt and Tahn-Skyyiah. It's the last steppingstone on our journey to defeating the enemy and bringing this war to an end, once and for all. The Tahni name for it is irrelevant, because once we move in and take it, we'll be using *our* name for it and theirs will only matter to the history books."

Well, *that* was probably hubris, but I had to give it to her, it made even my cynical soul stir with a bit of ooh-rah.

"We call it Point Barber."

Red icons jumped out at us from the inner system, clustered

around a habitable world, the second out from the primary star. It had twin moons, captured asteroids by the size and look of them, and each had yet more of the glowing red, which I knew meant weapons emplacements.

"As you can see, the whole system is heavily defended, both with fixed weapons platforms and the largest fleet we are likely to see in any battle of this conflict, larger than what we'll find at the Tahni homeworld. Because the enemy knows the same thing we do: we have to take Point Barber to win this war. Their numbers and type of their ground defenses are unknown as of yet, but we expect them to be at least as bad as what we found on Port Harcourt, and probably worse."

Another touch on her 'link and a wave of blue appeared on top of the red.

"Which is why the Commonwealth is holding nothing back."

I saw the largest of the blue icons and my hand shot up, almost of its own accord. I don't know how she saw it, but she did.

"Yes, Lieutenant?" Her voice was cold, as if she really hadn't wanted to be interrupted and least of all by me.

"Ma'am, are there *eight* cruisers on that display?" I asked.

"There are, Lt. Alvarez." She smiled, and a bit of the chill went out of her tone.

"I thought we only had five!"

"That's probably what the Tahni think, as well, Lt. Alvarez. But the shipyards have not been idle while we fought our war at ground level." Oh, good Lord, that sounded like a line she'd written for a presentation to the general staff. "We will have basically the entire fleet, which is another reason for the security surrounding this operation. If the Tahni were to find out we've left the Solar System undefended, this could prove to be the worst disaster in human history. That's the gamble we're taking, and we're throwing everything into the pot. We've received reinforcements from the Training Brigade at Inferno and we will be striking Point Barber with six full battalions of Drop-Troopers." She shrugged, as if the next part wasn't as important. "As well as five battalions of Force Recon."

The image shifted at her manipulation and we were looking at a view from far above a massive city, not nearly as big as Trans-Angeles or Capital City, but as large as Tartarus, the military base on Inferno, or even Hesperides, the capital on Eden, Inferno's more temperate twin sister. But the size seemed almost irrelevant compared to the strangeness of the design, the shape of the buildings, the arrangement of the streets and green belts. It looked as if it had been designed by a toddler savant, who somehow understood how to operate an AI architectural engineering program without actually grasping why humans used buildings or how they should be organized. Except for the spaceport, the design of which was dictated by practicality, since cargo shuttles and landers needed a large, flat area to put down and a certain sort and size of machinery to unload them.

And one other area, catty-corner to the spaceport, where the structures were boxy and ugly in their stark pragmatism. Deflector dishes surrounded the city, giving it full coverage from overhead bombardment, though I wouldn't have wanted to live in the clusters of what looked like communal housing at the outskirts. Probably where the females had their enclaves, if our intelligence analysts were right.

"This is the closest image of the capital city on Point Barber that we've been able to acquire from Scout Service drones before Tahni vessels detected and destroyed them. The city has a Tahni name, too, but we're calling it Target Delta, or Deltaville if you find that too impersonal. If you'll note the square structures near the spaceport, you've probably already guessed that these are their military barracks." The optical-spectrum image switched to a thermal filter and the buildings lit up in various shades of yellow, orange and red. "There's a lot of energy signatures in these buildings." She raised an eyebrow. "A *lot*. And that could mean older, second-tier forces with tanks and armored vehicles, or it could mean the largest collection of High Guard battlesuits and fire-support mechs we've ever seen. Together with the sheer number of deflector dishes and four separate fusion reactor power plants to feed them, this will be a ground battle until we clear the ground."

The deflectors and the thermal readings that I assumed were fusion reactors morphed into wire-drawing, each lit up red on the screen.

"Our targets will be the deflectors and the fusion reactors which power them. Our battalion will be split into four parts during this operation. Bravo, Charlie, and Echo will each be assigned one of the deflector dishes and the anti-aircraft batteries surrounding them. Alpha and Delta will be leading a strike on the fusion reactor connected to those deflectors, together with a full company of Force Recon. You'll hold the enemy armor off until the Force Recon units can take down the reactor." Her eyebrow quirked upward. "And yes, I am aware those missions are redundant, and yes, it *is* because we don't expect both of them to succeed in the face of opposition we expect. Ladies and gentlemen, I won't bullshit you. There *will* be heavy casualties. Some of you will not be coming back from this battle. Now is not the time to indulge in petty, personal differences. Put that shit behind you and pull together, because we need each other now more than ever."

I grunted, feeling like that had been a swipe directly at Cronje and me and I wondered how many other people got it.

She swiped her hand across her 'link and the hologram faded away as if it had never been.

"Point Barber is a big planet, but most of the ground

defenses are clustered around the capital, Deltaville. The Tahni aren't big on decentralization, and they figure, rightly to some extent, that gathering all their forces in one place will mean we have to go there to meet them. Conversely, this also means that taking this one city is the key to the success of the invasion." She held up a hand as if she'd sensed a question was about to be asked. "And before someone brings it up, yes, the high command *has* considered bypassing this planet and going straight on to Tahn-Skyyiah, and no, they aren't going to. Why? Complicated question involving morale, alien psychology, and a bunch of other things above my pay grade. It's not our concern. We have a job to do, and we're going to do it."

"We should just drop a damned rock on the bunch of them like the bugs they are."

Cronje. He'd said it way too loud, not like an aside to another Marine that I'd just happened to overhear, but like a challenge to Voss...and to me. I felt his stare boring into me, but I didn't bother to look up at him. It was what he wanted.

He wasn't through, either. I think Voss would have ignored him too if he'd just shut up right then. But Cronje was Cronje, and shutting up wasn't in his genetic code.

"I don't mind dying to kill these bastards, but no Marine should die trying to save them."

Now I did look up. I couldn't help myself, the same way I'd stared at drunks wandering down the street outside our house at night back in Tijuana, knowing they were going to trip or crash into a wall and yet unable to look away. He was still focused on me, though his words had obviously been projected at Colonel Voss.

"You have your orders," Voss said, her voice a gavel falling, and she might have been addressing all of us, but she was staring daggers at Cronje. "Follow them or you'll be replaced by someone who can."

———

The blinking icon on my 'link begged for my attention, but I resisted its temptation, giving into the lethargy that kept me in my bunk when I really should have been getting ready for tomorrow's simulation runs. I knew what it was. The notification on the screen told me that. I'd received an InStell message while we were on Port Harcourt, but it hadn't been cleared through the Fleet censors until we'd Transitioned. Now it waited impatiently to be opened and I just wasn't sure I wanted to know who it was from.

There were a vanishing small number of people who knew who the hell I was and cared enough to send an expensive transmission bouncing between relay satellites from one system to another via wormholes and Transitioning starships. It might have been one of the Marines from my platoon at OCS, or it might have been Trent, my roommate at Armor School. And they were all good people, but I wasn't in the mood for a long "hey buddy, how you doing?" message telling me how they were going to use their separation bonus on escort services and a brand new Sport Flyer when they got out after the war.

I didn't want to talk to anyone but Vicky, and Vicky wasn't talking.

"Fuck it," I murmured aloud.

I shared the cabin with William Cano, Fourth Platoon leader, but he was out with Kovacs, finding something illicit to drink, which was both easier and harder as an officer. Easier because you could get away with it, harder because you couldn't let the enlisted know you were getting away with it.

I touched the blinking icon on the screen, then cast the message to the big display on the cabin bulkhead across from the bunks. Dak Shepherd's image appeared and I sat up, almost gasping. I hadn't seen the man nor heard from him since Brigantia. I'd been a newly-minted corporal at the time, made a team leader for my sins so I could learn some responsibility for others. Then everyone in my fire team and half the company had died in the drop and I'd wound up stranded in enemy territory with no suit, no weapons, no support, nothing but an acute case of agoraphobia.

Dak had found me and taken me back to the civilian resistance against the Tahni occupation, and I'd met Maria, his daughter. She'd been twenty years older than me, widowed, her teenaged daughter lost along with her husband during the Tahni invasion, and she had no reason to feel anything but disdain for a city boy who could barely walk outside without having a panic attack. But she'd befriended me, shown me compassion, a human connection I'd been missing. And she might have saved my soul.

I couldn't save her. She'd died in the resistance attack to take down the deflector shield and allow the Marines to land. I'd almost died, too, and when I'd woken up in the hospital to find Dak waiting for me, I wished I had. But he hadn't blamed me for her death. Instead, he'd offered me a home. He'd founded the colony and he wanted me to have a place to go back to if I lived through this war.

I hadn't talked to him since, not because I didn't want to, but because I still didn't know what to say to the man. Should I tell him I found someone? That if I returned to Brigantia, I'd be bringing a replacement for his daughter? Should I tell him I'd gotten revenge for Maria? That I'd killed more Tahni than he'd ever seen on his world? She hadn't wanted revenge for her lost family, she'd wanted freedom for her neighbors, and she'd died for it. I doubt she would have cared, and I knew he wouldn't.

I touched an arrow-shaped button and the recording played.

"Heya, Cam," Dak said, his voice as rough and raspy as I remembered. "I hope this finds you well." He snorted and pulled off his brimmed hat, running a hand through his salt-and-pepper hair. "Hell, I hope it finds you alive. The official government net says you are, but you know as well as I do, they probably don't tell us about half the casualties you get."

That was the truth. Policy was that casualty figures weren't released publicly until the next-of-kin had been notified in person, which could take weeks or even months, depending on where they lived.

"But assuming I ain't wasting my breath, I called because, well, it's been too long. I saw on your file in the government site that you're an officer now." He smiled broadly, the expression sending the deep lines beside his mouth and eyes into sharp relief. "I guess that means you've gotten over that problem with trusting people."

I chuckled.

"Well, about that...," I murmured, suddenly wishing with all my heart that I could actually talk to the old man and not just pretend.

"I knew you would," he went on, nodding. "You have too much to offer to spend your life closed inside your shell, keeping the world out. That's no life for a man. It's no life for me. The real reason I'm calling you is that, I'm getting married."

It was almost as if he'd seen my mouth drop open, because he laughed at just the right time.

"Yeah, I know. I'm an old dog and I didn't think I'd ever learn any new tricks, but Hannah and I, we just sort of...got comfortable together. And my point being, if there's hope for me, if I can start over again, then you can...." He shook his head, searching for the right word. "...*start*. I don't know what you're going through, but whatever it is, however bad it gets, don't let it undo the good you've done. You can get through this and you *can* have a life when it's over. It's what Maria would have wanted for you. And if that life isn't here, just make sure it's somewhere you can call home." He reached out and cut the recording.

That was Dak. He'd said what he had to say and wasn't interesting in blathering on afterward like most people would. Most people didn't know how to say goodbye. I didn't turn the screen off, just left his image up there. It was a comfort, not so much the words he'd said, but the thought that there was someone out there who knew me that well and still cared about me.

Home, he'd said. He wanted me to have a place I could call home. But was home a place, or was it the people there? If I went back to Tijuana and found our old house, assuming someone hadn't already occupied it, it would have been nothing but a collection of mud and brick and wood without Momma and Poppa and Anton.

I don't know how long I sat there staring through his picture into the infinity on the other side of it, but only the knock on the hatch stirred me from the fugue. I blinked, unsure for a moment if I'd actually heard anything or if it was a waking dream, but the knock repeated. I pushed myself up from the bunk and opened the hatch, feeling a bit annoyed at whoever it was for not simply announcing their presence over the intercom.

It was Vicky.

"Hi," I said, stumbling over the word. "Is everything okay?"

"No," she said, her expression grim. "Can I come in?"

I stepped back from the hatchway and motioned her inside, then gave in to the paranoid urge to check the passageway behind her before I shut the door. She paced into the center of the compartment, arms folded over her chest.

"What's wrong, Vick?" I asked, wanting to touch her, wanting to wrap my arms around her but feeling a barrier between us I was afraid to broach.

"Cronje is insane." She turned on me as if she were making

an accusation, though at least I knew now the anger wasn't directed at me. "He's ranting and raving and calling me a traitor in front of the other officers, and Freddy isn't saying a damned thing to contradict him, either. I thought you two were friends."

"I thought we were, too." I leaned against the bulkhead, in one of the few spots not taken up by fold-down furniture. "I gotta be honest, Vicky, I'm not sure who my friends are anymore."

She reacted as if I'd slapped her, with a moment's shock followed by instantaneous anger.

"You *told* me to stay away from you till this blew over," she reminded me.

"It doesn't look like it's going to." I rubbed at my eyes, a dull ache developing behind them. "And we're about to drop into more shit than any of us have seen before, if you believe Colonel Voss."

"Oh, what the fuck does *she* know?" Vicky waved a hand in dismissal. "She hasn't fired a shot in anger this whole war. She started it as a staff officer and got her promotion to battalion commander because of her connections at Brigade Staff."

"I hadn't heard that," I admitted.

She sneered. "That's because your company commander doesn't get drunk and blather in front of his officers. Anyway, you're not wrong. It's not going away. Cronje is livid that Brigade forced him to drop the charges against you. He's mad at Freddy, too, for getting him into this mess, and Freddy's mad at me because I'm not going to throw you under the bus, but I think even he's beginning to see the problems with Cronje." She blew out a breath. "The bottom line is, I'm angry and I have the same bad feeling you do about this drop and I don't want to go into it angry at you, because I love you."

The words were a passcode, a key to the barriers that seemed to have grown between us over the last week and I pulled her into my arms and kissed her, all the negative emotions that had built up inside me turned into something else now.

"Come on," she said, pulling away but tugging me along with her by my hand.

"Where?" I asked, shaking my head.

She grinned. "My bunkmate is a Force Recon Lieutenant and she's got a thing with the *Iwo Jima*'s junior Navigation Officer. We'll have the compartment to ourselves for the night."

I followed, ignoring the nagging guilt. I should have been getting ready for the morning, but in the moment, nothing else seemed more important.

[10]

"Jesus H. Christ," Bang-Bang hissed.

I don't think he realized he was on the open platoon frequency, but I doubt he would have cared if he had. This was the closest I had ever come to shitting my pants from fear, and we hadn't even launched from the *Iwo Jima*.

"What is it, sir?" Majid asked, his voice tentative, like he wasn't sure he wanted to know. "What's happening out there?"

I had to remind myself that most junior NCO's didn't know the tricks I'd learned about accessing the Fleet tactical feed, and I wondered if I should tell him what Bang-Bang and I were seeing or just keep him in the dark. Then it might come as a surprise when he died, which I heard made it hurt less.

Because I knew with a more concrete certainty than I'd ever experienced before that we were going to die before we got anywhere near that fucking planet.

"Just a lot of ships, Majid," I lied.

I imagine if I'd just been looking at the optical feed from the drop-ship, it wouldn't have been as bad. Most of the details of a space battle are invisible to the naked eye, or even a camera with infrared and thermal filters. The Fleet tactical feed included lidar, radar, spectral analysis and gravimetic sensor readings, using the effects of moving mass on the Transition Lines within the system to build a picture of what was happening light-seconds or even light-minutes away before said light had a chance to reach us.

Most of the time, space battles, even the most pitched and violent ones I'd experienced, were spread-out affairs, with isolated skirmishes where a cluster of ships happened to emerge from T-space close enough to each other to use energy weapons but otherwise involving heavily-armored anti-ship missiles chasing down their prey while defensive weapons chipped away at their shields and sprayed ECM jamming their way.

Not this time. I had never seen this many ships, not even in interactive military fiction ViR-dramas about daring, human captains fighting imaginary battles against overwhelming odds. *These* odds were overwhelming, and I didn't know if our captains were daring, but they had more balls than I did if they could sail straight into this psychedelic vision of hell without running away screaming.

There was not one speck of darkness in the sensor display that I could have pointed to and said, "there's nothing there." Everywhere there were ships, ours and theirs, spread around us in a globular formation, enough that I could have sworn the *Iwo Jima* was the center of it, but I knew that was an illusion, like the models that showed our galaxy at the center of the universe. It only seemed that way because there was so much around us that any one of the ships could have been the center.

We weren't at the rear of the Fleet formation; I knew that much from the op order and our briefings. As always, the carriers brought up the rear, farthest away from the action but closer now than usual. They would normally have sat the battle out near the edge of the system, at the farthest Transition Points, ready to pick up the surviving missile cutters and run like hell if things turned bad. This time, they'd emerged from Transition Space just a couple light-seconds behind us, squadrons of Search-and-Rescue craft clutching the thin docking spokes stretched between their twin, redundant saucer sections, standing ready to pick up survivors stranded in space in the wake of the battle. Their number was endless, more carriers than I'd ever seen in one place, and I wondered if, like the cruisers, we'd committed every single carrier we had to this battle.

We were next, the troop ships, seven massive, bulbous cylinders, heavily armored and lightly-armed, riding flaring fusion drives inward toward Point Barber, their Marines strapped into drop-ships and ready to launch. I wondered if they felt as conflicted about it as I did, scared to be shed of the armor of the larger ship but eager to leave the huge targets before the Tahni anti-ship missiles had a chance to reach them.

If anything could make me feel more confident about our chances, it was the cruisers. Each of them was a mountain carved into a fortress and sent a-sail with the power of a star harnessed behind them, the work of the gods, not of men. And there were eight of them, more than had ever been in once place at one time in the whole history of humanity, more raw, destructive power than had ever existed before.

The missile cutters were mosquitoes flying around elephants by comparison, but there were clouds of them, uncountable. They popped in and out of existence like the subatomic particles in the quantum foam that I'd learned about in the physics annex I'd had to take for OCS.

And yet, for all that, the enemy's numbers were even greater.

The destroyer was the largest class of military starship the Tahni had, nowhere near as large as our cruisers but more agile, able to jump in and out of Transition Space quicker, though still glacial compared to our missile cutters. There had been two or three around in every system we'd hit in the course of the war, whether the Tahni outposts we'd struck at or the occupied colonies we'd freed. There were dozens of them here at Point Barber, formed up in clusters like fighters, burning toward us at high-g boosts, their missiles outpacing them because they were accelerating faster than a living being could withstand.

Their corvettes were slightly larger than our missile cutters, not quite as versatile, nowhere near as fast, but there were thousands of them; as many as the stars revealed by the infrared filters on the cameras. Their lasers and missiles crossed the silent blackness of the vacuum with the proton beams of our cutters, a spider-web pattern in the computer simulation, and people died. Not just a ship here and there, the two-person crew vanishing in a flash of vaporizing metal or a sphere of fusion fire, but dozens at a time, winking out of existence like bubbles popping as they floated into the sky and lost surface tension.

How many of those men and women had been sure they were going to be the ones who survived? How many of the Tahni felt the same way? Or did they even think about that? For all our intelligence analysts had discovered about the enemy, one thing missing from every briefing I'd audited was how they faced death. They were certainly *willing* to die, to give up their lives in service to an immortal, spiritual Emperor who manifested himself in a series of physical hosts. Which seemed weird, but then again, every religion seems weird from the outside.

Part of me wanted to think that any sexually-reproducing humanoid life form would be afraid of death, but I was about as far from a scientist as you could get without my knuckles dragging on the ground when I walked, so who was I to say? Maybe the Tahni threw their lives away and never had a doubt, never flinched. Maybe that's why they'd come so close to winning this thing.

But I could hear the Skipper's voice in my ear, laughing with an amusement that came from having seen it all happen before, so many times.

"It's always the same story," he would have told me, *had* told me or one of the other platoon leaders before during one of our company professional development sessions. "In every war, one side wants to paint the other as having some special fortitude, some fearlessness or fanaticism unheard of before in history. It's a way to make us feel better about ourselves, to explain why we haven't already won, why when we do, we'll have accomplished something incredible. So, if it's any comfort, feel free to imagine they're thinking the same thing about us."

The only thing that would have given me comfort was for all those damned red icons in the threat display to go away.

"Come on, Fleet," I muttered, careful to make sure my mic was cold. "Make yourself useful for once."

As if they'd been listening, the cruisers went into action. Their beam weapons spoke first, the raging flood of protons simulated by the white lightning discharge they would have shown in an atmosphere. That wasn't strictly necessary, I knew. The tactical computer systems could just as easily have made the cannon strikes checkered threads of white or yellow or crimson, but those wouldn't have been as dramatic, and this simulation was meant to invoke an emotional reaction as much as it was meant to convey the tactical situation. The crews watching their outgoing fire would feel more confident if their shots were the bolts of Zeus thrown down from Olympus.

And to the Tahni corvettes in their way, they might as well have been. Each bolt struck two or three of the smaller craft, erasing them from existence, a giant swatting at flies. More of them fell to point-defense Gatling laser turrets and pulse torpedoes and if all the fragments of ships could have been arranged into a solid surface, I might have been able to walk to Point Barber from here.

The Tahni forces saw the cruisers as well as I did, and their destroyers reacted with the glacial response time of capital-ship crews everywhere, waiting a solid thirty seconds before the first wave jumped in, a micro-Transition across a few light-seconds. Micro-Transitions were something that Attack Command pilots liked to brag about in the bars after a battle, telling the locals how dangerous they were, how hard it was to keep your lunch down when you hopped in and out of Transition Space with just a half second between the jumps. They went on and on about how the missile cutters were the most agile and versatile starships around because they could make multiple micro-Transitions in a fight.

The Tahni must have heard about the brag, because a hundred destroyers micro-jumped from hundreds of thousands of kilometers away to only a thousand kilometers in front of the formation of cruisers in the space of a second. I heard a gasp and realized it must have come from me, sheer disbelief at the audacity, the risk...the cost. At least a dozen of the ships collided, jumping out within a few hundred meters of each other, and I was absolutely sure I'd seen at least two pairs of them try to emerge into the same spacetime, all four disappearing into bursts of pure energy, not a speck of matter left of the ships.

But the rest...

Dozens of anti-ship missiles leapt out from launch bays, each the size of an assault shuttle, raging on plumes of annihilated antiprotons, defended by centimeters of boron honeycomb armor and its own deflector shield. What happened next was almost impossible for me or any other human to follow, and I wondered how advanced the targeting systems on the cruisers had to be to handle it. Lasers and proton cannons and pulse torpedoes fired almost nonstop, from the cruisers and from wave after wave of missile cutters popping in and targeting the enemy anti-ship missiles with their own, wasting weapons designed to blow up the destroyers to take out the biggest threat to the cruisers.

Then the cruisers opened up with their main guns, the massive railguns on spinal mounts, as if the flying mountains had been built around the guns. They weren't conventional railguns, or so I'd been told over and over by the Skipper, who seemed to have an appreciation for the weapons. The longer the conductive surface of the rails, the more velocity the shot had. So, the engineers who'd built the cruiser's spinal guns had worked out a system where ionized gas was ejected from the muzzle of the railgun before each shot and ran an electrical charge through it. The charged cylinder of gas added velocity to the shot like an afterburner and, more importantly to us grunts watching the show, it was a yellow lance of flame extending out from the nose of the cruiser, a fireworks show in the vacuum.

Where they struck, destroyers were ripped apart, cored lengthwise, their reactors spewing plasma into the vacuum in their dying spasms, just one more flash in a web of chain lightning stretching from one side of visible space to another as far as the sensors could see. It was simultaneously awe-inspiring and terrifying and my breath caught in my throat. It was thousands of kilometers away, but it seemed close enough for me to feel the heat through my armor.

I happened to be looking straight at the *Salamis* when she exploded. The cruisers were so huge, even the multi-megaton warhead from a Tahni anti-ship missile couldn't vaporize one completely. What was left of the ship looked like a half-burned log in the remnants of one of the bonfires the squad would make on Hachiman back when I'd been an NCO, the front half burned away, glowing at the molten edges of the hull armor. Nothing had lived through the blast, though. Even if the crew had been dressed in pressure suits and the vacuum hadn't killed them, the heat and radiation surely would have.

Talons twisted inside my gut at the thought of a thousand crewmembers burned to ash in a half a second. We Marines gave the Fleet a ration of shit for sitting back safe in their ships while we waded in the dirt and got shot at, but as many Fleet spacers had just died in the space of a heartbeat as Marines had died in any battle fought so far. They'd never had a chance, had nowhere to hide, no warning. They were just gone. And somewhere, a thousand casualty notification teams were going to have to find their next of kin and deliver the news in person, and a thousand families who never even thought of death as a possibility would have it delivered to their doorstep.

I tried to imagine how it would feel for them, but I couldn't manage it. Death had always been a reality for me.

"That's the first cruiser we've lost since the Battle for Mars," Bang-Bang said, this time remembering to keep it to our private net.

"It might not be the last."

The missiles were still coming in, so many of them I couldn't keep track of whether there were enough ships to intercept them all. And they weren't all aimed at the cruisers. One was easier to track, on an arcing trajectory around the cruisers, heading right down our throats.

The alarm wasn't one I'd heard before except in the drills we rarely practiced, the announcement that followed it tinged with real panic absent from those drills, which had been conducted with bored obligation.

"All drop ships!" the flight ops officer of the *Iwo Jima* yelled as if he had to pitch his voice loud enough to carry through the hangar bay instead of just over the intercom. "Launch now! Emergency launch! All hands to escape pods! Launch! Launch! Launch!"

Acceleration slammed me back into the padding of my armor and the view through the tactical display hookup went dark as it cut off.

"Shit!" I didn't know who had said it, couldn't focus on the readout in my Heads-Up Display with the pressure, but they summed up my own opinion perfectly.

Six gees, I thought. We had to be boosting at six gees, at least. No more than eight, because I was still conscious, but enough that I felt as if my ribs were about to give way, despite the padding inside the Vigilante battlesuit. I couldn't lift my chin off my chest and taking a breath seemed to require every bit of energy I had. I clawed at the controls positioned around my left hand and managed to switch the comm input to the drop-ship external cams.

It was a peek out a window compared to the feed from the sensor suite, but at least I wasn't stuck in the darkness of my helmet. Point Barber filled the view, a kaleidoscope of blue, green, and brown, and a muscle spasmed in the web of my thumb as I switched to the rear feed, needing to see what was happening behind us. The *Iwo Jima* seemed farther away than I would have thought possible from just a few minutes of boost and I could see her from bow to stern, her nose slowly lifting on a flaring maneuvering thruster as she tried to change course, a desperate and pointless move. She was built for cargo capacity, not speed and agility, and it would take her a solid five minutes to swap end for end.

The missile hit two minutes later.

A new sun swallowed up the ship, and I imagined I spotted the center of it, that one exact second when the fusion warhead ignited, a kernel of starfire at the heart of the *Iwo Jima*. It was a fantasy, an illusion of my fevered imagination and the pressure squeezing oxygen away from my brain. The fusion explosion was near instantaneous and it took a fraction of a second for the ship that had been my home as much as any other place for the last three years to vanish, disassembled on an atomic level, what wasn't ripped out of existence burned to vapors.

The *Iwo Jima* was gone. Everything I owned was gone with her, everything squeezed into a tiny locker built into the bulkhead of my compartment now just floating gas bound someday to fall into the atmosphere of Point Barber. The crew, the flight officers, the maintenance techs. They were dead.

And if the reality of that hadn't yet hit me, it was only because we were burning through the biggest space battle in the history of humanity in a lightly-armored drop-ship and very likely to join them any second.

[11]

"Kovacs," I said, remembering that First Platoon was sharing the drop-ship with us. Which wasn't as easy as it sounded. At the moment, I was so damned scared, I could barely remember my own name. "You hearing me, Francis?"

"Y...yeah." I didn't know if the hesitation was because of the pressure from the acceleration or from flat-out fear, and for once, I wouldn't have blamed Kovacs for either one. "I'm here, Cam."

I wanted to laugh but lacked the spare breath. He almost never used my first name, calling me Alvarez with the sort of disdain only an Academy ring-knocker could put into the word when speaking down to an OCS grad.

"Did you see the *Iwo* go up?" Which was sounded like a dumb question but wasn't. I'd been watching out the back cameras, but he might not have had time to switch before the blast.

"Yeah. Shit, Cam, do you think anyone else made it?"

Now that sounded like a dumb question too, because how the hell would I know? But again, it wasn't, because I could find out.

"Hold on," I told him, then switched my comms to the drop-ship crew's net. "This is Lt. Alvarez. Do you have IFF on any other drop-ships?"

Their answer took a moment, and I wondered if they were too shocked by the destruction of the troop ship to bother answering me, but finally, someone did.

"Alvarez, this is Lt. Abanks." Abanks sounded almost normal despite the pressure of the boost, inured to it by experience, I suppose. "We have positive IFF transponder readings on nine of the twelve drop-ships from your battalion, plus another six from Force Recon." He hesitated. "And twelve of twenty assault shuttles on launch prep when the...," he trailed off. "When the missile hit. According to the troop manifest, the full complement of Alpha, Bravo, Charlie, Delta and Echo companies launched and are under boost."

I frowned. That was all of us, wasn't it?

"Who didn't make it, then?"

"Battalion Headquarters and staff."

Shit. Colonel Voss, Major Anderle, her XO. Sgt.-Major Martelle. All the staff, all the communications gear and drones.

"Do you have comms with any of the other birds?" I was sure of the answer, but I had to ask anyway.

"Negative. Even if there wasn't active jamming, there's so much ionization, particulate scatter, and radiation out here, no one could get a signal through." A pause. "I'll let you know if I hear anything."

"Thanks, sir." It took me a second to remember to add the honorific, not that he would care. Fleet lieutenants were the equivalent of a Marine captain, which was confusing and based on a fixation on tradition that I didn't understand. I switched back over to Kovacs. "Delta is good to go," I told him. "The other companies too. But we lost Battalion."

"Oh, man," he hissed. "Does that mean the Skipper is in charge?"

"By date of rank. But that won't mean anything unless we make it to the ground. Listen up, Francis, we have to be ready for an early drop."

"That could kill us all," he reminded me. I didn't need the reminder, but he hadn't been around for Brigantia.

"So could staying on this bird if she gets shot out of the sky. Point Barber is a little under Earth standard. I think we could get most of us down and operating if we don't drop before 500 meters, so let's plan on that, right?"

"Right." He sounded relieved to have someone else to give orders, which I also couldn't blame him for.

"Get with your platoon sergeant and get your people ready. Don't let them think about the *Iwo* or the rest of the flight to the planet. There's nothing they can do about it except panic, and we don't need panic." *More panic*, I added silently.

"Will do. Thanks, Cam."

I focused on the front camera feed, allowing myself just a few seconds to consider how close all those explosions seemed, how many enemy ships were in front of us, trying to kill us. Then I switched over to Bang-Bang and told him what I'd told Kovacs.

"You dropped early once," he said. I was impressed. He must have looked up my history. It was a very platoon sergeant thing to do. "Didn't go so well for the other people in your bird."

"And it'd be worse this time, with a planet crawling with enemy and a not a single human colonist to be found within twenty light years. Improvise, adapt and overcome, though."

"Ooh-rah, sir."

"Third Platoon," I said to the Marines, "listen up."

They needed calming, I thought, but they needed me to be honest with them, too. I'd let Bang-Bang give them the details, but they needed to hear from me, if for no other reason than to let them know I wasn't gibbering like an idiot.

"We've lost the *Iwo*. She took an anti-ship missile." I paused, knowing they'd be cursing inside their helmets, not wanting them to miss the next part. "But we have nearly the whole battalion intact and all of Delta. I can't promise you for sure we're going to make it to the planet—that's up to the Fleet boys running interference for us. But I *can* promise you that if we do, the operation is still a go, and we are just the Marines to pull it off. Gunny Morrel is going to give you some last-minute guidance on what to do if we have to drop early, and I want you to listen to him like your life depends on it, because it does. Are we clear?"

"Clear, sir!" Kries yelled it out first, then the rest echoed it.

Warmth spread through my chest, not just at the trust they were showing in me but at the balls it took not to give in to the fear. And it was quickly replaced by a sick feeling. I was giving them false hope. But it was the only kind I had available, and it would have to be enough, because all I had left to do was stare out at a battle I couldn't affect, at the very finger of chance writing her twisted tale through the fire and destruction around us and hoping she'd miss me.

"Uh-oh," Abanks said in my ear. It's never good when your pilot says something like that. "Everybody hold on back there."

Like we had a choice.

I tightened the muscles in my gut even more than they already were and the six gees turned into zero, followed by a thunderous hammering against the hull, the sound of the maneuvering thrusters changing our trajectory. And then God stomped me into a paste and I blacked out.

I don't know how long I was out, but I woke to the sound of someone retching over their suit comm pickup, then two more someones who couldn't take the sound and I was lucky I wasn't one of them. We were accelerating again, though not as hard, and somewhere, an alarm blared, letting us know we were taking laser fire. The ship went into a spin on a staccato chain-fire of steering jets and the angular momentum of the spin didn't just add to the three or four-gravity acceleration, it squared it or maybe cubed it. I was never very good at math, and worse at it when my inner ear was screaming obscenities at me and swearing to kill me if we both survived this.

I had no concept of what had happened or how hard we had wound up boosting, and I wasn't about to press the flight crew for information while we were spinning to try to keep a long-distance shot from a laser from burning through our armor. We were running from something I couldn't see, and couldn't have focused on even if I'd found the right camera to watch it. Light flashed around us and something exploded, and I just had to clench my teeth and hope to hell it wasn't the ship coming apart.

"Oh, yeah!" Abanks crowed, and steering jets took us out of our spin as if the drop-ship was celebrating with its own drum-beat. "Thank you, Assault Flight!"

He whooped and then so did I as a dagger-sharp assault shuttle burned past our right wing, another on our left. And then we were in the clouds. I hadn't even noticed because it was a coal-black night over Deltaville and only the absence of stars had provided a clue we'd entered the atmosphere, but the clouds shut out the nightmare battle and I almost thought we were safe.

But the presence of an atmosphere was a cruel trick by God to make it even plainer exactly how much danger we were in. Lasers weren't invisible threats only revealed by distant alarms, they were sheaths of crackling fire rising up through the clouds like reverse lightning, seeking us out and finding something, if not our bird. The cumulonimbus lit up, not with the violence of a thunderstorm, but with the death of a human flight crew. I could only pray it wasn't one of the drop-ships, and felt like shit doing it, because that would mean it was one of the assault shuttles that had just saved our asses.

More lightning crackled downward, our own birds striking back, followed by the firecracker flare of igniting rocket engines as missiles streaked out of a weapons bay and sought out enemy defenses, or maybe hunted down a Tahni dual-environment fighter.

This is insane. How could anyone hope to survive this?

I couldn't stop thinking it, over and over. They'd sent us into this knowing what could happen, knowing how much it would cost. Who'd made the decision? Had it come from the High Command, Generals and Admirals who hadn't heard a shot fired in anger since the Pirate Wars, or maybe since the First War with the Tahni? Or *never*?

Had it come from President Gregory Jameson, that slick-haired weasel puppet of the Corporate Council? The man had never spent a day in combat, had never so much as set foot on a colony world, much less a military ship. I was half convinced he didn't exist, that he was an AI simulation, a long con run on the few citizens who bothered to vote by the people who held the real power.

Would anything change from this war? Would Earth pay any more attention to the colonies now? Would the people who buried their nose in the scansheets as they walked from their train to the Zocalo in Trans-Angeles even give a shit who had won? Would they even know or care about the Marines and Fleet pilots and crews who'd died today?

And I could only afford to wallow in that self-pity for about five more minutes until I had to lead a bunch of kids who had no dreams beyond living through the day into the biggest infantry battle on another world in human history, and try to pretend I could make that dream come true. How the hell did the Skipper do this? How had he done it for decades? Top had been doing it even longer, but all she had to do was teach the kids to survive. He had to lead them into hell and pretend they'd come out the other side.

Turbulence tossed us like a feather on the wind and I couldn't be sure if it was the incredible heat and ionization of the air or if we'd felt the concussion of a missile warhead, and wasn't sure if I cared. Belly jets roared and pushed us into a trajectory no airframe was meant to follow, and only the incredible power of the fusion-fed turbines kept us in the air.

How much longer? Mother Mary, how much longer?

I should really learn to keep my mouth shut. Another concussion, closer this time, and just above the roar of the rush of superheated air, the patter of something smacking against the hull rang through, like hail on a roof. The bottom fell out from beneath us and left my stomach somewhere a thousand meters higher, and we were in a spin and I couldn't tell which way was up.

"Drop!" Abanks screamed in my ear. "Emergency drop!"

"Emergency drop!" I echoed the order without thought. "Third Platoon, drop now!"

I didn't have time to check altitude or position. I just yanked the lever and the ship spat me out like a watermelon seed into a night afire with explosions, engine flares and the actinic glare of energy weapons. The plane had been in a spin and now I was, cartwheeling into the sky with very little idea of where the ground was or my position in relation to it.

Luckily, the suit knew, and the jacks implanted in my head shared the knowledge with me as if it was something I'd known all along, like an instinct I'd been born with. I hit the thrusters and cried out at the pain of the sudden cessation of the spin, the deceleration pounding me into the suit's padding with bruising force.

The suit's jets slowed the drop, but I couldn't make out a

damned thing through the helmet's optics through the sea of static discharge and particulate haze, so I checked the altimeter and the dead-reckoning map instead.

It was bad, I decided in that split-second, but it could have been worse. We were about ten kilometers off-target of our drop zone and more importantly, just over 550 meters up. Which meant a painful, potentially damaging landing but not a deadly one. At least if we could avoid being blown up on the way down.

"Third platoon!" I said, counting on laser-line-of-sight to reach them, since no microwave transmission was going to make it intact through the static charge crackling in the air, sending yellow halos off the metal of my suit like St. Elmo's Fire. "Form on me! Execute Emergency Landing Fall on impact!"

The ELF was something we trained with rarely and never used. Until today. The theory was, if one of us had an emergency drop that wasn't at some impossible altitude like the one we'd faced on Brigantia, but something just over recommended safe drop, we were supposed to hit in the ELF form. It was based on the way our predecessors, the paratroopers of hundreds of years ago would try to land, the appropriately named Parachute Landing Fall, or PLF. Balls of the feet, side of the calf, side of the thigh, side of the hip, side of the back, to spread the impact out over as great a surface area as possible. For us, it meant avoiding critical damage to the armor before we took it into battle.

I had no fucking idea if it would work in practice, because it wasn't something you *could* practice to full effect. No one wanted to drop a Vigilante at a hundred meters over optimum altitude, then let a clumsy Marine break their legs *and* damage an expensive piece of military hardware in the process, so all practice was done either at recommended drop height or in a simulator.

I always did great at it in the simulator.

I'd thought the fog would clear as I dropped lower, but it went all the way down to the street and I had to make last-second shifts in my suit's attitude to keep from bouncing off the side of a two-hundred-meter-tall building, something shaped vaguely like a wedge of quartz I'd seen as a hallway decoration in the Marine Headquarters on Inferno. I blew out a breath, thinking I'd cleared it, but I abruptly realized the thing broadened out substantially as I neared the base and I had to dodge again, losing track of my altitude and nearly slamming into the ground flat-footed.

The Emergency Landing Form was not as easy to pull off in real life as it was in the simulators, mostly because the Vigilante's feet were very flat, and it took a shitload of effort to make the damned thing topple over sideways. I pulled off something close to textbook...well, in the general area of the textbook, anyway. As long as that included skipping the whole leg part and falling straight on my armored ass.

Stars filled my vision and other yellow flashes I thought might have been residual effects of the hit turned out to be my armor's damage control systems informing me I was a moron who shouldn't do that again. But when I rolled to my feet, the suit worked, and I guess that was as much as I had a right to expect.

The rest of the platoon came down in the street around me, some of them remembering to do an ELF, some just hitting flat-footed and falling to their knees. Where First Platoon had come down, I had no idea and probably wouldn't find out until we reached the objective.

"Squad leaders, status," I snapped, feeling the temptation of taking a minute to simply revel in disbelief at our own survival or descend into terror at what we had passed through and realizing we had the time for neither.

"First squad," Valerie Medina reported, her words clipped and precise, "all Marines present, all suits operational. Delp has minor damage to his left hip actuator, Slattery has a warning light in her right knee motivator."

"Second squad, all Marines present, all suits operational, sir." Bradley Houghton was the youngest of the squad leaders and he sounded a bit shaky. He also didn't offer any more details, but that was all right, I'd never remember the exact damage to everyone's suits, anyway.

"Third squad...," Christian Majid trailed off, his voice breaking. "Sir, we lost Private Carroll. He dropped but then... something hit him. I couldn't see what it was. He went offline a few seconds ago and I'm not picking up a transponder, so he must have landed somewhere out of line of sight." He sucked in a ragged breath before he continued. "Umm, all others present and operational."

Shit. There was nothing we could do about it. Carroll could have come down anywhere, and going to search for him now would kill the mission.

"I'll let Search and Rescue know as soon as we have comms again," I said, because what else was there to say?

"Fourth squad all here," Kreis told me. "Hoagland has a frozen ankle joint but she can still run on it. Everyone else is good to go."

"My suit is operational, sir," Bang-Bang told me, his voice neutral. He'd slipped into his game face and he wouldn't be showing any emotion until the game was won.

One MIA, probably dead, and we'd just landed. But it could have been so much worse...and it probably would be before the night was over.

"First squad," I said, "take point. Bang-Bang, you're on drag." I waved an arm forward. "Move out, Third. We got a war to win."

[12]

The streets of Deltaville were quiet.

Above us, lightning crackled from cloud to cloud, and explosions glowed orange and white like the sun breaking through the haze here and there, but the fog was so thick, it all seemed a world away. Down among the residences and shops and temples, there was no sign of habitation at all, as if the Tahni had simply decided to abandon the planet in the face of our invasion.

I knew better than that, knew their method of operation. They'd had hours of warning that we were coming between the time we'd Transitioned into the system to the first of us setting foot on the planet. The civilians were well disciplined enough to stay off the street, to stay out of the way.

Except at Port Harcourt. Except at that warehouse, at the bunker.

I shoved the thought aside, pushed back the images of dead Tahni juveniles, following their fathers, brothers, and uncles into harm's way, trying to act as living shields for their military. When had they started doing that? Had they figured us out, figured out that we didn't like killing their noncombatants?

Well, some of us don't like it.

Maybe Cronje had been right, maybe I'd just been falling for their trick, letting them get away with it. But those kids hadn't volunteered to be living shields, even if their adult male family members had. And for me, it all came down to Demeter. We'd been furious with the Tahni for deliberately slaughtering civilians at Demeter, but if we did the same thing, how could we blame them?

And yet...civilians died in war. Any war from the beginning of time right up until the latter half of the 23rd Century.

Something moved down a side street to my right, and I barely kept myself from roasting it. It was an animal. Something furry, about the size of a sheep, wearing some sort of harness around its shoulders. It saw us and ran back the way it had come, letting out a high-pitched squeal.

"What do they call those things?" Bang-Bang asked me.

"Kuwari or quori or something like that," I told him. "They're like pets or service animals, I think. Someone from Charlie told me they taste really good grilled."

I checked the mapping display and tried to force my thoughts back to the mission. Recriminations and regrets were a luxury for after the battle.

"We're two streets over from a sort of central courtyard," I announced. "That's the Delta Company rally point. If everyone else made it down, that's where they'll be. And if there are already Marines there, they might be under fire, so don't blunder right into an electron beam or a coil gun round, Delp."

"Yes, sir," the Marine walking point affirmed. "No wandering into electron beams today."

"Cut the chatter, Delp," Bang-Bang snapped, not so much in anger but from habit. He was a platoon sergeant, after all.

I snorted dark amusement. Just a few months ago, he'd been a raw nerve, a kid snatched out of a regional detention center in

Toronto after an adolescence spent in one petty crime after another had culminated in something serious enough to make enlisting seem the lesser of two evils. He'd shown something of a natural talent for the Vigilante, but he'd been skittish and uncomfortable around officers in general and me in particular, maybe because of my reputation. Now, he wasn't afraid to yank my chain a little, which was an improvement, though it didn't make up for his propensity to let the local girls buy him too many drinks and then getting into fights with their boyfriends.

"Take a right at the next cross-street, Delp," I said. "Then right again."

This would have been faster if we'd hopped a block at a time with the jump-jets, but I was running totally blind, with no idea where the enemy was deployed, and nothing says 'shoot me' quite like a platoon of battlesuits flying through the air over an enemy city. So, we walked. Or rather, we loped, the overpowered artificial musculature of the Vigilantes taking us four meters at a stride, the pounding of our footpads on the pavement a chorus of jackhammers. It wasn't exactly subtle, but it was fast enough, and with practice, we'd developed a talent at holding formation while galloping at full-speed.

It had become second-nature to me, which was why I was able to run full-out while letting my attention wander to the sensor readouts in my helmet, why I saw the thermal signatures just before Delp yelled out on the platoon net.

"Battlesuits!" It was a mix of the panic of encountering the enemy, and the eagerness for a fight every good Marine felt when the real guns started firing.

But these weren't the enemy, and I knew it from their heat signature even before the IFF transponders began registering.

"Hold fire!" I commanded, pushing forward to the front of the formation in just a few steps. "Hold fire! Those are ours!"

The two platoons of Vigilantes faced each other at the intersection of the two streets, plasma guns still raised and at the ready, mute, inexpressive visages showing no recognition. It reminded me of cleaning robots colliding where their routes overlapped, neither willing to yield to the other.

"Cam?" Francis Kovacs said, a familiar voice in my headphones. "Is that you?"

"Of course, it's me," I shot back. I stepped closer to the First Platoon leader, by useless instinct. He could have heard me just as well twenty meters farther away. "Glad you made it down. We've got one Marine MIA, might have been taken out by ground-to-air fire. You?"

"We lost two." Kovacs's tone was grim with a plaintive note to it, as if he was asking God why this would happen to *his* platoon. "Did you see where the others landed?"

"No. We didn't even know we'd find you here. We were heading for the rally point. It should be just one more street over. You want us to take point?"

"Sure, yeah."

I hadn't really needed to ask. Kovacs wasn't a coward, but he was more than happy to let another platoon do the heavy lifting. I wondered if it was because he didn't have confidence in his ability as a combat leader, or if he thought taking casualties would look bad on his record. But I might have been letting my own bias against Academy grads cloud my judgement of the man.

"Okay, then. Staggered file until we hit the courtyard, then staggered wedge formation. Move it out, Third."

I knew something was going down at the rally point before Delp hit the intersection. There was a constant background crackle from the air battle raging above us, but the sonic sensors on the Vigilante were sensitive and sophisticated enough to differentiate the concussive reports reverberating off the curved faces of the buildings surrounding us from the blasts overhead. I opened my mouth to give Delp a warning, but shut it again. He knew what to expect just as well as I did. Instead, I moved up again, wanting to get a look at the situation before the rest of the force stepped in it.

The courtyard was separated from the residential and small business district by a wall, curving and twisting adobe four meters tall, broken in places by gaps big enough to let in pedestrians or small vehicles. Actinic flares of light flashed through the gaps, tiny windows into what was happening on the other side, and I knew if I tried to maneuver two platoons through, I was funneling them into what might be pre-registered firing arcs.

"Third!" I commanded, running just a few meters behind Delp as we approached the wall. "Over the wall! Hit the jets and follow me!"

Delp went first, probably trying to make sure I didn't take over his position at point, but probably regretted it when an electron beam came just a few centimeters from spearing through his helmet.

"Shit!" he blurted, firing out into the blackness at the source of the shot.

We'd jumped into chaos, a raging firefight that surged and swirled and tossed like waves against a rocky coastline, and information flooded in at me faster than I could process it. I let my consciousness go slightly out of focus, allowing the important details to penetrate the filter while the rest washed over me, ignored.

The courtyard was huge, bigger than I'd thought it would be from the maps we'd been given, probably three kilometers on a side. Paved paths described a spiral course through swathes of tall grass, or something similar to grass that filled the ecological niche on Tahni worlds, while odd, geometric sculptures sprouted up seemingly at random. On the far side of the square, probably four or five klicks away, the fusion reactor complex rose above the curvature of the ground in a series of geodesic domes surrounded by gigantic water pipes for cooling. The whole thing was lined with a retaining wall and surrounded by bunkers, bristling with KE gun turrets and looking fairly unassailable. Beyond it were the massive, concave dishes of the deflector shield generators protecting the military base and the spaceport, crackling plasma energy surrounding the dishes in a halo of raw power climbing into the sky to meet the proton bombardment from the cruisers in orbit.

And beneath the battle raging between the gods in heaven, demons and angels fought for control of the world below. Faceless, metal beings breathing fire, tangling and running and leaping in a fatal ballet out of some reimagining of Dante's Inferno using 23rd-Century technology, Vigilantes taking the place of the heavenly hosts for my purposes, while Tahni High Guard battlesuits stood in for Satan's hordes.

The IFF signals were all over the place, dribs and drabs from every company in the battalion. How they'd wound up here was testament to the truth of that old saying about battle plans and how long they survived after enemy contact. But I recognized some. Most of Fourth Platoon was there, and Cano was in the midst of them, and if he wasn't exactly leading or directing, he was doing a damned good job of fighting for his life.

There were at least two companies of High Guard facing them, pouring into the square from the direction of the fusion plant, some jetting in even as I watched, outnumbering the Marines nearly two to one before First and Third joined the fight. And if we didn't exactly even out the numbers, we certainly evened the odds.

"Third Platoon," I ordered, my brain working separately from my instincts, my finger touching the trigger and blasting a

High Guard suit in the chest with a gout of plasma, sending it tumbling backwards away from the Marine it had been about to finish off. "Volley fire, target the incoming enemy suits with your missiles! Now!"

We couldn't use the missiles against the closest of the enemy. They were too tightly engaged with our own people, and while the weapons had a fail-safe against fratricide and would disarm automatically if a friendly IFF signal was detected, even an on-target hit against an enemy suit could damage the Marine engaged with them. But there were two more platoons of High Guard suits jetting in from the power plant, and they were handy targets.

I had picked out an enemy suit before I even touched the pavement, and I braced there for a split-second, giving the missile a nice, fixed platform to launch itself from before I touched the jets again. I squirted off the spot just as a pair of electron beams bracketed me, throwing up a steam explosion of dirt and rock, chunks of debris pattering off the helmet of my Vigilante, and barely registered the impact of my first missile before I tapped down on one flat, rounded foot and launched another.

Two platoons of battlesuits launching their complement of missiles in volley fire is an impressive sight, and not one most Tahni get to see twice, certainly not the ones trying to join the fight in the courtyard. A chain-fire line of explosions lit up the edge of the courtyard and nearly two dozen of the enemy battlesuit troopers tumbled to the ground in sprays of torn-up sod or pinwheeled out of the air, their jump-jets failing catastrophically.

Our arrival proved too much for the Tahni force and the suits began to disengage, pulling out of the skirmish and jetting back toward the reactor complex, leaving behind nearly two-score of their dead and disabled. And at least ten or twelve of ours. I scanned through the IFF signals of the dead, not just to figure out our strength but in a desperate search to make sure none of them were people I knew.

It was selfish, but I wasn't so long away from the disaffected PFC fresh off the streets who had taken months just to make friends among my platoon. I'd seen too many of them die already and I had to make sure Vicky wasn't in one of the mangled, twisted, vaguely humanoid metal shapes on the steaming ground. But she wasn't among the living or the dead, and I had to hope she'd landed somewhere closer to our objective and. . .

"Cam, Francis!" I heard William Cano's voice before I picked his suit out from amongst the shambling mess left after the attack. "Goddamn, I am glad to see you guys. When I saw your dropship go down, I thought all of you were dead."

"I was kinda convinced of that myself," I told him. "Who's in charge of this clusterfuck?"

"We got half a squad from Charlie, three separate fire teams from Third Battalion, and Marines from all over the freaking place. I think the highest ranking is Sgt. Manley from Fourth Battalion and he's a squad leader. But it's most of a platoon."

"Sgt. Manley," I said to the NCO, "I'm Lt. Alvarez, Third Platoon, Delta Company. We're going to designate this gaggle Fifth Platoon and you're the acting PL. Until we can get all of you reconnected with your units, we're going to drag you along on our mission to take down the primary power coupling for the Deltaville fusion plant. You cool with that?"

"Since I can't call anyone to complain," Manley said, "I guess I'll have to be cool with it."

"Designate your squads and squad leaders. Our No-Later-Than time to move out from the rally point to the fusion plant is in ten minutes from now, according to the op order."

"Are you taking over the company, Alvarez?" Kovacs asked.

I bit back a curse when I saw he'd asked it on the general net, where all of them could hear it. I switched to our company's command net before I answered.

"I'm listed as next in command after the XO on the op order," I reminded him, then shrugged, though neither of them could see it. "Either of you want to do it? Honest, guys, I have no idea which of us has more time in rank, but I have more combat experience than anyone else in the company except Top and the Skipper. If you got a problem with this, tell me now...or at least sometime in the next ten minutes."

"No, no problem," Cano said. "As far as I'm concerned, you're in charge until we find the Skipper or Lt. Bradley gets back."

That seemed to decide Kovacs. I couldn't see his face, but I'd served with the man long enough now to know how his mind worked. The Academy grad was resenting the idea of following the orders of an OCS officer, but the part of him who wanted a spotless war record to further his career was calculating how much of a liability it would be if he insisted on leading our company and then fucked it up, either by a failing of his own skills or just from blind chance. If Cano had expressed any doubts, I think Kovacs might have objected, but now the die was cast.

"Yeah," he said, though the words lacked conviction. "If the Skipper doesn't show up in the next ten minutes, I'm fine with having you take over."

"All right, then," I told them. "Francis, go ahead and get your platoon into a defensive perimeter on the other side of the wall." I pointed back toward the decorative barrier between the courtyard and the residential district.

I searched the opposite direction for anything that could be used as cover and discovered a parking area just the other side of the courtyard, filled with what I thought were industrial machinery, though I couldn't have told you their purpose from just a cursory glance. But they were heavy and metal and looked to be thick enough to stop an electron beamer.

"Billy," I told Cano, using the nickname he hated but that everyone still used anyway, "take Fourth Platoon to the other side and use those big, green metal things for cover, watch any approaches from the industrial district."

That covered the north and south approaches. East dead-ended into a lake, maybe two kilometers in diameter and perfectly round enough that I thought it had to be some sort of big retention pond. The Tahni could attack from that direction, but they'd have to ride their jump-jets the whole way, which would make them sitting ducks for our missiles.

"Bang-Bang, set up watch on the lake over there, missile launch pattern in depth if anything tries to come that way."

"Good copy, sir." If Gunny Sgt. Morrel was rattled by the exploding drop-ship or the changes to the operation, it certainly wasn't evident in his voice. He seemed as calm as if he was escorting the platoon to session in the simulator pods.

As for west, that end of the park or courtyard or whatever it was to the Tahni, butted up against a large, dome-shaped building I couldn't identify from its location or construction, but I knew it needed investigation. It was probably three hundred meters in circumference and streets or walkways radiated out from it in a 180-degree arc opposite the courtyard.

I switched over to the general net, remembering that Sgt. Manley wasn't keyed into our command net. "Manley, your platoon is coming with me. We're going to check out that building. Detail two squads to guard the western approaches and send two in with me."

"Will do, Lieutenant." Manley might have taken offense at the detail, but his reply was mild and business-like.

No one bothered to ask why I was going with them, and

why I hadn't just stuck Manley's hodge-podge platoon to guard the eastern approach, because they knew the answer. I didn't trust the NCO yet and wasn't planning on counting on him and his Marines to carry out any combat operations until I'd vetted them. And there was ten minutes' worth of vetting to be had.

Our notional Fifth Platoon moved out with the sloppy, awkward confusion I expected from Marines who'd never trained with each other, and Manley lumbered out ahead of them, trying to lead from the front because he was a squad leader and not any sort of officer. I let him because I didn't have the time to turn him into one.

"There's an entrance over here, sir," Manley told me, gesturing with his plasma gun toward an oval doorway set in the side of the dome.

I'd been surprised at how similar some of the Tahni architecture was to ours. Doors were doors, and if they had little touches like kick plates to open them with a foot instead of a hand, they still served the same purpose and swung inward or outward or sometimes withdrew into a niche in the wall. There must have been a practical reason why they didn't construct them to dilate like a pupil or slide up into the ceiling or something weird like that, and I was sure some university egghead would get a government grant someday to launch a multi-year study into the socioeconomic significance of Tahni architecture, because that was the sort of thing the Commonwealth liked to waste money on instead of useless things like reforming the foster care system or trying to rebuild the squatter cities.

This particular door would no doubt cause much consternation for my notional researcher because it was reminiscent of every depiction of a medieval castle door I'd seen in fantasy stories or historical epics, oval at the top, squared at the bottom, constructed from wood planks banded by metal. All it lacked was the big metal ring at the center to pull it open, since the

Tahni liked to open doors with their feet. This one was four meters tall and nearly as wide, so I had to think the kick plate at the bottom was an electronic switch, but I did my part to show my respect for a different culture and slammed the flat of my suit's right foot into the door.

The mechanism didn't have the chance to do the polite thing and open the door for me, because my kick knocked it off its hinges and sent it tumbling inward. Light spilled out from inside the dome, and I took a step through the entrance. And stopped in my tracks.

I would have figured the dome would be divided into dozens of separate rooms, given its size, but it was a single chamber, huge and cavernous. The light came from panels stretched out across the ceiling in a fractal pattern, and beneath it, bathed in its amber glow, hundreds of Tahni females danced.

Well, it *looked* like a dance. If it had been humans, I would have said they were dancing. The sounds they were making seemed like a chant, and though some of them broke off their dance and their chant at our intrusion, others kept it up, as if they were lost in some sort of trance. The chant had no rhythm that I could recognize, but it did repeat, and the dance spun and leapt and lunged with it, bare feet kicking up spray of something that could have been sand or sawdust. The females wore clothing woven of multihued strips and the strips whipped around with their motion, turning each of them into a kaleidoscope of motion and color.

"What the fuck is this shit?" Manley blurted, squeezing through the door behind me.

The rest of the ad hoc platoon was stuck behind us, shuffling in place, their spiked, metal foot pads scraping against the pavement. I could feel their impatience but I stood in place. Either this was a trap of some sort or it was exactly what it looked like, a shitload of young Tahni females doing some sort of communal dance, and either way, I didn't need thirty battlesuits busting through the door into the middle of it.

"Is this some kind of religious ceremony, sir?" Manley asked me.

I wished he could have seen the look I gave him, because he deserved it.

"How the hell would I know, Sergeant?" I replied. I was scanning the interior of the dome while I spoke, and the display told me exactly what I expected. Other than four hundred and thirty-two Tahni females, there was nothing in the chamber.

Then something changed. The females who had kept dancing and chanting despite our entrance finally seemed to notice us, and their waving, spinning motion took on a particular focus, heading our way. I thought of the females who had attacked us on Confluence and began to back away.

"Out," I told Manley and the others, my voice taut. "Back out now."

"I've heard about the Tahni females, sir," Manley said. "They're worse than the males. We should burn them all down before they can try anything."

Looking at the black eyes shining with feral rage, coming ever closer, I could sympathize with the sergeant's fear. But I couldn't let myself be controlled by it. That was why they'd put the bars on my shoulders, or at least that's what I told myself.

"Negative, Sergeant Manley," I told him. "Back out of here and do not fire. Get the platoon back and set up a perimeter fifty meters from the entrance. Now."

"Yes, sir."

I could hear the skepticism in his tone, but he followed orders just the same and chivvied the loose collection of Marines back into their positions. I stood just outside the door, watching the females get closer, their ranks surging forward like a wave on the beach, slowly advancing. I took a hop backwards out of the doorway and aimed my plasma gun at the pavement just outside, firing before the civilians could rush after me.

The blast melted the pavement into black, steaming tar, heat rolling off of it, sending the Tahni females retreating from the exit despite their furor, religious or otherwise. It should keep them back for a few minutes, I thought. And a few minutes was all I needed.

"Cam!" I heard Vicky's voice before I noticed the incoming Vigilantes on the IFF screen, and relief flowed through my chest like a cup of hot coffee on a Hachiman night. "Thank God you're here!"

She'd brought most of two Alpha Company platoons with her, and the other, I noted, was Freddy Kodjoe's. He was there, near the middle of their tactical movement formation as they jetted in, touching down in the center of the park, but he said nothing to me.

"Vick," I sighed the name. "I thought maybe we were all that was left of the battalion."

"Not yet," she said, her relief at finding me turning into urgency, "but we may be soon if we don't get to the reactor complex."

I didn't think it was possible for a Vigilante battlesuit to fidget, but she was proving me wrong, shuffling from one foot to another, her plasma gun pointed off in the direction of the power plant.

"What do you mean?" I asked her. "Why would they be at the plant already?"

I had a sudden, cold panic at the thought I'd gotten the timing wrong for the rally point, been late for the battle.

"Just about the whole battalion mis-dropped," she told me. "Half of Alpha Company, most of Bravo and the Headquarters platoon for Delta all landed right on top of the fusion reactor complex. They're pinned down by a whole battalion of High

Guard and at least that many Shock-Troopers. We have to get there now!"

I blew out a breath and shook my head. This whole thing was turning into a giant clusterfuck.

"I got good news and bad news, Delta," I transmitted to the rest of the company. "The good news is, we don't have to wait the whole ten minutes..."

[13]

It seemed as if every Tahni High Guard trooper in the whole universe had decided this was the hill they wanted to die on. The reactor complex was built on a rise, or perhaps the Tahni had piled dirt and sod over the underground parts of the complex and let the hill grow around it, surrounded by raised steppes, either from natural erosion over the decades since its construction, or by design for defense or aesthetics.

Or religious, cultural, or sociological reasons, I silently completed the words of every intelligence report I'd read about Tahni culture. They did a lot of shit we didn't understand and rather than admit we had no idea what their real reasons for, the junior officers who wrote the reports always included that caveat.

Whatever the reason for the steppes, they were the only thing keeping the Marines who'd dropped into the complex alive against the hundreds of Tahni battlesuits swarming over them, flying in from every side, hornets to the hive. Well, the steppes and one other thing.

The coil gun rounds burst out from the ranks of the Marines clustered together in their natural earthwork fort, splitting the air with the sheer force of their passage, sending out visible shockwaves like the ones I'd seen at the tail of aerospacecraft flying supersonic in an atmosphere. Plasma guns were impressive weapons, but their effective range was short by comparison, a shotgun blast versus a hunting rifle, to put it in terms Dak might have used. The coil guns mounted on the Boomers were weapons meant for assault shuttles or the point-defense turrets of a warship, and being this close to one of the smallest and least fearsome of such armaments gave me a brand-new appreciation for how insanely powerful the main gun of a cruiser was.

Thunder rolled out over the plain, the eponymous signature of the Boomers, and tungsten slugs the size of my fist obliterated two or three Tahni battlesuits with one shot. And the projectiles didn't stop for the effort, either plowing meters into the ground if aimed downward or, if shot upward into the High Guard troops jetting in from all around, blasting straight over the horizon to land in parts unknown.

If it had been me, or any other Marine charging into that sort of artillery, I would have pulled back, strategized, come up with a new approach to bypass the guns. But the Tahni were defending their home, a world near the heart of the Imperium, and they threw themselves into the fire with no regard for their lives like the elite soldiers they were. High Guard, so I had been reminded before by Captain Covington, didn't refer to the altitude at which they operated, but their status as warriors. They were the best the Tahni had to offer.

And most of us were hood rats, the dregs, the ones so desperate to avoid a sentence in punitive hibernation, or a death sentence by the gangs or just desperate to get *out* that we were willing to let the government implant jacks into our brains and send us past the edges of human space to do something as insane as fight an interstellar war.

Yet here we were, on their turf, coming down their throats. It was enough to make even a cynic like me a little patriotic.

We'd been running, our rounded, spiked footpads digging divots into the pavement with each step, leaving tracks behind us that would take industrial equipment months to repair, but once we'd cleared the last line of buildings, we could see the enemy and I knew it would be a matter of seconds before they saw us.

"Hit the jets!" I ordered, somehow in charge of all this. Whose brilliant idea had *that* been? "Third, you're the tip of the spear!"

Which meant First squad was the point of the tip, and Private Delp was the...well, he was the poor son of a bitch who was going in first. And it should have been me. I felt it every time, but more now than ever. I should have been the one going in first, the one running point. But someone had to be in command, and I'd been stupid enough to volunteer, so I ran behind Third Platoon, still too far up for the book recommendation for someone commanding the equivalent of a light company, but as far back as I could allow myself.

Cano and Kovacs were just behind us and to either side, Vicky and Freddy behind them and Manley bringing up drag, the whole lot of us roaring into the air in a formation like a gaggle of geese heading south for the winter.

"Don't shoot at us!" I yelled into the general brigade net. "Check your IFF! Drop-troopers on the hop!"

Which wasn't at all dignified, but incoming friendly fire always has the right of way and I would have looked damned silly getting killed by my own people after surviving the second hairiest drop of my career.

I wasn't sure if the warning worked or the defenders were just too busy shooting at the hordes of bad guys to even notice us, but the coil guns didn't kill us and I considered that a win.

"Target at your discretion," I directed, watching the battle-ground pass below me like I was taking a virtual tour of it, "and volley fire."

Volley fire on the hop was about a hundred times harder than on the run, but I figured there were enough Tahni troopers out there, any missile we launched was bound to hit something. I had two missiles left after our last fight, and I was so absorbed trying to direct the battle that I wasn't conscious of firing them, was just suddenly aware of the ammo indicator flashing red at me to let me know they were gone.

I definitely noticed the effect they had. We had five platoons, more or less, nearly a hundred suits firing at once, and the results were spectacular. I'd watched a time-lapse video of a field of wildflowers blooming somewhere in the Rocky Mountains on Earth, somewhere I'd never had the chance to visit and probably never would. The field had been barren, rocky, lifeless, and then sprouts of color had flashed to life, here and there at first, but eventually covering the entire expanse of what had been dirt.

The chain of explosions blossoming across the side of the steppes reminded me of those flowers, beautiful and miraculous and short-lived, though not as short-lived as the Tahni High Guard troopers at the heart of the blasts. The enemy knew we were here now, and staying in the air would, I suspected, prove to be a bad idea.

"Down," I snapped. "Take them on the run."

Electron beams were burning out at us, starting high and arcing downward with the trajectory of our flight, just a fraction of a second and a few meters behind, hounds baying at our heels. We had the Tahni in a crossfire and our plasma guns were adding to the destruction, bits of the heart of a star burning through whatever they touched, and yet it wasn't enough. I felt like I was killing a High Guard suit every other second, knew the others had to be doing the same because there were just too many to miss, but too many to miss also meant too many to beat. The knowledge rubbed against the soft skin of my mind, a burr stuck in my shoe on a long hike, that I couldn't take the time to remove because this section of trail was too dangerous.

Why am I thinking in hiking metaphors? I never hiked once in my whole fucking life until Basic. I blamed Scotty. He used to go on and on about how his dad would take him and his brothers hiking in the Bloodmark Mountains back on Hermes until I felt like I'd been there myself.

I missed his ramblings about Hermes, missed having him as a sort of cool older brother for the platoon. Bang-Bang was more of a typical Gunny, loud and harsh and overbearing in a fatherly sort of way, and he was good at his job, but he wasn't Scotty. There wouldn't be another Scotty. And I could have really used Scotty right now, could have used a Marine I trusted implicitly to lead Third in combat while I tried to direct this impromptu group of dribs and drabs, someone I wouldn't have to check because I would know exactly what they were doing.

Bang-Bang was doing the right thing, keeping the platoon in formation, keeping their fires focused and their lines as clean as possible as we all touched down, doing a better job than Manley or Kovacs, one of whom should have known better. Kovacs' platoon was bunched up at the center like scared kids huddling for support, and there wasn't time for their platoon sergeant to straighten them out, much less their half-assed company commander. They paid for it, though, before I could even open my mouth to warn them, two of them dropping almost as their feet touched the ground, lit up like torches in the night by the atomic sledgehammers of the Tahni electron beamers.

My gut tightened at their deaths, at the IFF transponder signals going dark in a remote corner of my IFF display, and heat kissed my skin as if it were me burning up at the blast of heat and hard radiation.

"Fucking spread out!" The words burst out of me like the plasma blast I fired without consciously aiming. "Close with them and limit their arc of fire!"

If we could get close enough, the whole mass of them couldn't shoot at us without hitting their own people. And if that didn't stop them from trying, it would still mean more dead Tahni, less for us to have to engage.

"Manley, Kovacs," I ordered, the words and the decision behind them taking up the better part of my conscious thought, the plasma gun firing as if on its own, its flare surprising me nearly as much as the impact of the blast on an enemy suit, "hit the jets, fall in behind the defenders and bolster their lines. Cano and Morrel, curve around the left flank, Sandoval and Kodjoe go right and squeeze them between us."

I had to get Manley and his rag-tag platoon somewhere he wouldn't have to make any more leadership decisions, and Kovacs was already down four Marines, and probably wouldn't have been much use in this dynamic a battle-space anyway.

Goddammit, I said 'battle-space' again. The Skipper would kick my ass for that.

I trusted Vicky, of course, and I was going to keep an eye on Third because, whether Bang-Bang was competent or not, they were my Marines. Cano...well, Billy was Billy, and if he wasn't the best platoon leader I'd ever encountered, he was going to have to be good enough. And Freddy was competent, if uninspired, and I at least trusted him enough to let Vicky watch out for him.

If the makeshift company didn't split exactly like a well-choreographed dance routine, they at least managed to make the move close enough to each other that the enemy wasn't able to focus fire on any one element. And I found I couldn't focus my eyes on any one of the enemy suits in particular. They faded to ghosts in my peripheral vision, a secondary problem beside the movements of my own Marines.

Was this what the Skipper saw when he led Delta into combat? Because it was uncomfortable as hell, something akin to that mild feeling of motion sickness that tugged at my gut when I was travelling fast in one direction and looked aside just far enough to where my peripheral vision could pick up the forward motion while my eyes were mostly fixed to the side. I had the terrible intuition it would fade if I gave too much thought to it, so I just shoved the mild nausea aside and let the image form an active map in front of me, using the data from the display and the feedback along my interface jacks, the intuitions that were actually data flowing back along the lines into my brain.

The gestalt of all that data input was like a new sense, a spatial awareness of where everyone around me was, their trajectories, their status. It forced me to withdraw from the more immediate sensations of my suit's footpads slamming into the pavement, of the pavement transitioning to clay, then sod, and the subtle difference in the sound and vibration as the surface changed. The High Guard suits were everywhere, and if they didn't happen to be shooting at me, it was only because they were still too involved with the group defending the earthen steppe nearly a kilometer up ahead of me, their backs to a wall of dirt and rock, their Boomers arrayed in a semi-circle like old paintings I'd seen of early settlers on the frontiers of Earth defending against raids from the natives.

And if the endless ballet of move and counter-move on the ground and in the sky above us wasn't confusing and distracting enough, the very air seemed to crackle with the constant discharge of energy, the static electricity of hundreds of electron beams and plasma blasts and coil gun shots crisscrossing in grid-square lines of destruction. The helmet optics did their best to minimize the flare and flash, to make them just one more bit of information rather than the apocalyptic web of death I knew from unhappy experience of a battle such as this outside my suit. But there was too much of it, too much pure energy in the air to be survivable, it seemed.

And many didn't survive. I saw IFF transponders blacking out on my display and forced myself to think of them only as game counters, not people I'd met, Marines I'd worked beside for months. Jurgensen went down from Third squad, Third Platoon...*my* platoon. I didn't see him die, didn't personally witness the damage the electron accelerator did to his armor, didn't hear his final scream, but I could imagine it all. It was present in my head, a replacement for the sterile and impersonal disappearance of the vital blue line beside his name on the display.

I was going to have to write the notification to his parents.

Notifications. They're not together. Cleveland Metroplex. Both of them non-workers on the dole their whole lives. But that doesn't mean they loved him any the less.

The thought was almost clinical, distant in a way that frightened me. I was planning out the messages in a small compartment of my thoughts, like it was a job I had to do, one more chore to be accomplished after the battle, like clean-up and PMCS. It wasn't that I didn't care about Jurgensen, it was simply an overload of information, too much input for me to process it all, much less allow myself an emotional reaction to any of it. Vicky could have died before my eyes in that very moment and I wouldn't have had the luxury to grieve until the battle had ended.

She didn't, and neither did I. I hadn't died yet, in this one, solipsistic reality where I wouldn't die, where I couldn't, where all the twists and turns of reality conspired to keep me alive. It was easy to believe in the wild idea now. I hadn't died when the wild shots from the street had hit our house, Momma had. I hadn't died in the desert crossing, Poppa and Anton had. I hadn't died crossing in front of that train in the Underground, the cartel enforcer had. I hadn't died at Brigantia or in all those battles after, and maybe I couldn't. But even in my crazy, combat-stress-induced fantasy where the universe revolved around me, I could be hurt and I knew how badly it sucked, so I still dodged and moved and hopped and shot and maybe prayed just a little.

One of Vicky's Marines went black, then another from Manley's platoon just before they reached our defensive lines, but the second they did, something shifted. I'd had different trainers call it different things: the Flux, Momentum, the Tide, the Big Mo. But you could tell when it happened, when the battlefield began to tilt in one direction or another. Maybe it was just adding more guns to the base of fire at the defensive position, or maybe it was the enemy figuring out that the rest of us were going to catch them in a pincer movement, but the Tahni front lines moved back, just a few dozen meters at first, and then a hundred. They left their dead and disabled behind them, smoldering and blackened, side by side with our own, the metal coffins so melted and slagged that it was difficult to tell which side they belonged to.

It began as an organized withdrawal, but it quickly turned into a retreat, the Tahni High Guard pulling back down the hill, seeking cover wherever they could, behind rows of cracked and crumbling buildings, lots packed with construction equipment, even behind the burning wreckage of their own aircraft. It was easy, down here, to forget the war up there, but it was still going on, the sonic booms nearly constant overhead, the night banished in the glowing aftereffects of the destruction of our aerospacecraft and theirs, of warheads detonating either at their targets or prematurely, brought down by ECM jamming or counter-missile fire.

"Strike Cover," I called, just a prayer into the night wind, "this is Strike Delta Three-Zero, need air support. Do you read? Over." I even used proper comms procedure, which we didn't bother with much suit-to-suit, because the Fleet types were sticklers for it.

Nothing.

Yeah, I didn't think so. I could have tried to launch a commo drone to get a line-of-sight linkup with one of the assault shuttles, but the odds of it surviving more than a couple seconds once it climbed up a hundred meters were almost nil.

Plasma blasts chased the High Guard troops back to cover, and it looked as if Cano and Freddy wanted to pursue as well, caught up in the momentary victory and thinking they could run the enemy to ground if only I set them loose. But I couldn't. I knew better.

"All Delta elements," I said, the words seeming to come from somewhere outside my body, "pull back to the defensive lines now."

"We got them, Cam!" Cano insisted. "They're on the run!"

I shuffled to a halt, aware again of my motions and position, my conscious mind finally catching up with my instincts, and stood for just a moment, staring at Billy Cano.

"They're on the run *now*," I told him. "If we go running headlong after them, they'll make a stand and we'll be strung out and bent over. Now get back to the defensive lines until some other stupid bastard volunteers to take charge of this bunch of yahoos."

"Right, okay," Cano said, his tone going meek, as if he understood what he'd been about to do.

I didn't fly the kilometer up to the earthwork, as tempting as it was to save time. The Tahni were out of sight from the ground, but there was no use tempting them with an airborne target. Sod crumbled under my steps, and I had the unreasoning fear the whole side of the hill might collapse under the weight of us. It was nonsense, the whole thing was built up around the walls of the fusion plant, the dirt anchored by age until it would have taken earth movers to rip it out, but it was the sort of fear that took hold when I let my mind wander away from the mission, the abject terror that I'd missed something, that something would go wrong and kill us all and it would be *my* fault.

I topped the hill and found myself staring into the yawning muzzles of half a dozen coil guns for just a moment before the Boomers shifted their aim. The raised wall of dirt had been crystalized to glass by the heat of the electron beamers, and the brittle surface crunched under my feet, the slivers sharp enough to slice through flesh, and I was grateful mine was shielded by the armor.

"I'm Lt. Alvarez, Third Platoon, Delta," I announced to no one in particular, lacking the time and the mental energy to read through all the IFF transponders scattered across nearly a kilometer along the earthen step. "Who's in command?"

I was hoping like hell it was the Skipper, because I was just *so* ready to not be running Delta, but even more I was also just wishing it was someone superior to me in rank, because I was not even going to try to command what amounted, in sheer numbers, to a light battalion. I should have remembered that old saying about being careful what you wish for.

"I am, Alvarez," Captain Cronje said, and if he didn't snarl the words, it might have been because he was too damned relieved at having the siege on his position lifted. "Not surprised to see you scurrying out of the rubble. Cockroaches are born survivors."

His IFF shone like a demonic halo as he shuffled across the crystalized dirt, cracking off shards that glittered by the light of the fires, the flashes of artificial lightning in the sky. I wanted to snap something very insubordinate at him, but one of us had to be a responsible adult and it wasn't going to be this asshole.

"Did anyone from Delta Headquarters make it?" I asked, instead, maybe from sound tactical thinking, maybe from sentiment, or maybe just the desperate hope *someone* here was higher in rank than Cronje.

There was a pause, a hesitation that was harder to detect when the other person was inside a helmet and I was only hearing their voice instead of seeing their face, but I caught it just the same.

"Captain Covington and First Sergeant Campbell took Lieutenants Burke and Patel with them, along with the Delta Company Boomers." His rasping sigh shouldn't have made it past the static filters, but it did. Or maybe I just imagined it. "He left the rest of us here to hold off the Tahni High Guard while they went into the reactor complex to finish the mission. And that's exactly what I intend to do."

[14]

"How long ago?" I asked him, glancing aside at the looming curve of the power plant's central dome as if I could see them, as if I could make out the external signs of their attack over the chaos and the flames and the explosions rising up all over Deltaville.

"Five minutes. Not nearly long enough to have reached their objective." His tone was scolding, preemptively so, as if he was trying to justify his decision before announcing it. "He thought we could hold off the enemy long enough for him to get there, but I saw a force of High Guard and Shock-Troopers bypassing our position to the south."

"I could take the rest of Delta Company and reinforce him," I said immediately, taking a step as if to go right now, urgency pulling at me. Five minutes was an eternity in combat, despite Cronje's dismissal.

"Negative," he said, the denial flat and broaching no argument. "We're going to do just what he said and stay here in a good, defensive position."

"Sir," Vicky said, and I finally noticed she'd moved up onto the steppe beside us, "Captain Covington ordered me to go out and find the rest of the battalion in order to complete the mission. He'd clearly taken command of the battalion in the absence of Colonel Voss and the XO. He never said anything about keeping the Marines here."

"And he's *gone*, Lieutenant!" Cronje reminded her. I couldn't see his face, but I could picture it, soft-edged, round, and florid. "He left *me* in command here, and *my* orders are for the entire battalion to maintain a defensible position until such time as we can contact the Fleet for air support. Leaving this position without air cover is suicide!"

"You aren't seriously going to let Captain Covington die out there with no reinforcement, are you?" I blurted. It was stupid, I knew it even as the words tumbled out. I wasn't going to accomplish anything by antagonizing him. But some things can't be kept inside.

"I know you're a worthless hood rat from the Underground with a problem taking orders from your superiors, Alvarez," he replied, anger and disgust dripping from his tone, "but I'm in command and no one is going anywhere! Unless you'd like to try again for the court-martial you deserve."

I stared in silence at the optical display on my helmet's interior screen, my guts seething, the muscles in my shoulders bunched up as if I could reach through the suit and punch the asshole in the face. I did nothing, said nothing for a long second. Somewhere to the east, I thought I saw a lightening on the horizon that might have been the approaching dawn, or could just have been part of the city on fire.

"Lt. Sandoval," I said, finally, broadcasting on the battalion net so every single Marine could hear it, "what were Captain Covington's last orders before he sent you out to find us?"

"He told me to bring in any battalion elements I could locate," she said without hesitation, "and bring them to his location so we could complete our assigned mission."

"It doesn't *matter* what...," Cronje tried to interrupt, but I cut him off. He probably didn't think I could do it, that he had the command override on his suit that would let him take control of the battalion comm network, but I'd learned the secrets of the Vigilante from the best, from a Warrant who knew them better than the men and women who'd designed them.

"Lt. Kodjoe," I went on, finding Freddy Kodjoe on the IFF overlay a few dozen meters away from our position, "do you concur that these were Captain Covington's last orders?"

That was a risk. Freddy hadn't given me any indication he'd changed his attitude toward me or what had happened. I was making a bet with myself that the Freddy Kodjoe I'd known at OCS wouldn't lie, no matter what he thought of me now.

"That's what the captain said," he confirmed, proving me right. He added, "It's all going to be in the mission recordings on our suits," as if he was trying to apologize to Cronje for agreeing with me.

"Alvarez...," Cronje began, but I cut him off again.

"I'll just take my platoon," I volunteered, hating myself for it, for having to bend over for Cronje, for putting my platoon at risk and letting him sit here in relative safety. "You'll still have plenty of troops to hold off the High Guard." *Plenty of troops to keep your ass safe,* I didn't say but thought as loud as I could.

He didn't answer immediately, and I imagined I could see the gears grinding in his brain, considering if this was his best chance to be rid of me once and for all.

"Go," he told me. "If you want to commit suicide, I won't be the one to talk you off the ledge."

"You're not going to just send one platoon, are you, sir?" Freddy asked, something between disbelief and horror in his voice.

"Shut up, Kodjoe," Cronje snarled at the man. "Get your

platoon arrayed on the defensive perimeter. That's a fucking order."

Vicky and Freddy were still talking, arguing with Cronje, but I didn't wait around for him to change his mind, switching to the platoon net and shutting everything else out.

"Third Platoon," I ordered, "follow me on the hop. We're staying low and hugging the side of the hill until we're over the top."

Maybe I was leading them to their deaths, and to mine, but one of my first trainers had told me, the mission always came first. The mission, he'd said, the troops, and then you. And if the troops and I had to sacrifice to accomplish the mission, well, that was why we were Marines in the first place.

"First squad, you're in the lead," I went on. "And remember, Delp—no electron beams to the face. That's an order."

"Sir," Bang-Bang said, something hesitant in his voice. I checked the feed and saw it was private between us.

"What is it, Gunny?" I stepped to the inner edge of the steppe, ready to launch, ready to get away from Cronje before he could try to stop me.

"Are you sure this is the smart play?" he asked. He was making it sound canny, like the question of an old Marine NCO trying to check his platoon leader's foolishness, but I was a former NCO myself and I knew the tone. Bang-Bang Morrel was scared.

"If there was some point in my life where I might have decided to make the smart play," I assured him, "it would have to have been before I volunteered for the Marines. Ooh-rah, Bang-Bang."

"Ooh-rah, sir." And if there wasn't enthusiasm in that voice, at least there was acceptance.

"Over the hill, Marines!"

The fusion plant, seen from the top of the tiered hill, reminded me of the images I'd studied in my history classes at Officer's Candidate School of ancient, walled cities like Constantinople. Instead of spires and towers and vaulted cathedrals, though, this alien fortress was a collection of domes and spheres and a power transmission column, crackling with the raw energy of a star held in a dungeon somewhere within the depths of the Earth. Cooling pipes two meters tall ran from outside the city, bringing water in from inland seas, and if we could have sabotaged them, it might have been the easiest way to disable the plant. But they were centimeters thick, and probably had a short-term liquid-nitrogen backup system, and we just didn't have that kind of time.

In the midst of the fairy-story city surrounded by the crenelated retaining walls lay the gap the invaders had used to infiltrate, a cargo entrance at the end of a broad, paved road passing through a natural canyon carved from the surrounding hills. Cargo trucks were lined up on either side of it, some of them with empty beds, others piled with freight. I couldn't tell what it was, wouldn't likely have known even if this had been a fusion reactor on a human colony. I knew what the twisted, humanoid metal shapes scattered on the road alongside the trucks were, though. Too small for battlesuits, they were the remains of Tahni Shock-Troopers, probably stationed at the facility as guards. They might have been an effective deterrent if Force Recon had hit it, but the Skipper and his half-company had ploughed right through them and left at least two dozen of the armored infantry dead behind him.

"Go," I urged Delp. "Kreis, set your squad up around the entrance and pull security until we're inside."

Waiting on the side of the artificial hill, suit down on one knee, while Kreis deployed his people and Medina probed cautiously into the yawning cavern of an entrance, I felt startlingly alone. Not just because we were one platoon against a whole planet, but because of who *wasn't* with us. I wasn't sure what I had expected. I suppose I'd had some fantasy about the rest of the platoon leaders seeing what a fucking coward Cronje was being and defying him to come with me to complete the mission. I suppose I should have known better.

"Clear!" Sgt. Medina called from the mouth of the tunnel.

I was happy to get out from beneath the writhing, war-torn sky.

The entrance bore the marks of a battle, with more of the Shock-Troopers lying dead just inside. Light panels on the walls and the ceiling still sparked where the impact of Tahni KE gun rounds or our own plasma blasts had blown them out of their frames and left live wires exposed. The malfunctioning panels threw strange, shifting shadows across the unfinished cement walls of the tunnel, five meters tall and ten wide, large enough to allow two cargo haulers abreast.

I'd felt horribly exposed a minute ago, and now I felt just as horribly confined, and I almost missed the distraction of having to control a company now that I was back to a platoon.

"We got a casualty up here, sir," Medina told me.

"Hold up," I ordered, slipping through the tight formation we'd been squeezed into by the confines of the tunnel.

It curved just ahead, and around the curve, the battle had grown fiercer. The enemy had been waiting there. Not Shock-Troopers but High Guard. Their dead were stacked high, one atop another, as if the Skipper's force had piled them to the side so they could pass. Metal was ripped and burned and sheered away, had melted and reformed into something wavy and surreal, and I couldn't tell where the metal ended and the burned flesh beneath began.

The Tahni suits were stacked like rubbish, but the one Marine Vigilante had been left where it lay, respectfully. An electron beam had pierced the helmet, leaving a twisted mass of metal, and mercifully, I couldn't see what was left inside. The IFF transponder was dark, but I could still read the ID. It was Lt. Cassandra Burke, the Second Platoon leader.

I barely knew her, less than I knew Cano or Kovacs. She'd seemed pleasantly gung-ho about the Marines and the war, like a fan at a soccer game, and the few times we'd talked, she'd never mentioned anything personal, just reminisced about her days in the Academy, as if it had been the crowning moment of her life. I thought I'd heard her say once that she was from Australia, and I vaguely knew where the continent was. They had kangaroos there, I thought.

Did she have a boyfriend in Australia? Parents? Brothers and sisters?

"Get going," I told Medina. "Hurry, but keep your eyes open."

If this had been the first skirmish, it almost assuredly wouldn't be the last. Cronje had told me he'd seen a sizable force heading up the road around them, and I knew this wouldn't be the only entrance into the reactor facility, just the easiest one for us to use. The enemy would have come in the other side and sent a scouting force ahead to look for us. Covington had met them here, and he hadn't killed them all. Some had to have retreated back further into the complex to tell the others, to get them ready to meet the Marine force. And we were several minutes behind, ten or twelve at a minimum.

Too far.

The cargo tunnel seemed to go on forever, and really did stretch for over a kilometer, putting us beneath the dome of the reactor, maybe beneath the edge of the tokamak. We reached the cargo loading area and found the scene of the next battle, a bigger one. The space was huge, almost a kilometer on a side, and two more cargo trucks were parked side by side in the middle of it. Freight containers were stacked fifteen meters high at the outside walls, and had been much further in, I deduced from the rows of them that had been toppled like the dominoes the old folks used to play in front of the bars in Tijuana. Some still burned, struck in the crossfire, while others were simply scattered across the cavernous chamber as if kicked there by a titan.

And more bodies. Always more bodies. Ours and theirs, and if there were more of theirs than ours, twice as many littering the cement floor of the storage chamber, well, they could *afford* to lose more. This was their world, and we'd had to bring everything and everyone with us we were going to have.

It won't be enough.

The thought nagged again at the frayed edges of my thoughts, a dolorous conviction that this was it, the place where my luck ran out, where my solipsistic theory fell apart. This world was *not* centered on my existence, and I would make that discovery suddenly and violently.

Just the way most of Second Platoon had. They had, I figured, been left back as a rear guard, to allow the main attacking body to press on to the objective. That was the only reason I could think of why every wrecked and smoldering Vigilante I scanned came back as from Second Platoon. Except Lt. Bradley. He was the company Executive Officer, a First Lieutenant. He'd been a friendly guy with an easy smile and I barely ever saw him. The few times I had, he was complaining how he was buried in clerical work and felt more like a file clerk than a combat Marine. I guess he'd felt like one at the last.

He'd probably volunteered to lead Second after Burke went down. He'd probably volunteered to stay behind with them, too.

"Any survivors?" I rasped the words, my mouth dry. I took a

sip from the water nipple beside my chin and it didn't seem to help.

"I don't see any, sir," Bang-Bang said. "Not all of Second is here, but...I don't know how many survived the drop."

"Keep moving, Delp. All of you, keep your intervals. I know we all want to bunch up down here, to feel like we're all protecting each other, but that's not how it'll work if they ambush us. Ten meters minimum, and spread out across the tunnel as far as you can."

I was an idiot, a school teacher lecturing children on fire safety while the building burned down around them, but every superior officer, every trainer at OCS, every NCO I'd had always insisted shit like that was necessary, that it calmed the troops. It had never done a damned thing for me, and I thought maybe the whole thing as a mutually-agreed-upon practical joke foisted on platoon leaders by our trainers.

I moved forward, past the trailing fire teams of First squad and even with Sgt. Medina, not so much from lack of trust as impatience. I wanted the show to kick off, and it would happen sooner for me if I were near the front. While I walked, I called up the plans for the fusion plant we'd been issued with the Op Order. They weren't the actual blueprints, of course, just a generalized layout extrapolated from similar facilities we'd seen on other Tahni worlds.

They were surprisingly big and primitive compared to Commonwealth plants, and their weakness, the one spot we knew we could take them out with conventional hyper-explosives or even the coil guns from a Boomer, was the central solenoid for the magnetic field coils. Everything else was buried too deep inside the shielding, but the solenoid could be reached even by something the size of a Vigilante. And reaching it meant going straight ahead until this tunnel hit the central service hub, a vertical passage that stretched from the shielding over the tokamak to the cooling pumps near the surface.

That was where Captain Covington would be headed, and the Tahni knew it. It would be the logical place to leave their main force, and I expected, when we reached it, we'd either find the battle still raging or maybe that we'd already lost. If that were the case, I'd have to hope he had, at least, whittled down the enemy numbers and do my best to carry out the objective myself.

I got my answer before we even reached it. The suit's sonic pickups were more sensitive than my human ears would have been if they'd been unencumbered by so many centimeters of BiPhase Carbide armor, and they were flashing red in frantic warning hundreds of meters before we reached the hub.

"We got fighting up ahead, sir," Delp told me, redundant but trying to be helpful.

"Send out a spy drone," I told him.

I couldn't see his face when I gave the order, but I was willing to bet he'd rolled his eyes. We all carried a couple of the tiny, remote-controlled quad copters, but we rarely had the opportunity to use them for anything useful. Most of our operations were too dynamic to let the comparatively-slow spy robots do their work, and in the ones that weren't, jamming was a constant issue.

But we had them, and doctrine dictated I try to use them. And for once, I was willing to give doctrine a shot.

The drone separated from the top of Delp's backpack, hovering just above him for a moment before it shot forward and around the slight curve in the tunnel. I tied into its signal, whispering a prayer for clear images and useful intelligence. Murphy, as it turned out, is an atheist.

"Loss of Signal, sir," Delp reported with an air of I-told-you-so to the words.

The drone's small, weak antenna couldn't burn through the jamming, and laser line-of-sight wasn't useful when we didn't have a direct line of sight. And if we *had* been afforded a direct line of sight, we wouldn't have needed the fucking drone and I felt like an idiot again.

I shrugged. It had been worth a shot.

"Sgt. Morrel, Sgt. Medina," I said, wanting to rush ahead and help the Skipper but knowing I was just as likely to get everyone killed without a plan, "when we hit the hub, I'm guessing the Tahni are going to be on the far side of the circle, close to the surface entrance tunnel. That's going to put the bulk of whatever's left of Delta between us and them. Bang-Bang, I want you to take First squad and circle counter-clock-wise. Kreis, you follow the hub wall clockwise, and both of you lay down suppressive fire for the rest of the platoon. I'm going to take Second and Third squads straight across, if possible, and break through the enemy position. Any questions?"

"None that wouldn't get me in trouble," Bang-Bang murmured.

"Yeah, I know it's nice and vague," I admitted, "but the alternative is to send in a couple scouts to get shot at and hope one comes back alive to tell us the enemy is expecting us and we're fucked. So, again, any questions?"

There were none.

"Delp," I told the point man, "when you hit the hub, don't stop moving. Not for a second, not until and unless you reach cover or get behind our lines."

"Gotcha, sir," he assured me, not sounding very confident at all. "At least I won't have to worry about the Article-15's."

"Look at the bright side, Vince," I assured him. "I'll be right behind you, so there probably won't be anyone left to press charges anyway."

The power plant's hub was something I might have expected to find on a starship, a vertical passageway, open to the sky, extending right through the center of the tokamak's torus, the shielding grey and massive around the magnetic coils just a few levels below us, and through the center of it, reaching upward from the bottom of the fifty-meter drop into the middle of the coils, the central solenoid that powered the fields. Around the edges of the passage, a service walkway curled like a strand of DNA, the ramp wide enough to allow cargo jacks to haul freight capsules from the warehouse to replace parts of the reactor at need.

We emerged near the top of the hub, just eight or ten meters from the rain shield, a plastic awning on thin, metal struts that was the only thing separating the open roof from the outside weather. The opaque awning seemed to block out the air battles above us as well, conspiring to confine our reality to the few hundred square meters of hell beneath it.

This was the battleground, the place where all that was left of our comrades and our enemies had retreated to or advanced toward, and I don't believe I had ever seen so many battlesuits crammed into so small of a space. Captain Covington wouldn't have chosen this place, not if he'd had options. He would have recognized it for the chokepoint it was, would have seen how it totally negated the maneuverability and versatility of the suits. But this was where the objective was, and if it was where the enemy was, too, well...the mission came first.

I nearly stumbled over the torn and smoking corpses of two Vigilantes before I'd taken three steps into the hub and didn't even have the time to run their transponders to see who they were before one of my own had joined them. It wasn't Delp. He'd done what I said, kept moving, even in the face of a blinding firestorm of raw energy, a wave of overwhelming heat. But Muller, the Alpha fire team leader, had paused at the first of the dead Marines. It was forgivable...by me, but not by the gods of battle. An electron beam lanced through his chest and he was dead in the space of a second.

The reality of our situation hit me like an intuition, laying itself out in a mental lap. The enemy was concentrated two levels below us, just above the base of the solenoid, taking cover behind a half a dozen freight containers abandoned on the walkway, still mounted atop cargo jacks, their caster-style rollers blown out from beneath them either during the battle or on purpose beforehand. The Marines were up one level from the Tahni, and if they had the high ground, that was more than balanced out by the fact that they had no cover and their numbers were down to less than platoon strength.

"Move!" I screamed at the others, wanting to take the time to explain our position but knowing we'd all be dead in the seconds it would take. "Hit your jets and follow me!"

This was the part where we could all get killed between one heartbeat and the next, and the wrong decision could cost us the battle and our lives, and I had to make it in a fraction of a second. I could have led them into a charge directly at the enemy, counting on surprise to let our inferior numbers overwhelm them, and maybe I should have, but instead, I took them into our lines, supporting the position of the Marines who were already there just from an instinct that they wouldn't figure out who we were in time, that they'd catch us between their fire and the Tahni.

I snapped off a shot in mid-air as I jetted down to the Marine position, and a dozen more followed it, a volley perfected in endless training, the rain of starfire pinning the Tahni down, suppressing their fire long enough for us to make it across the gap and touch down alongside the Marines. As I did, I noticed I'd been wrong. The Marines *did* have cover, of a sort. The remains of seven Vigilante suits were piled in front of their position, a fortification built from our own dead. They'd taken one hit after another until they were almost fused together into a solid mass of metal and flesh and it was all I could do to tear my eyes away from them and scan the IFF transponders of the ones left alive.

The highest-ranking of the survivors was Top. First Sergeant Ellen Campbell had taken more than one hit, and her suit was coated a carbon black over the matte grey. God alone knew how badly she was hurt inside it, but she limped over to me, unfazed by the electron beams impacting the wall behind us.

"Alvarez," she rasped, her voice matching the battered condition of her suit, "about time you got here."

"Sorry I'm late, Top. Where's the Skipper?"

"Down there." She pointed to the base of the solenoid with her plasma gun. "He took the last two Boomers down there about three minutes ago to try to destroy the solenoid. We laid down suppressive fire, but the Tahni managed to get suits down to take him on and I ain't heard a thing from him since."

"If they got the Boomers," I said, "how the hell are we going to take this thing out?"

"Plasma guns ain't gonna do a damned thing to it," she agreed. She was slurring her words. Not a lot, just enough to let me know she was hurting, maybe already woozy from pain meds. This wasn't good. "It's designed to *handle* plasma."

I could barely hear her, even with the volume in my earphones turned up all the way. My Marines were crowded into a space barely thirty meters across, their plasma guns blasting every few seconds, the volleys timed with the rest of Delta to keep a solid wall of fire going toward the Tahni. The concussion of the constant wave of superheated gas going outward along with the lightning-crack of the occasional answering electron beam was like trying to hold a conversation in the center of a thunderstorm.

"I've got to get to him," Top told me, shuffling forward, her armor half-toppling like she was drunk. "I'll pull him out of there..."

"Top," I said, putting my Vigilante in front of hers, blocking her way. "You're in no condition to go down there, and neither is your armor."

"We going in to get the Skipper?" Bang-Bang asked, huddled beside me, crouching down slightly to stay behind the dead Marines.

"Negative," I told him. "*We* aren't going anywhere. You are going to stay up here and lay down covering fire. I'm taking one fire team with me down there to relieve the Skipper and carry out the mission."

"Sir!" he protested. "You're the only officer here!"

"And the mission is shutting down this fucking reactor, Sergeant," I reminded him. "I'm not needed up here directing fire against a distraction, I'm needed to finish the fucking mission. That's why the Skipper was down there instead of up here." I motioned at the Tahni. There were about three platoons of them over across the hub, maybe sixty or seventy meters away, equal our strength. "When I say, I want you to..."

The sky exploded.

That wasn't what *actually* happened, of course, but at the time, it was close as I could come to understanding it. One second, the white, plastic awning stretched across the top of the reactor hub, and the next, it was sheathed in flames, burning fragments raining down around us. And on the heels of the burning awning were High Guard battlesuits, and a wave of missiles aimed not well, but in our general direction.

I had less than a second to act and no time at all to think, and the only coherent thought blaring in my head was not to be caught sitting there.

"Jump!" I bellowed on the general net, not wanting to leave out anyone who might have tagged along from another company.

I took my own advice and hit the jets, heading straight up into the teeth of the Tahni force, firing my plasma gun as I flew, all thoughts of taking out the reactor forgotten in a desperate attempt to just survive the next few seconds. In retrospect, it must have been a missile. They were crashing down on top of us, hitting the service walkway, blowing burning fragments out of the concrete walls, and one must have detonated just a bit too close.

Red flashed in my visor, useless warnings telling me what I already knew. I'd been hit, my jets were out, and I was falling.

It was nearly fifty meters down, way too far to survive, and I was going to hit hard enough to shatter my spine and fracture my skull, and there was no way in hell anyone was going to get me to a stocked medical bay on a ship in time to save my life. But something was just beneath me, something grey and metal, with the face of a golem, boosting up on reactor-powered jets. It was a Tahni High Guard battlesuit, one from the two platoons who had been just below us. He'd launched himself to strike at us before we could attack the incoming force, and I caught him in mid-air, arms going around his thick neck, the articulated claws on my left hand digging into the softer metal at the thing's shoulder joint and hanging on with every ounce of energy my suit had.

His jets weren't powerful enough to keep us both airborne, and we began to descend, slower than the fall had been but just as sure. He thrashed and tried to shake himself free of me, tried to smash his back up against the wall and scrape me off, but I threw the weight of my suit to the opposite side and dragged him away from it. We fell and the shadows descended to swallow us up. I had fleeting glimpses from above, frozen images of High Guard suits fighting Marine Vigilantes, and what I saw made no sense to me.

There were too many Vigilantes, seemingly as many as the High Guard, and there couldn't have been. I glanced at the transponder readout and saw an IFF signal from Vicky's platoon, guessed at that instant what had happened. The Tahni force Cronje had been fighting had bypassed his position and headed here, and at least Vicky's platoon had pursued.

We weren't alone, but I was still riding a Tahni battlesuit to the ground floor. He managed to toss me away just before we hit bottom and I crashed to my back, the wind going out of me despite the cushioning inside the suit. It bought him a second, maybe two before I could move, and it would have been enough. He had the emitter of his electron beamer lined up with my head and would have ended me,

Except a plasma blast from my right ended him first. His head vanished in a supernova of burning gas and he stayed upright, frozen like a statue, his gun still pointed at me, his dead finger probably still on the trigger.

"How the hell did *you* get down here, Alvarez?" Captain Covington asked.

He was leaning against the far wall, both his legs burned off above the knees, surrounded by a pile of our dead and theirs.

"Jesus Christ, sir," I hissed, looking at him. The suit's legs were longer than ours, of course, but his own had to have been taken off at least somewhere near the top of the shins, and the thermal bloom would have cooked him higher than that.

"Don't worry, son," he said, his voice sounding curiously detached, like he was watching all this from orbit and relaying a transmission down to a remotely-piloted suit. "The pain-killers in this thing are pretty powerful. Not feeling a thing."

"Is there another way out of here, sir?" I asked, stumbling over to him, trying not to trip over the dead.

"There's a service tunnel back that way," he said, motioning with his off hand to our left. I peered down that way and noticed a slight lightening of the stygian darkness. "But it doesn't matter, I'm not walking anywhere. We need to take down this reactor. From what's going on up there, I'm not sure how much time we have left."

"Take it out with *what*, sir?" I wondered. "The Boomers are gone."

I flinched at a thunderous detonation just a few dozen meters overhead, edging closer to the overhang that protected the Skipper's position. It had been cramped and close down here before a dozen battlesuits had been trashed and scattered in every conceivable place I could put a foot down flat. I was nearly standing right on top of him, and I tried not to look at what was left of his legs, afraid I would see through the ragged, melted armor into the ravaged flesh beneath it.

"Take it out with *me*," he said, not a note of concern in his voice for the chaos above us.

"What are you talking about, sir?" The pain-killers could be getting to him, I thought.

"Remember Warrant Officer Mutterlin?" he asked me, seemingly apropos of nothing. "Mutt, back on Inferno? In the armory?"

I did, of course. He'd taught me everything I knew about the inner workings of a Vigilante, and he'd probably saved my life a dozen times over, though he'd never know it.

"Yes, sir, but what...."

"It's a shame we couldn't bring Mutt with us," he went on, rambling a bit, I thought. "But the man got severely space-sick, not a damned thing the drugs could do about it. But he probably did better teaching new Drop-Troopers the secrets of the suit than he would have repairing damaged Vigilantes after a battle. And of course, if he'd been on the *Iwo*, he'd be dead right now. But he taught me something he didn't tell too many Marines, something that could have got him in big trouble." He chuckled with just a hint of insanity behind the sound. "You see, Cam, this isotope reactor we wear on our backs, well...it's quite the little firecracker. It *wants* to explode and the R&D teams had to spend quite a few years figuring out ways to *keep* it from exploding. So, if you know the way around all those safety procedures, it's not impossible to make the damn thing explode."

"Sir," I blurted, "there is no fucking way I'm going to let you..."

I don't know what clever and assertive remark I'd been about to make, but I didn't get the chance. The battle above us spilled down into our laps and I threw myself over Covington's prone form as a High Guard suit crashed down only meters away, trailing fire. Two more were heading for us and I fired at one of them reflexively, but they went down to plasma fire from above, and two Vigilante suits touched down beside us. Their IFF transponders announced their identity bright and clear, yet I had trouble believing it.

One was Vicky Sandoval, and the other was Captain Cronje.

"Come on, Alvarez, Phillip," Cronje snapped at Covington and me, gesturing with one hand, the other aiming a plasma gun upward. "Every fucking High Guard and Shock-trooper in the city is heading for this reactor. We have to get the hell out of here now."

"My God, sir," Vicky gasped, finally seeing Covington's legs. "Come on, Cam," she urged me. "Help me grab him. Together, we can fly him out of here."

"You two get him," I told her. "My jets are damaged. Readout says they might be usable again once the turbines cool down, but I'm ground-bound until then. Get him out of here and I'll try to get out on foot."

A missile struck the wall only ten meters overhead and cement and insulation sprayed out in a gout of fire, spattering our armor with flaming debris just ahead of a cloud of dust. The only reason I wasn't thrown to the ground was because I was already leaning over Covington, sheltering him with my armor, but Vicky was on her side and Cronje's back had gone up against the shielding of the solenoid. He pushed himself up, firing back at the High Guard troopers on the service walkway above us. If it had extended all the way down here, getting out wouldn't have been a problem, but it ended ten meters up, disappearing through the wall into another section of the plant.

"Come on!" Cronje said. "We're getting out of here now, Sandoval! That's an order!"

"What about Captain Covington?" Vicky demanded. "We can't leave him and Cam down here!"

"Then you stay with them, you crazy, worthless bitch!" Cronje screamed back at her. "The rest of us are getting the hell out of here!"

I should have been shocked when he boosted out of there,

not even stopping to help fight off the Tahni troopers, just heading straight out through the ruined awning. I should have been outraged at a Marine officer leaving his troops behind. Instead, I was numb, unsurprised. This was the end, the one I'd been expecting.

"Get out of here, Vicky," I told her. "You have to make it."

"No," she told me, the words flat and broaching no argument. Another Tahni battlesuit dropped down on us and she stood her ground in the midst of a lightning-storm of electron fire and returned it with her plasma gun. "You think I risked my career to get that piece of shit Cronje to come rescue you just to leave you down here? If you stay, I stay. That's how it's going to be."

"Jesus," Covington murmured, pushing himself up on his hands, getting what was left of his feet beneath him. "Get a room, you two."

Then he hit the jets and flew straight at the central solenoid, and I knew exactly what he was going to do.

"Vicky, in here!" I yelled, grabbing her armor by the shoulder plastron and shoving her toward the narrow opening in the far wall, concealed in the shadows even from my thermal and infrared, absolutely no light shining through it.

She nearly tripped over the bodies of Marines, but turned the stumble into a lumbering run, and disappeared into the darkness. I was right behind her, the narrow walls like the mouth of a great beast swallowing us both, and a claustrophobia I had never felt before clawed at my gut, but I didn't look back. I didn't even look back when light brighter than a sun exploded behind us, flooding the maintenance tunnel with an impossible, shadowless glare that seemed to penetrate even the blind face of my helmet.

The concussion hit just as we emerged from the other end of the tunnel and into what might have been a pump room for the water coolant system. I say might have, because I had about one second to notice the details of the chamber, to take note of the water pipes and other equipment before the blast tossed me across the room. I hit the opposite wall and I hoped the crunch I heard was concrete breaking and not my bones. The stars, though, they were all mine, floating in front of my eyes, blocking the much less interesting view of bits of the roof collapsing down around us.

"Get out," I croaked, not even able to see Vicky through the flares in my vision, much less tell if she was even conscious, much less on her feet. "The building's coming down."

"This way," she said, but I couldn't even make out where she was to follow until I squeezed my eyes shut for a second and tried again to focus them.

She was heading for a cargo door, sealed with some sort of rolling, metal curtain. I whispered a prayer that it wasn't too well-built, and for once, God seemed to be listening. Vicky's battlesuit ripped through the thin metal as if it wasn't there, strips of it peeling away in her wake and I could, at last, see the grey light of dawn. And a slightly brighter glow from behind us, from the west.

We lumbered out on a gravel road and I turned around to look. Where the central hub had been was a column of glowing smoke rising into the air, beyond a fire, not quite a nuclear explosion or we wouldn't have survived it. The plasma had vented catastrophically and taken the central reactor tokamak with it.

Taken Captain Phillip Covington with it.

"He's gone."

The words hissed out of their own volition, like the air escaping a balloon. They seemed to take a part of my soul with them.

"The Skipper's gone."

[16]

"Lt. Alvarez."

The voice crackled in my headphones, distorted and stat-icky, and I knew, on some level, that it wasn't the first time I'd been called. I still didn't reply, staring at the rising cloud from the explosion, trapped in a mental loop. There were certainties in the universe, laws that couldn't be violated. The speed of light in a vacuum in real-space, the inverse-square law, the conservation of mass...and the immortality of Captain Phillip Covington.

Nothing could kill him. He'd outlive the heat-death of the universe, just a few basic particles, radiation, and Phillip Covington. Everyone knew that. And now he was dead. He'd done it himself, so maybe the truth was that the Skipper was the only one who could kill the Skipper.

"Cam," Vicky said, and I could almost feel her hand on my arm, even though it was impossible.

Her voice broke the spell, and I blinked, reality coming back into focus. We were still standing on the gravel service road, still facing the roiling black cloud that was Covington's tombstone, but it wasn't just the two of us anymore. A Vigilante suit was standing at the top of the earthen wall separating the service road from the rest of the reactor complex, faceless and anonymous yet I knew from the IFF it was Sgt. Manley. He must have come with the rest of the force under Cronje, but I wondered why he hadn't pulled out when the captain had ordered him to.

"Lt. Alvarez," he said again. "Are you all right?"

"Yeah," I rasped, staggering as I tried to turn and face him, the weight of the day, of the death, of the many times I'd almost died all catching up with me at once. "What are you still doing here, Sergeant?" I hadn't meant for it to come out so harshly, like an accusation.

"We were all looking for you, sir," he said, as if that explained everything.

"We?" I repeated.

I hadn't noticed the other two suits pounding over the hill behind him, but I knew who they were instantly.

"Cam," William Cano said, relief heavy in his voice. "Thank God. I thought you'd bought it in the explosion."

"Where's the Skipper?" Kovacs wondered. "Did you get to him before everything blew?"

"The Skipper...," I trailed off, the words fighting and clawing to stay inside my chest, unwilling to come out. I forced them, knowing it had to be said. "The Skipper *was* the explosion. He overloaded his suit reactor to take out the solenoid. The rest was the plasma breach once the electromagnetic field shut down."

"The Skipper?" Kovacs put such utter devastation into the question that I felt bad about all the things I'd thought about him.

"Captain Cronje," I said, fighting down the flare of anger the name invoked. "Did you see where he went?"

"He just yelled at us all to get out," Cano told me, "then he was gone. He took his company with him, I think, but we weren't leaving till we found out what happened to you and the Skipper."

"Fucking bastard," Vicky muttered and I checked to make sure it was on our private circuit. "He took my platoon with him."

"Where is everyone?" I asked. "How many effectives do we have left?"

"We got everyone in a defensive perimeter at the front of the power plant," Cano said. "Our platoon sergeants are getting a head count and checking everyone's suits. We came to find you and…," he trailed off. "You know, the Skipper."

I sighed, the weight of a thousand worlds settling onto my shoulders.

"Show me."

It wasn't as bad as it could have been. The reactor battle had been a knife fight in a closet and I was surprised so many had survived it. Though from the looks of it, not everyone had. The perimeter was a semi-circle extending out nearly a kilometer from one side of the main entrance of the reactor, around to where the main road curved toward the city and then back to the other side, but there wasn't more than three platoons' worth of suits in the line.

More were clustered near the yawning half-oval that was the plant's main entrance, and one of them was Bang-Bang Morrel.

"God *damn*, sir," he said, loping away from the pack when he saw me and the others approaching. "I thought sure you'd bought the farm."

"It was a near thing," I assured him. "What's the butcher's bill? For my platoon and the whole company," I amended.

"Well," he said, some of the relief going out of his voice, "it's not good. We lost Majid, Muller, Kim, and Villanueva."

Shit. Each name was a punch in the gut. They'd trusted me.

The fact that we'd had a job to do and no choice in the matter didn't make anything about it better.

"Garcia and Hewson are going to make it, but they're out of action." Bang-Bang motioned at the half a dozen suits near the entrance. A couple of them were standing, but the rest were seated, and the only reason for a Vigilante to be sitting down was if its legs were damaged. "We got a few others who have minor injuries or burn-throughs, but they can Charlie Mike."

Continue the Mission. I knew the phrase, but it was old-old military slang, something before even Top's time.

"The rest of the company...," he began, but a familiar voice interrupted him.

"The rest of the company ain't much better," Top said.

She was one of the suits that was standing, but I thought it had to be a near thing. Her Vigilante looked like some near-sighted High Guard trooper had been using it for target practice, and if there was more than twenty square centimeters of her suit that didn't have a crack or burn or crater in it, I couldn't find it. I didn't know how bad it was for her inside the armor, but at least she sounded more coherent now than when the pain-killers had first hit her.

"You have three full-strength platoons if you shift some things around," she told me, "and only two platoon leaders for them."

"But there's three of us, Top," Kovacs said, sounding as if he thought the pain meds were clouding her thoughts. "Me, Cano and Alvarez."

"No, *Francis*," Top said, using the officer's first name in a deliberate shot at his thick-headedness. "There's two of you, because Lt. Alvarez is now acting company commander."

"How did you know?" I asked. I hadn't been looking forward to breaking the news to her.

"He's been my boss for almost five years," she reminded me. "You didn't think I'd know?"

The delivery of the words was flat, emotionless, but I knew the hurt was there, even if she wouldn't let herself feel it yet.

"He accomplished the mission," I told her.

"I know. He always did."

"You're wrong, Top," Vicky said. I turned physically at the pronouncement, even though it made little sense in the suit, wondering what she was saying. "There's three platoon leaders," she clarified. "Cronje took my platoon with him, and I'm not inclined to go chasing him down on my own."

"Okay," I said. "You take Third platoon. Manley can fill in as squad leader for Majid. We'll sort things out, rearrange what we need. Top," I turned my attention back to the First Sergeant, "you ain't going anywhere until your suit gets patched up." *And you with it*, I thought but didn't say. "How about you stay here with the other wounded and damaged and set up a perimeter. As soon as I can get a call out to the air cover, I'll call in a dust-off for you."

"I ain't hit that bad, junior...," she began, but I cut her off.

"I know you could tough through it," I assured her, "but someone has to stay and look out for the wounded, and I figure you're the best to do it. Am I acting company commander or not?"

Her sigh was a burst of static in my headphones.

"Goddamnit," she murmured. "All right, you win."

"But where are we *going?*" Kovacs wanted to know. "I mean, what the hell are we going to do now?"

I grabbed at patience and made sure I was on the private command net before I answered.

"You did read the fucking Op Order, right, Francis?" I asked him. "The jamming is still in place and we don't have air superiority yet, right? So, we're supposed to hook up with Battalion at the Tahni spaceport and give them support. If they've already taken it, then we get further orders from there"

"Oh, yeah," he said, abashed. "Right. But I thought Battalion all died when their drop-ship got hit."

"They did, but someone will take over," I told him. "Just like someone had to take over here."

"Yeah. I guess so." He didn't seem convinced.

"We got you, boss," Cano assured me, or maybe he was trying to reassure Kovacs.

"Bang-Bang," I said to Gunny Morrel. "Top is staying here with the wounded. That means you're acting First Sergeant."

And God, how badly I wanted it to be Scotty. Not just for my sake, either. He should have had the chance.

"Copy that, sir," Bang-Bang said with more confidence in his acceptance than I had in the decision.

"Get the company reorganized into three platoons," I told him. "We move out in five mikes."

It was nearly ten kilometers to the spaceport from the fusion plant, and it might as well have been on another planet. The power plant was an isolated pocket of dead calm in the midst of the storm, protected from the chaos of the overhead fight for air superiority by anti-aircraft batteries we hadn't even tried to take out. There were too many of them and we didn't have the troops for it. The assault shuttles would spare some missiles for them once the jamming was down and Force Recon could target the batteries with laser designators.

Outside the cover of the missile batteries, the clash overhead was a constant roll of thunder and the city was afire, and thank God we didn't have to march through it. The road from the power plant to the spaceport was largely empty, a few smaller industrial storage buildings popping up here and there without any real rhyme or reason to their placement, just another of the mysteries of Tahni city planning. The Fleet pilots hadn't even bothered to blow them up, having better things to shoot.

The road was nice and broad, allowing the company plenty of room to spread out into a tactical travel formation, multiple, mutually-supportive wedges, the only obstacles abandoned vehicles, the only visible surface threats the storage buildings. I could have sent a squad into each of them to check for concealed enemy, but I opted for speed over excess caution and we pressed on, not flying or hopping, but running at a steady thirty kilometers an hour.

Pavement cracked under the steady drumbeat of our foot-pads, one after another of us stomping down onto the same spot, and it was easy to let the rhythm hypnotize me, to fall into it like I was a private again and all I had to worry about was my own ass. I missed those days, the days when I didn't have anyone beyond myself to be responsible for, when my world ended at the tip of my nose. It had been lonely, sure, but it had also been comfortable. People could die and I wouldn't especially care, wouldn't mourn them beyond a passing gratitude that it hadn't been me.

People were still dying. People always died in war, and nothing you could do would stop that. But now, I cared about them. Now, I *hurt*. Now, I worried. Vicky was a hundred meters away from me, leading my platoon, and I had to accept the fact that she could die at any second, and I wouldn't be able to do anything to save her, and I knew just as surely that if it happened, part of me would die with her. I also knew I'd keep on fighting because that had become who I was. I was a Marine now. I'd been a loner, an outcast, an outsider, a criminal...and now I was a Marine. I couldn't go back, and yet I wondered if there was still a way I could go forward.

After the war, I reminded myself. *First things first.*

The illusion of separation from the battle began to dissolve as we neared the spaceport. If none of our assault shuttles had struck the targets there, it wasn't for lack of trying. One of them tumbled in while we were still three kilometers away, a coil gun round knocking it out of the sky. The explosion when it hit was nearly anticlimactic compared to the halos of light, the flights of missiles, the staccato beat of gunfire and the sharp, intermediate thunder cracks of energy weapons constantly rolling out across the flat pavement of the chains of landing fields.

There were buildings between sections of the port, maintenance, emergency services, storage, whatever any spacefaring race needed to have next to the field where landers and cargo shuttles and dual-environment spacecraft needed for their takeoff and landing. A Fleet pilot would probably know all the details, but to me, they were just obstacles and potential hiding places for enemy troops.

Not that I expected any enemy troops to be hiding in isolated buildings, given the utter, devastating violence rolling off the center of the spaceport. The terrain wasn't *quite* flat, and, together with the curvature of the planet, I didn't have a good look at the battlefield until we were just a hair over two klicks away. When I saw it, I almost ordered Delp to stop where he was and turn the whole fucking company around.

"Oh, sweet mother," Delp murmured, either forgetting he was on the general net or not caring. "That doesn't look good at all."

I didn't bother yelling at him and I wasn't paying enough attention to notice if his squad leader did, because I was too busy agreeing. The enemy defense was arrayed around the main spaceport facility, but the buildings themselves were important only in the overhead cover and likely the localized power generator they gave to the anti-aircraft turrets. Coil guns and missile launchers scanned back and forth with each pass of an assault shuttle overhead, their sensor dishes following the action like a fan at a tennis match.

By themselves, the turrets would have been insanely vulnerable to ground attack. Even with the bunkers dug into their flanks, covering those approaches with KE gun turrets, a platoon of Drop-Troopers could have taken them down in a half an hour.

I suppose that's why had the mecha.

Sweet Jesus, I hated those things.

Imagine if an assault shuttle and a Vigilante battlesuit made sweet love and had themselves a mutant child, and that's not even half as bad as the reality of a Tahni mecha. It was the Tahni version of mobile artillery support, only in their minds, mobile meant walking on two legs. I don't know why that made it more intimidating to me than if it had been a tracked vehicle, but it did. The thing was powered by an antiproton reactor and bristling with weapons: long-range missiles, a coil gun, multiple KE turrets to take out infantry, and the capper, a proton cannon that could smack an assault shuttle right out of the sky. Right now, it was aiming lower, the actinic flare of the proton cannon smashing into the dirt of a retaining wall about a kilometer away from the spaceport facility, doing its part to smash it to powder, right alongside the KE turrets of the bunkers, making sure anything that showed itself above the wall would be no more than a fond memory.

It took me a second to pick out the Marines, even though they were a kilometer closer. A light company of Vigilantes was huddled on the other side of the retaining wall, following the shallow curve it described around the grass courtyard at the front of the spaceport, separating it from the pavement of the landing field. They were clearly visible on thermal, not at all on optical in the dim, grey light of dawn, all of them covered in dirt, huddled as low as they could crouch in the armor. I could feel their fear from a kilometer away. Or maybe that was just me.

Something else moved between the Vigilantes, something smaller and crouching lower, lacking any clear thermal signature and only visible from the movement. I wouldn't have spotted them at all without the IFF transponders glowing over each of their positions like a giant arrow pointing downward. They were Force Recon Marines, and what the hell they were doing here, I had no idea, but I felt for the poor bastards. Deltaville was a screaming nightmare for me wrapped in a Vigilante, and I couldn't imagine going out into it with nothing but light body armor and a tiny peashooter of a Gauss rifle.

"What the fuck are we gonna do, Cam?" Kovacs asked, the horror in his voice matching my own.

Then High Guard battlesuits flowed out of a cargo entrance on the right-hand side of the main spaceport building, heading up a service road out to the edge of the grass courtyard. They were trying to flank the Marines and even if there weren't enough of them to take out the Drop-Troopers on their own, all they had to do was force them into the open and the mecha and the bunker turrets. And the decision was made for me. There was no way I could let them be slaughtered.

"Vicky," I said, both because I trusted her more than Cano or Kovacs and because I trusted Delp to run point, "stay low, stay fast...and take us in."

We ran toward the sound of the guns.

[17]

"You don't see us," I chanted under my breath, a prayer, a command, and a wish all in one. "You don't see us. You don't see us."

There was nothing else to do, no strategy to take. We were out of missiles, out of time, out of options. If that mecha caught sight of us while we were too far away, while we were running across the open plain with no cover, no chance at dodging, it could wipe out half of us in seconds.

My only hope was that the Tahni were too focused on what was happening in front of their noses, too concerned with the flanking charge to check their long-range sensors. And it seemed as if they were. Five hundred meters passed by in seconds, and we were halfway to the wall, and it looked so damned close. But we couldn't run straight at it. Vicky's platoon, what had been my platoon, curved to the right to meet the incoming threat. I wanted to scream at them to just get to cover, but I couldn't because she was doing the right thing.

And then they noticed us. We were too close to ignore, but close enough, *gracias Dio*, that the mecha couldn't target us with its missiles. But that fucking proton cannon...

The Tahni mecha pilot depressed the weapon as far down as it could go, but it was intended for air defense use, so the blast of charged particles smacked into the edge of the earthen retaining wall first, which was the only thing that kept it from wiping out all of Third squad, Third Platoon. Instead, it just killed Sgt. Manley. One instant, he was running full tilt, the next there was nothing left of him except a blackened scar and a burning haze of sublimated metal.

"Move!" I yelled, useless and redundant but I couldn't help it. The word burst from my lips and I couldn't think of a single order to give that would save the rest of us.

At least not one I could give to someone else. I hit the jets, just hopped a couple dozen meters up, high enough to get the damned mecha's attention the only way I knew how, by shooting at it. The plasma burned away a centimeter of armor over its chest, but it had centimeters to spare and it returned the favor with a tantalum slug the size of my fist.

I could have died right there. Most Drop-Troopers would have. But there was a feeling I'd developed, a sense of where I should be, and it told me to give the jets an extra half-second burst before I headed down. The slug from the coil gun passed centimeters beneath my feet, where I should have been if I'd just let the natural arc of the blast take me back down.

I touched down already running and didn't feel the slightest twinge of fear from the near-miss. I wondered if that was because I'd just been overloaded with adrenaline in the last hour—*had it even been an hour, yet?* It hadn't been much, but it had bought us extra seconds, and a second in combat was forever. The company was behind the cover of the wall now, and more importantly, the mecha couldn't take any more shots at us without risking hitting his own troops.

It had been stupid and reckless, and I couldn't take chances like that anymore as a platoon leader, much less a company commander and *blah, blah, blah*. Fuck it. If they were going to stick me with this many Marines and tell me to keep them alive, I was going to do whatever it took.

"Stay low," I ordered, probably repeating what the platoon leaders were already saying but not caring. "Don't let them force you over the wall. Curve wide if you need to, but don't go up."

Delp was the first one to hit them, the first sign the High Guard troopers had that we were there. I was too far away with too many troops in-between us to have a good view of the contact, but I saw the flare of his plasma gun. An electron beam slashed wide and then the rest of First squad was curving around Delp, firing their plasma guns in a rolling volley as they went.

Four of the enemy went down in as many seconds, and the rest broke. I hadn't expected them to run, given how fanatical the High Guard had been at the reactor, but maybe having the mecha and the bunkers as a backstop was enough to make them feel confident that they could withdraw and still win this battle. It wasn't a bad assumption. We were hitting them with everything we had, throwing every force available into this attack, but the margin for error was thin and it had already been cut to the quick. Let the battle for Deltaville drag on too long, give the defense ships time to organize a counterattack in orbit, and the war would be over, all right. We'd lose it.

The quickest way to end a war is to lose it. I couldn't remember who had said it, but I remembered hearing it at OCS, along with a lot of other pithy quotes on the subject.

"Don't pursue," I cautioned Vicky, not that I expected her to. "Delta, fill in the lines beside the rest of...." The rest of who? I hadn't even figured out who we were relieving. The IFF signals were all over the place, but I thought it was Bravo Company, by a narrow margin, and Captain Geiger was the only officer present above second lieutenant. "...the battalion," I finished, though it seemed an exaggeration.

"Is this Delta?" I knew the voice, with or without the IFF transponder. Captain Geiger didn't come out to meet me, no less intimidated by the threat of the mecha than anyone else, but she moved over to offer me a spot behind cover when I arrived. There was a habit Drop-Troopers developed after a while. At first, I thought it was just me, but Scotty had assured me it was universal. When I talked to Geiger, I didn't see her suit's featureless grey helmet, I saw her face as if it was projected over it.

"Where's Captain Covington?" she demanded.

"I'm afraid he's KIA, ma'am," I told her. "So's the XO. I'm acting company commander for the moment. Delta took down the fusion plant and since the jamming hasn't lifted, I brought us here hoping someone would be carrying out Battalion's primary mission." I hesitated. "Have you seen Captain Cronje? He still has most of Alpha with him, last I saw."

"No, I haven't," she told me, and I wasn't sure if the bitterness dripping from her words was because of the news of the Skipper's death or disgust with Cronje's absence. "Besides us, you're all I've seen of the battalion." She motioned with her suit's left hand at a line of Force Recon troops hugging the side of the retaining wall, nearly buried under loose dirt. They looked more scared than I had ever been. "We picked up most of a platoon of straight-leg Recon troops who barely got out of an emergency landing in their drop-ship, and that's it. And this is a major clusterfuck, Alvarez. We're never going to take out that fucking mecha without air support and we're not getting air support until we take out the anti-aircraft batteries."

"And we're not taking out the anti-aircraft batteries with that mecha there," I finished for her.

"Exactly."

"We're here for you, Captain," I said, the shoulders of the Vigilante shrugging along with mine. "What's the plan?"

"We have three Boomers left," she told me, motioning down the line to my left, where the fire support suits were kneeling awkwardly, their coil gun tubes digging into the dirt as they tried to stay behind cover. "I've been holding them back, but now that we have you, I have no choice but to try."

She hesitated and I knew I wasn't going to like what she said next.

"I'm going to send everyone over the top," she decided. "It won't be pretty, and we're going to lose a lot of people, but it'll give the Boomers time to target the mecha."

"Shit." I hadn't meant to say it aloud, but there it was.

"I know," she admitted. "But I'm all out of ideas."

I was about to agree, but then I discovered that I wasn't.

"The reactor. We took out the main fusion plant," I said, talking myself through it as much as explaining it to Geiger. "That means the air defense turrets are being powered locally. Probably something right in that building."

"So?" she demanded, stress and impatience turning her voice ragged.

"So, we can take out the local reactor and shut down the anti-aircraft turrets, then let the shuttles take out the mecha."

"There's no time for that! The longer we fuck around here, the more likely they're going to lose patience, take their chances and just send that Goddamned thing walking this way and pound right into our lines!"

"No, they won't," I assured her. "If they had the will to take those sorts of chances, the High Guard wouldn't have retreated when we hit them. They would have sent the mecha in right then. They're happy to sit there and wait us out, because they think time is on their side."

"And you think it's not?"

"Just give me a few minutes," I pleaded. "I have a guy who can help with this."

"You have five mikes to give me a plan," she said. "After that, we're going over the top."

"Yes, ma'am."

I fought against a pre-military instinct to run to William Cano and lean in close for a private conversation. It wasn't necessary with the armor and private, line-of-sight comm nets, but it was still hard to resist.

"Cano," I said, "you were training as a reactor tech before you got in the Academy, right?"

I didn't have to see his face to imagine the confused frown dragging down his rounded, pudgy features.

"I was," he admitted, "but I'd only been taking classes for a year. I wouldn't be able to work on one."

"And I don't need you to," I cut him off. "I just need you to tell me what they have powering those air defense turrets and how to find it and take it out."

"Oh, uh, well...," he dithered and I bit back an impatient curse. We didn't have time for this, but I knew pressuring him wouldn't help any. "It would be fairly small, like the size of the reactor on a shuttle. Most of it would be underground, but the cooling system would have to be at least partially above ground. Probably liquid nitrogen and they'd need a hook-up outdoors where they could refill it. Hold on a second." There was inspiration in his voice and I wanted to encourage it, so I stayed silent and let him do his thing.

His thing, as it turned out, was launching a spy drone. It rose from his backpack like some sort of oversized, prehistoric mosquito, and I was about to tell him it would get shot down in a heartbeat, but Cano surprised me with his ingenuity. He flew the quad-copter parallel to our lines, using the retaining wall for cover, taking it off to the left, the opposite way from the service road the High Guard had come down. I tied into its feed, hoping to get something useful from it before the troops in the bunkers saw it and wasted a KE gun burst to take it out.

The retaining wall ended at a drainage ditch, maybe two meters deep and the same across, and he kept the drone beneath the edges of the depression, riding the concealment as far as he could until the thing had to pop up at the left corner of the building. Cano gave it a burst of speed, trying to get behind the cover of the wedge-shaped walls, but I thought I caught just a half-second glimpse of three huge transmission dishes out beyond the left edge of the building. The place was a mix of the pragmatic lines of a Tahni military base with the artistic designs of their cities, angular and curved in ways that made no practical sense to my human aesthetic, broad at the base and narrowing sharply at the roof in what seemed to me to be a huge waste of space.

One thing made sense, though, rising above aesthetics and art, rising out of the pavement at the rear, left-hand corner of the building. There was a wire fence around it, probably for safety, to keep someone from accidentally running into it with a cargo loader since the Tahni didn't seem to worry about crime or vandalism. I wasn't a technician, nor had I even taken a few classes in it like Cano, but I could still tell the machinery was some sort of high-pressure valve meant to deal with something super-cooled and potentially dangerous.

"There it is," Cano said, and if he could have pumped his fist without looking like an idiot, he would probably have done it, from the tone of triumph in his voice. "There's the liquid nitrogen fill valve."

"And no one's guarding it," I mused. "All right, bring the drone around the other side of the building. When they notice it, I want them to think we were trying to spy out the positions of the High Guard troops."

I didn't wait to see. I'd had five minutes and about four and a half of them were up.

"Captain Geiger," I said, "do any of these Recon troops have demolition charges?"

The question was nearly cut off by a proton blast that ploughed a furrow a meter deep in the top of the wall, spraying molten dirt ten meters behind us. She didn't answer me immediately and I assumed she was either stunned by the explosion or was busy finding out, the question not having come up before. One of the straight-legs high-crawled the few meters from his position on the wall to come to a knee beside us. I couldn't see his face through his helmet's visor, but he was tall and rangy and his IFF transponder told me he was Gunnery Sgt. Eduardo Vazquez, platoon sergeant for Fourth Platoon, Alpha Company, Third Battalion, 187th Marine Expeditionary Force (Recon), for all the good that did me.

"I've got a demo pack," he said, his voice rough and hoarse, as if he'd been screaming orders for hours and had little left to give. He hefted the shoulder bag to show me exactly which pack was the one in question. "What do you need?"

Heavy KE turret fire showered the Gunny with dirt and he didn't even seem to notice after the concussion from the proton blast.

"Captain," I said, "here's what I want to do. My company is going to head right, charge straight into the High Guard positions while you and your armored troops lay down suppressive fire. That should distract the mecha, the battlesuits and the turrets in the bunker long enough for Gunny Vazquez to take his demo pack around the other way and set the nitrogen fill valve to blow. Once the liquid nitrogen tanks for their reactor flush, it'll shut down automatically." I touched a control by my left hand and sent a copy of the drone video to her and Gunny Morales.

"Do you think you can do it, Gunny?" Geiger asked him once she'd had a chance to check out the video.

"Shit, ma'am," Vazquez sighed, "I'd do anything to get the hell out of here right now."

"If this shits the bed," I told Geiger, "we'll take out the High Guard troops and your Boomers can still try to get a shot at the mecha." *And it's just as likely to not work as if we'd gone with your plan*, I didn't add.

"Right," she said immediately. "Let's do it. Lt. Alvarez, Gunny Vazquez, get your people ready. This kicks off in three mikes."

Shit. Three minutes.

"Yes, ma'am," I said and loped back down the line, feeling absurd with my suit hunched over, the fingers of the left hand scraping the ground like a gorilla.

I could have given the briefing over the comms without moving at all, of course, but it didn't feel right. This was as close to a suicide mission as I'd encountered since I'd become an officer, and some things needed to be said face to face.

"You know," Vicky said, "it's been over a year since the last time you almost got me killed, and I was hoping we were all done with that phase of our relationship."

"Not my fault," I insisted, talking fast because we didn't have much time. "And you would have liked Captain Geiger's plan even less."

She, Cano, and Kovacs had clustered around me near the right end of the wall, again with that instinctive need to be close to the person talking to them. I didn't bother saying anything about it. I might as well have asked them not to breathe.

"Third is on point, Vicky," I told her. "I'll be right behind you. Billy, you're next and Francis will ride drag. Remember, the point of this is to tie them up, attract attention. Hit them hard, but don't try to break through and leave them behind us. If we can't kill them all, we have to keep their focus on us until the Recon troops can set the charges. Not only will that take out the turrets, but I have a suspicion a lot of the EM jamming is coming from those dishes I saw behind the spaceport offices."

"What about the mecha?" Kovacs asked. He was, I thought,

trying not to sound scared, but it wasn't working. I wasn't sure if he was scared for his own life, his Marines or maybe just scared of fucking up. Maybe all three. "If it comes after us while we're tied up with the High Guard, we're all dead."

"We just have to hope he doesn't want to kill his own people." It wasn't a firm foundation to build a hope on, but it was all we had. I checked the countdown on my HUD. "Get your platoons in order. We have less than one minute."

"Hey sir," Bang-Bang said. I checked his IFF and found him near the rear of our lines, ready to bring up drag like a good Top Kick should. "I'm new at this shit and all, being First Sergeant, but I feel like I should be the one to tell you, most company commanders don't ride the horse that far in front of the saddle."

The laugh burst out of me in spite of the situation.

"Where the hell did you say you were from again, Bang-Bang?"

"Me? I'm from Greater Chicago."

Which was only slightly less massive and entangled than Trans-Angeles.

"Then how the hell do you know anything about riding horses?"

"Virtual reality, sir. My dad rode a horse once when he was a kid and he made me learn how on a simulator. He made me swear once I got out of the Corps, I was going to move somewhere I could ride one for real."

"Shit, maybe we'll be neighbors. But as for where I fight from...I may be an acting company commander, but this isn't going to be a chess game. It's a fist fight. And I throw the hardest fucking punch."

"Uh-huh." He didn't seem convinced.

"If you're that worried, I guess you'd better make sure nothing kills me."

"Alvarez," Geiger said, maybe ten seconds earlier than I thought she would, "it's time. You ready?"

"Yes, ma'am." I switched to the company net. "Delta, move out."

That was when it hit me. Up until that point, things had been going too fast, just one thing after another since the second we'd been within sight of the spaceport. Taking the first step along the retaining wall, sending Vicky and Bang-Bang ahead of me leading *my* platoon, the whole company following *my* orders, not just as a temporary measure because we were separated from the Skipper, but because he was dead...that just brought everything together in one package and slammed it into my chest. The *Iwo* blowing up, the drop-ship on fire, the isolation, the fusion reactor, Captain Covington's sacrifice, each of them a body blow, setting me up for the knock-out punch.

I kept going, mostly because I knew Vicky would take over if I didn't. Maybe she'd do a better job of it, but I didn't want to make her or the others think the less of me for not stepping up when it was my turn. I loved her, but I wasn't thinking of her as my lover at that moment, I was thinking of her as a sister Marine. She had the right to expect me to pull my weight.

I don't think the Tahni force expected the attack. I think they were ready for Geiger's over-the-top assault, because when she and her Marines began laying down covering fire, the response was overwhelming, an unending barrage of every weapon the enemy had, like the planet itself was exploding behind us. But nothing jumped up to meet our flanking maneuver, no rounds came in above us. The first we saw of the enemy was when we hit the service road.

The High Guard troops were in about company strength, maybe a little more. The Tahni equivalent of a company was smaller than ours, so maybe this had started out as two companies before the casualties they'd taken. They were behind the cover of some sort of industrial machinery, tracked vehicles with rollers and jets attached to tanks that I thought maybe had something to do with surfacing the landing pads. The machines were scored and burned and twisted, but they'd protected the High Guard troopers from the brunt of our fire...from the lines on the wall. They did nothing to stop my flanking force.

Delp was on point, but the rest of Third Platoon was spreading out to the side into an echelon right as we swung up the curving road to hit the High Guard troops, and the first shots were unleashed in an almost-simultaneous barrage at under a hundred meters. High Guard suits disappeared in flares of burning metal and we'd achieved surprise if we could keep it.

Behind me, back in Kovacs' platoon, two Marines went down, their IFF signals fading to black, maybe the mecha, maybe the bunkers finally figuring out where we were and what we were trying to do. I couldn't even take the time to read their names, to grieve for them. They were gone and all I could think was that his platoon was down six Marines now, nearly a whole squad, and I would have to keep that in mind before I tasked him with anything else. It felt cold, calculating, someone else's thoughts intruding on mine.

And I was utterly lost running even as far back as the rear of the lead platoon. The battle was taking place on another planet, displayed on the screens of a simulator and I ached to fire, to target the enemy and kill them, but by the time I reached the enemy, they had retreated or already lay dying. I'd expected the High Guard to retreat toward the mecha. It would have made sense for them to take the fight into the mutually supporting fields of fire from the artillery piece and the bunker turrets, and we'd planned for it. We were going to stick close so the enemy couldn't target us without killing their own people.

I guess that's why they're called aliens, because they didn't think the way we expected them to. Instead of heading out into the courtyard and support, they ducked into a side entrance to the spaceport administration building and I was left with my first major decision and about three seconds in which to make it.

"First and Fourth Platoons," I barked, "split off and go around the rear of the building. First, look for another entrance and see if you can flank them. Fourth, head to the other end and support the Recon team."

And that was it, our fates decided by a guess, a hunch with a fifty-fifty shot of being right. I should have gone with First and Fourth, should have preserved my ability to call the plays, but I made another guess. The action was going to be inside and so was I.

I hadn't noticed how light it was getting outside until the shadows of the interior shut out the gathering dawn. The helmet optics kept it as clear as high noon, but there was a qualitative difference between actual daylight and enhanced imaging, just another of the little things I had come to notice during my time in the suits. The entrance was broad and four meters tall and led to what seemed to be a garage for industrial vehicles like the ones lined up outside. Maybe the Tahni had pulled them all out to provide cover, because the garage was mostly empty, a single resurfacing vehicle sitting partially disassembled in a corner.

Which left plenty of room for the rear guard of the Tahni troopers to turn and make a stand. If the chaos of battle seemed confusing in the open spaces of the port, it was incomprehensible inside the confines of the garage. Thank God it was Third going through that door and Vicky and Bang-Bang in charge of them. The natural thing to do, the thing I would have expected from most platoons, would be to pile up, to get on First squad's ass and use them as human mine detectors, but I'd trained them better than that.

Second and Third squads split off left and right just through the door, spreading wide and opening up fields of fire for themselves. The Tahni weren't quite as practiced. They'd narrowed their front by using the opposite door of the garage for cover, but that also meant only two of them could fire on us, and two electron beamers versus eight plasma guns abreast was no contest. A Marine in First squad took a hit, and their damage flashed red on the IFF display, but the High Guard suits simply disappeared, along with half the doorway.

On the other side of it was...something. I couldn't have sworn what the Tahni used the rooms for, but they were broad and open, and my brain wanted to call them business offices, for all that they bore little, if any, resemblance to the business offices I'd seen on Earth or the colonies. It could have had, I reflected with a snort of dark amusement, religious, cultural, or sociological significance. Right now, what it had was a platoon of enemy battlesuits huddled in the corners of the room behind furniture comically undersized for their bulk, as if they were all searching for someplace to sit.

They were spread out more this time, and our front lines had another full second before their capacitors recharged, but this was something else we'd practiced and no one had to give an order, not Vicky or Bang-Bang or me. First squad ducked to the side as they entered the room and Second moved forward, firing their plasma guns then moving to the opposite side of the room. If we'd been Force Recon, we'd have been diving for cover, but there was no cover to be had here for us. Electron beams would have cut through anything in this building, including the walls. Another hit on another Marine, not fatal, not disabling, and four Tahni troopers died in the space of three seconds, while the rest retreated out of the building.

And I couldn't help but wonder what their endgame was. They were giving up lives to buy time, but to buy time for what?

We all got our answer to that question when the front wall caved in and the Tahni mecha waded into it like a toddler crashing through a house made from building blocks. And I knew immediately I had fucked up, had forgotten that part about them being aliens. What made sense for us didn't make sense for them. The mecha *should* have stayed out front and concentrated fire on Geiger and her people. Any human would have. But they didn't. They took their biggest weapon to what they considered the most imminent threat, and they'd mouse-trapped us in the middle of a building, willing to risk killing their own people and destroying their own facilities to get us.

It was my fault, and I'd be the one to set it right.

"Get everyone out of here!" I yelled at Vicky, and I hit my jets.

The mecha was leaning forward, its weight on its front foot, slightly off-balance because it had never been built for agility, just enough brute force to carry around an antiproton reactor and a shitload of weapons. I rammed my shoulder into the thing's trailing leg, my teeth clacking together with the impact, and ran the jets so far into the red I could almost hear them screaming for mercy.

It didn't knock him over. I hadn't thought it would. I just wanted to buy time, and that I did. He lost balance and had to slam his trailing foot to the ground, which, unfortunately, took me to the ground with it. The armor was tough. It could take a huge beating and keep working, but unfortunately, us humans had to be inside it.

Every time we got a new guy in the platoon, they would always wind up asking why we had to be in the suits, why the Marines didn't just put an AI program in the suit computers and let it do the fighting, and *someone* would have to repeat the same explanation that Captain Covington had given to the platoon leader who had given it to everyone else. It was the old story about how automated weapons had been tried during the Sino-Russian War and had turned against their own side. It might have just been because the computer systems weren't sophisticated enough back then, but no one with the power to change things had ever trusted them again, so us poor, vulnerable humans still had to pull the triggers.

When my back hit the concrete foundation of the building, I could really have come up with some great arguments for automated weaponry. I'd had cracked ribs before, and I was fairly sure I had them again. The pain sucked the breath right out of my chest, replacing it with white fire, and I wanted more than anything else to just lie there on the ground and rest, to let someone else do the rest of the fighting.

That wasn't an option for a few reasons, the main one being that if I stayed on the ground, the mecha was going to squish me flat. The massive oval of its foot pad hovered above me and I punched the jets again, sliding through oceans of debris but getting out of the way of the stomp. The mecha's foot pad cracked the floor beneath it, shaking me right through the BiPhase Carbide of my armor. I had to get up, and even though the Vigilante would do the work, the only way it could react was by me using the muscles that I would have needed if I'd been just trying to move my own body and not the three-meter suit of armor. And moving fucking hurt.

I rolled to my feet, screaming into the privacy of my helmet, knowing no one would hear, and turned to face oncoming death. Instinct screamed at me to get distance, but experience yelled just as loud that I should stay close. The mecha was an artillery piece, and its heavy weapons were designed for distance fire. Neither the proton cannon nor the coil gun turret could depress far enough to reach me, but the damned KE guns could.

Tantalum needles cracked off my armor, no single one of

them able to penetrate, but the combined effect of hundreds of the things enough to wear my protection down and kill me, given time. Thankfully, even though my plasma gun wouldn't penetrate the mecha's armor over anything vital, there was one target I was fairly confident about servicing.

I blasted the thing's right-hand KE gun with a plasmoid, the ionized gas melting the infantry-defense weapon to slag. The Tahni pilot must have really liked that gun because he seemed to take its loss personally. His leg was the size of a tree trunk, and when it impacted the left shoulder of my suit, it threw me four meters, straight through the back wall of the building.

It didn't hurt as much as I thought it would, if I could honestly say I had a coherent thought at all. Stars filled my vision, and even the HUD in my helmet couldn't penetrate them to tell me where I was or what was happening, and everything felt numb. Drugs. I was drugged, the pain-killers were kicking in. That was why it didn't hurt, though it damned well should have. I was propped on a knee, though I didn't remember getting up, and someone was screaming into my ear. Several someones, and I couldn't separate them into anything comprehensible.

"Alvarez!" It was Geiger, and she didn't seem happy. "The Recon troops are pinned down! Two platoons of Shock-troopers came out of the bunker to intercept them. There's no way they're going to get those charges set!"

Well, shit. Should have known better than to count on straight-legs. When the hell had they ever accomplished anything except grabbing the glory? I somehow managed a reply to Geiger, though I can't recall the specifics of it. It was something reassuring, I suppose, some promise that Delta would get the job done. That was what the Skipper would have said, or at least my drug-addled mind hoped it was.

"Vicky!" I said, the word half a command, half a prayer. "Status report!"

The mecha was coming. It took the thing two steps to come through the wall.

Her reply was staticky, slipping in and out, the laser line-of-sight comms interrupted by particulate debris.

"...taking casualties!" she said. "We have linked up with First and Fourth Platoon and we're pushing them back..."

And then I was too busy to talk. The mecha swiveled on its jointed hips, trying to line up its remaining KE gun and I gave it a plasma blast because why the fuck not? I wasn't saving the gun for a special occasion. It hit something on the mecha, though I couldn't tell what. Probably nothing important, because it was still taking giant, swooping steps towards me, determined to stomp me into the ground if it couldn't shoot me.

Where was I? The question bounced back and forth in my brain; the part numbed by the pain-killers laughing at the inanity of it. I was on Point Barber, in Deltaville, at the space-port, getting my ass kicked by something three times my size and ten times my weight. The part that was still trying to accomplish this mission understood the importance of the question.

Where was the liquid nitrogen pump house? Where was I in relation to it? I was the only one left who could take it out. The Recon troops were pinned down, Geiger was pinned down, the rest of Delta was tangled up with the High Guard. If I had concentrated—if I'd been *able* to concentrate—I could have seen them on my sensor readout, somewhere behind me and off to my left. They were fighting for their lives and Vicky was leading them when I should have been, and I felt like I'd failed them, but there was still work to do, and I could feel sorry for myself later.

I turned and ran. Or rather, limped. Not from any injury to me, though there were plenty of those, but from damage to the suit. Just a bad motivator in my left hip joint, but the timing was worse than the problem.

The liquid nitrogen fill valve. It was there, only fifteen meters away. The transmission dishes loomed behind it like a boundary marker, making sure I wouldn't miss it even in my drug-addled state. I knew the odds were against me reaching it before the mecha reached me, but I ran, just the same, because there was no other choice.

So close, so close I could touch the wire fence, and that damned thing reached down with an arm meant to dig fortifications and swatted me aside like a bug. Drugs or no, the pain was too much and I blacked out for the half a second it took me to plow into the dirt. My eyes opened just in time to watch that stupid-ass mecha, unable to stop with all the built-up momentum he'd used to catch me, barrel right through the coolant pumphouse.

I thought for one, pain-clouded second that I was back on Hachiman, with its white-out blizzards and its freezing fogs coating every metal surface with ice. But it was no snowstorm that sprayed ice across the legs of the mecha, it was a high-pressure stream of liquid nitrogen. And the armor on those legs began to crack and splinter away...

I had, perhaps, ten seconds until the combination of the pain and the armor's attempts to fight it made my fight to stay conscious a losing battle. I don't know how I aimed, because my vision swam with stars and double-images, but the thing was so close, how could I miss? I pointed my plasma gun at the joint of the mecha's left leg and hip and touched the trigger.

Normally, it would have little effect, but normally, the armor there wouldn't have been supercooled by liquid nitrogen. The leg blew right off the torso in a spray of vaporized metal and that titan fell, collapsing onto its side. The pilot would probably abandon the thing, I thought, and I wished I could spare the time to put a grenade up his ass, but that would have required me to be conscious. The mecha was down, the reactor would be shutting down in seconds, the jamming would be lifted, the air defense turrets unpowered.

Mission accomplished.

I passed out.

[19]

It was not, unfortunately, the first time I'd woken up shivering and damp in the cold, hard plastic of an auto-doc. At least this time, they hadn't had to grow any new parts of me. Probably.

I blinked, rubbed rheum out of my eyes and blinked again, finally able to see. Gravity. Not *exactly* Earth-standard, which meant I wasn't in Transition Space on a ship. The lid of the cylinder was unlocked and I pushed it open, gasping at the sudden influx of cold air. The room was small, the walls plastic sheeting, and the medics moving from auto-doc to triage bed to auto-doc were wearing field utilities and not their white, shipboard uniforms. Point Barber, then. An aid station.

I tried sitting up, prepared for it to hurt, but it didn't. However long I'd been in the auto-doc, the nanite bath had done good work. I was fairly sure my ribs had been shattered and while I hadn't exactly been coherent enough for a complete self-assessment, I probably had some internal injuries as well. No one tried to stop me from climbing out of the cylinder, so I assumed it was all good now.

I didn't wait for any of the harried, overworked medical staff to contradict the impression. There was a row of wire basket shelving against one of the walls, each filled with clothes, though none of them were labelled. I guess that would have been too much to ask when they were busy trying to save lives. I knelt down and began shuffling through them, hoping mine would be in there, hoping I would find *something* before someone came along and made a joke about my naked ass hanging out.

"You ain't gonna find your stuff in there."

I craned my neck around and saw the hulking, shaven-headed orderly resetting the controls of the auto-doc I'd been confined in. He wasn't looking at me, still concentrating on his work, but he continued, just the same.

"Anyone who comes in unconscious," he told me, "we cut their clothes off."

"How long was I in?" I wondered, shifting my focus from finding my clothes to finding clothes my size. Because I wasn't staying here long enough to get someone to pick me up.

"Thirty hours, ten minutes, fifteen seconds," he said, reading off the display as he reset it. "Three cracked ribs, three compound fractures, punctured and collapsed lung, ruptured spleen, dislocated shoulder and a sprained left knee."

This one. I pulled out a set of utility fatigues and checked the tags just to be sure. Yeah, this should fit. I wished for under-wear, but you can't have everything and I wouldn't really want to wear someone else's used underwear, anyway. I straightened and began pulling the clothes on. They felt weird and uncom-fortable against my skin, still slightly damp and clammy from the biotic fluid of the nanite suspension, but not as weird and uncomfortable as walking around naked.

Boots. I needed boots. It took another half a minute to find some close enough to my size to strap them down tight and make do. I stood from securing them and found the gorilla staring at the name-plate on the chest of my fatigues.

"Captain Emil Johansen, huh?" he asked, an eyebrow shooting up. "That's you?"

"It is now," I assured him. "Any idea where Fourth Battalion of the 187th Armored might be?"

"Not a one," he admitted. He jerked a thumb behind him toward the door flap. "But there's a shitload of armored Marines and all their equipment down at the end of this row of tents. You can probably find out there."

"Thanks, man."

The inside of the aid station was air conditioned. Deltaville was *not*. Stepping through the airlock-style door of the tent, I was hit by a wave of humidity and I hoped like hell this was summer, because if it was winter, this planet would be pretty much uninhabitable the rest of the year.

After the heat, the next thing that struck me was the frenzy of activity. In the thirty hours I'd been under, I guess the city had been pacified, at least enough to start work on a temporary base. Construction bots were scuttling everywhere, tracked undercarriages clicking and clacking along as they poured build-foam into prefab metal molds, laying down the dome structures that would serve until something more permanent could be built.

And we would be here permanently, I thought. At least for a few decades if I was any judge. There was no way we'd let the Tahni run their own government until we were damned sure they wouldn't go back to building up their war machine and come right back after us for revenge. At least I *hoped* we'd learned that lesson in the first war.

It took me another twenty or thirty steps before I realized we were out at the spaceport, not too far past the battle where I'd gotten my ass kicked. My first clue was the screaming roar of jets and the descending wedge of a cargo lander, coming down nearly on top of the construction before it curved around and landed somewhere less than a klick away. My second was when I reached a gap in the construction and saw the remains of the administration building. There wasn't much left of it, just a bare, forlorn framework standing watch over piles of debris. I couldn't see if the mecha was still back there. I liked to think it was, waiting so I could come back and take a look at it and see how badly I'd fucked up, but realistically, the engineers had probably hauled it away.

How many of the Marines from my company were out there, their armor still laying broken open under the afternoon glare, monuments to my stupidity? Was Vicky there? Delp? Kreis? Suddenly, I almost didn't want to find the battalion.

Past the construction were more plastic tents, and guarding their approaches were a squad of Force Recon and a single fire team of Vigilantes. I didn't recognize their unit designator, but that didn't mean anything. Just about everyone had been involved in this invasion. I stepped up to one of the Recon grunts, figuring it would be easier to talk to him than a Drop-Trooper in their suit.

Her, I judged, checking the name plate on the chest armor of the Marine.

"Sgt. Suharto?" I read the name and rank, hoping I hadn't mispronounced it.

"Yes, sir?" she asked, her voice tinny and unnatural through the external speaker of her helmet.

"Know where Fourth Battalion is set up?"

"I'm kind of iffy on where the battalions are, sir," she admitted. "But Brigade HQ is the third tent down thataway." She pointed down the road with a knife hand. "Good luck, they're all running around like a chicken with its head cut off."

I laughed softly, thinking I was probably one of the few Drop-Troopers who knew exactly what that saying meant.

"Thanks, Sergeant."

I could see what she meant before I even reached the tent. Supplies were being hauled in on cargo jacks, puttering slowly up the cracked pavement, maneuvering around battle damage with robotic instincts, a line of ants heading into the largest of the plastic tents, dropping their loads and then filing out the other side. Beneath the shelter from the punishing mid-afternoon glare, Fleet engineers and Marine grunts were offloading the pallets, taking necessary supplies this way and that, some to lines of Vigilante battlesuits awaiting service, others to the mess hall or the aid stations.

There was the normal yelling and cursing, shouted orders, and incredulous questions in return, all struggling to make themselves heard over the rumble and clank and scrape of the cargo offload. The normal sounds of a Forward Operating Base, though on a scale I hadn't seen before, twice as big as any I'd seen in previous operations. It stretched out for kilometers, curving along the perimeter of the landing field, and overhead, assault shuttles on Combat Air Patrol circled at different altitudes. While I walked and stared, one of them broke its pattern and screamed off to the west, hell-bent for leather. Probably called in for air support by a patrol.

There was still resistance somewhere out there. There probably would be for months and I hoped I wouldn't have to stay around to deal with it. That had become a nightmare scenario talked about in hushed tones by the platoon leaders when no one else was listening, the possibility of our company being left behind on one of the conquered worlds to crush any enemy forces still fighting long past reason. No one wanted to miss out on *the* battle, the invasion of Tahn-Skyyiah, the Tahni homeworld, the one enemy planet we all knew their name for.

Captain Covington had always chuckled when he'd over-heard those bull sessions, told us that he would make sure that didn't happen. But he was gone now. Maybe that meant what-ever was left of Delta would be stuck here. I resigned myself to the idea with dolorous acceptance. Given how badly everything else had gone, how truly massive of a clusterfuck this battle had become, nothing else bad that happened would surprise me.

I was so busy moping, I nearly ran straight into Vicky as she came out one of the flaps of the command tent.

"Oh, damn!" she exclaimed, eyes going wide. "I was just coming to check on you!" She held up arms filled with utility fatigues and a pair of boots. "I had to have these fabricated because, well...all our shit was on the *Iwo*."

I looked around, then realized I was wearing someone else's name plate and figured, the hell with it and pulled her into a kiss.

"I am so fucking glad you're alive," I told her, leaning my forehead against hers.

"Of course, I'm alive, dumbass," she said, smiling through the words, thumping the heel of her hand against my chest. "Who the hell do you think called Search and Rescue to pull you out of your suit? What the hell were you thinking, going up against a Goddamned mecha by yourself?"

"There wasn't much thinking involved," I admitted. "Shit just sort of happened." I sobered. "What was the damage? How bad is Delta?"

"Not nearly as bad as it could have been," she said, and I couldn't tell if she was relieved or just trying to make me feel better. "After the mecha came through the building, we ran into the main force of the High Guard, and Third took a couple of casualties. Kreis and Pena were wounded, their suits deadlined, but they're already out of the aid station. But your boys, Kovacs and Cano came through for us and flanked them. I think Cano lost two KIA in the fight, but I don't remember their names." She winced apologetically. "I'm sorry I don't know more, but Captain Cronje showed up again about ten hours ago and started acting like nothing fucking happened. I've been busy policing up the mess and putting my platoon back together."

I clamped down on the anger roiling in my gut at the mention of Cronje's name and forced myself to concentrate on what was important.

"Where's Delta?"

"Come on," she urged, tugging at my arm. "I'll take you to them." She cocked an eyebrow at my stolen uniform. "But maybe you should change first, Captain Johansen."

I smiled lopsidedly, any anger I felt fading at her touch.

"My friends," I told her, "call me Emil."

———

Delta was somber as a tomb.

They were gathered in the makeshift maintenance tent, their Vigilantes broken open and stripped bare, and some made half-hearted attempts at trying to scrub away carbon scoring or clean debris from the joints, but mostly they were staring, enlisted, officer and NCO alike. They stared at the armor, at each other, some talking in muted tones, a few popping caffeine chews or sipping half-heartedly at coffee. It had the air of a funeral...a mass funeral, for all the Marines we'd lost, nearly three full platoons. Almost all of Second, the whole Headquarters platoon and enough Marines here and there from First, Third and Fourth to make up another.

I registered an instant of shock at the open door of the tent, wondering why no one had taken charge of them, tried to get them doing something productive to take their minds off of it... until I realized with just as brutal a shock that there *was* no one to take charge. Battalion was gone. Brigade was juggling a dozen running chainsaws with one hand tied behind their back.

I padded into the center of the tent and still, no one noticed me.

"Where's Top?" I asked, and the question seemed unreasonably loud, like in Boot Camp when one of the DI's had thrown a metal garbage can down the length of the barracks at zero four thirty and woken us all from an exhausted sleep.

Marines jumped up from the folding stools, ration boxes and cargo containers they'd been using as seats and every eye went wide.

"Cam!" Billy Cano exclaimed, hurrying over to me, looking uncertain, as if he couldn't decide whether to shake my hand, salute, or give me a hug. He compromised with a slap on my shoulder. "Jesus, man, I'm glad you're all right. When we found you, it looked like that mecha had stomped you flat."

"It just about did," I told him, not wanting to sound off-putting but also not that interested in talking about the battle right then. "Where's Top?"

"She went to find First Sergeant Taylor, sir," Bang-Bang told me. The big man was unusually subdued, and I wasn't sure if it was from the general downbeat mood in the bay or maybe from embarrassment at the fact that he'd let my platoon get away with being part of it. "Sgt. Taylor is filling in for the Battalion Command Sgt.-Major," he added.

"I think there's going to be a Brigade-level meeting in a couple hours," Kovacs put in. He was fidgeting, scratching at a callous on his palm. "She's like, getting ready for it." He pointed between himself and Cano. "We, uh...I mean, we haven't been told if we're supposed to go. I think it's for company commanders. I guess that means, you should go?"

I fought very hard not to roll my eyes at the man. Instead, I looked back and forth across the tent, forcing all of them to meet my glare. I had a decision to make. If someone else had stepped up and tried to take charge, I might have hesitated. But they weren't.

"Okay, listen up," I snapped. I know we're all kind of in a funk because of what happened to the Skipper, and Lt. Burke and Second Platoon. But take a listen out there." I jabbed a finger at the wall of the tent. "Shit's still going down. Patrols are going out; shuttles are making fire support runs. We could get called out there. The fucking battle ain't over and we can't be sitting on our asses waiting for the shuttle to take us back to the ship because the ship doesn't even fucking *exist* anymore."

That hit them between the eyes. Kovacs seemed to deflate, his shoulders sagging.

"So, here's what we're going to do. Until and unless someone comes along and tells me they have a new company commander for Delta, I'm going to have to assume I'm still in charge for now. I want full PMCS done on every single Vigilante we have left. I want a full report ready from the platoon leaders by the time I get back from the brigade meeting." I nodded toward Bang-Bang. "You're acting Third Platoon leader until we get a replacement or they send us a company commander and I jump back in."

"Yes, sir," he said, back straightening with the responsibility.

"Any suits we have that are deadlined, I want a full report on what's needed to repair them." I paused, frowning. "By the way, where's my suit? They didn't have to cut me out of it or anything, did they?"

"No, sir," Bang-Bang said, the corner of his mouth turning up. "It's over in the corner. Needs a new left hip actuator. I'll put it in the report."

I let my gaze linger on the Vigilante. Its surface was scored and scorched, bearing the scars of not just this battle, but every one of them, a Dorian Grey portrait of my soul.

"All right," I concluded, nodding. "You know what to do. Get your heads back in the game, boys and girls. We took a hit, but we hit them back and we came out on top. We'll have a memorial for the fallen after we get our shit sorted. Their war is over. Ours is not."

[20]

"There you are," Top said, straightening from a portable holographic display table and cocking an eyebrow at me. "I wondered how long they were going to keep you in the aid station for a few cracked ribs."

"Among other things," I reminded her. I checked around us, making sure none of the other NCO's and junior officers present were listening to us. They buzzed around the Brigade command tent, drawn to the crumbs of data Intelligence dropped on us like flies to shit. "Are you okay?'

"I just had a few burns," she said, waving it away as if third-degree burns over a quarter of her body was nothing. "They didn't even bother with the auto-doc, just slapped a few smart bandages on me and let me sleep it off."

"I'm sure," I said, letting the skepticism drip from my words, "but you know that's not what I meant."

Top was good at the act. She'd been Top for so long, she might forget sometimes that Ellen Campbell was down there, buried under layers of armor that didn't come off after a battle. But something tugged at the corners of her eyes, lines of stress and grief she couldn't hide.

"It's war, child," she told me, her voice quiet, her tone weary and showing, for once, her age. "You can roll sixes all day long, but you still have just as good a shot at snake-eyes with every toss."

"He didn't toss snake-eyes," I said. "He made a choice."

"The mission, the men and you. The mission always comes first."

The words were automatic, a rote recital for all that they were true. She was putting off the real truth with the platitude, but it was coming. She pushed away from the display table, leaving troop dispositions to some baby-faced first lieutenant in Fleet Intelligence blacks, and leaned heavily against a support pole, a muscle twitching in her cheek.

"He knew what was coming," she told me, finally. "He knew we were getting close to the end. This had been his life for so long. I wonder if he didn't want to see the end of his usefulness."

"If he was looking for a dramatic way to go out," I said, "he sure as hell got it."

"You should talk, boy," she snapped, and I could see the few seconds of vulnerability had ended and she was back to being Top again. "You took that mecha on by yourself. It might not have been as blatantly suicidal as overloading your own reactor, but it's right up there."

"If I'd run," I reminded her, "he would have come after the rest of the company, and they needed to deal with the High Guard." I shrugged. "I was the one whose plan put us in that position, I wasn't going to let anyone else pay for it."

She laughed, harsh and barking.

"You sound just like him." She checked the display on her 'link. "Meeting starts in twenty mikes. You want to go find a seat?"

It was just another tent, of course. All we'd have for the next couple days would be tents, and maybe a few Tahni buildings we took over. I'd heard scuttlebutt that we were trying to avoid that because command was afraid the Tahni might have left IED's in the buildings that could be command detonated from sleepers they'd left among the civilian population, but rumors were like venereal disease in wartime—everyone had one and was doing their best to spread it.

They'd found chairs, somewhere. Guess that shows military priorities. We'd been on the planet less than two full days, at least one of our troop transports had been blown up, but we still managed to bring down office supplies in one of the first shipments.

The men and women under cover of the tent looked grateful for the chance to sit down, and if we'd set up showers already, they hadn't had the chance to use them, or their cots. I felt guilty for having slept, even if it had been inside the auto-doc and under sedation. I recognized the weariness and fatigue in the faces, but I didn't recognize the faces themselves. I had a passing familiarity with the staffs from the other battalions in the brigade, at least the ones who attended the briefings to which the Skipper had dragged me along, but I knew none of these Marines.

The significance of that sent a chill up my back.

Muted conversations buzzed around us, but I didn't take part in them, just sat down beside Top and listened, catching snippets of the talk.

"...fucking wouldn't surrender," someone was saying. "Just wouldn't surrender, even when they were down to their last soldier. Made us kill them all."

"I don't trust the so-called civilians," a woman's voice declared. "Too damned many of them look like retired military. I think we need to put all the males in some sort of detention center. Not that the females can't be just as bad..."

"...couldn't do a damned thing about it. Major Bray was

there one second, then the next, she was gone. Not even an explosion. Never saw her again."

I'd had enough of listening and began trying to shut the conversations out, but I was rescued by the rest of Fourth Battalion's company commanders filing into the tent with Geiger at their lead. Her company XO was there as well, and I figured he must have taken over the company for her since she stepped into the battalion commander's shoes.

The plastic chair creaked under my weight as I pushed out of it and stood to meet them.

"Alvarez," Geiger said, nodding a greeting. "Glad to see you up and around. That was some damned epic shit back at the spaceport. I don't know if you heard, but that pretty much turned the battle for us, taking out the reactor. It freed up the spaceport for landers to come in and drop support for the Vigilantes." She snorted a laugh. "It was also crazy as hell going up against a mecha by yourself, but it was damned epic shit."

I didn't sigh with frustration, but it was a fight.

Then I discovered I was wrong. Not *all* of Fourth's company commanders had come in with Geiger. Cronje pushed through the flap door of the tent while I was still letting out the breath I'd been holding. His piggy little eyes darted between Geiger and me, tongue darting across his lips like a lizard.

"Always a surprise to see you, Captain Cronje," Geiger sneered, squaring off with the man as if she were ready to fight him. "I don't suppose you'd care to share with me where you and your company were while we were trying to take the spaceport." She raised an eyebrow at him. "That *was* our battalion rally point after initial objectives were accomplished, or did I misread the Op Order?"

"We got cut off," he said, and I wondered if the excuse sounded as weak in his ears as it did in mine. "After that fiasco at the reactor, we *tried* to get to the spaceport, but there were High Guard patrols everywhere..."

"And I'm sure your armor camera footage will confirm that," she snapped.

"I'm sure his armor footage would confirm all sorts of shit." I'd meant to say it under my breath, but the anger and frustration that had built up a day at a time over the last few months had reached overload and there was no holding it back. "Like how he left Captain Covington to die."

"You watch your fucking mouth, *Lieutenant!*" Cronje exploded, surging toward me.

I set my feet and waited. This was what I'd been wanting for weeks and if he wanted to do it in front of Brigade and everyone, then fuck it. But of course, someone stepped in the way, because it *was* in front of Brigade and everyone, and when you get a bunch of officers together, there's going to be at least one do-gooder. This time, there were three, and they grabbed Cronje by the shoulders and held him back.

People were staring, I noted, but not commenting, not interfering. After what all of us had seen these last couple days, no one cared that much. I saw Top's lip curled in something between a sneer and the feral smile of a wolf.

"Calm the fuck down, Greg," Geiger told him. "You don't have any friends here and Colonel Voss is dead, so don't expect your connections with her staff to protect your ass anymore."

Cronje reacted as if she'd slapped him, then he blinked and I saw in those dark little eyes the realization that she was acting battalion commander and he was pushing very close to the line. He pulled away from the captains holding him back and fell into one of the chairs, arms crossed over his chest, looking away from the rest of us.

"Brigade!" a woman's voice rang out from the tent flap. "Attention!"

Cronje looked ridiculous having to jump back up two seconds after sitting down, which made me smile. I didn't recognize the major who had called us to attention, but I did know General Terrence McCauley. The brigade commander was short, almost ridiculously short in a day when such things could be adjusted genetically before birth, and his upper body was massive, his arms long enough I thought his knuckles might hang down past his knees if he let his shoulders sag. He looked rough and ready, as if he'd walked into the tent straight off the battlefield. He hadn't, of course. Generals didn't suit up and drop from four hundred meters, they landed in secure LZ's long after the real fighting was over. But he had that fucking look down.

"At ease," he growled. "Have a seat."

It wasn't that he was angry, he was just maintaining an image. Gruff, hard-edged general who hadn't forgotten what it was like to be a combat Marine. I didn't know if he had ever seen combat, but if he had, it hadn't been in *this* war.

I sat down beside Top, with Geiger next to me and the whole battalion a row back from Cronje, as if the man had the scabies and everyone else was afraid of catching it from him.

McCauley stepped up behind a folding table that was standing in for a podium in these primitive staff conditions and leaned against it. The table creaked with the pressure and I half-expected the man to go crashing forward when it collapsed. God might have a sense of humor, but apparently it didn't run to slapstick, because the table held.

"One Hundred and Eight Seventh Armored," McCauley said, "your planet, your people, your government has asked much of you, perhaps more of you than has been required of anyone in this whole war, and you have answered the call. I can swear before Heaven that I have never been as proud of any Marines as I am of you."

Jesus Christ, my head hurt from trying to keep my eyes from rolling.

"You may think I'm exaggerating," the general said, as if he were reading my mind. "You may think this is general-speak, the sort of speech I'd give to the politicians—and I may repeat it to them, eventually. But I swear to you, it's the God's honest truth." He shook his head. "Some of you may not know the details of what happened in the Battle for Point Barber, so let me tell you. No fancy holographic presentations, no charts, just my words to you."

I settled back and decided to rein in my natural cynicism and give the man a chance.

"Before we even reached the planet, we lost two Fleet cruisers, the *Salamis* and the *Actium*."

"Fuck," someone muttered somewhere behind me, and I couldn't help but agree.

I'd seen the *Salamis* go up, but the *Actium* too...

"The *Leyte Gulf* took major damage, but she's still spaceworthy and repairs are already underway in orbit. Some of you are already aware that the *Iwo Jima* was destroyed in the middle of launching drop-ships, but we also suffered the loss of the *Tripoli* after she launched. The remaining troop ships were able to Transition back to the edge of the system, but it was a near thing." He let his head hang over the table as if in prayer. "I don't have a count for the number of missile cutters and assault shuttles downed, but the numbers run into the hundreds. Drop-ships...into the dozens. But I can tell you how many Marines have died. I'll never forget the number. I'll see it in nightmares for the rest of my life."

His eyes came up and scanned across the room, meeting each of ours, the eyes of every officer and NCO in the room.

"843 Force Recon," he declared, "and 1,096 Drop-Troopers."

I grunted, the pain spearing through my chest a phantom remnant of my broken ribs. That was over a battalion's worth of us, gone in a matter of hours. And if fewer Force Recon straight-legs had died, it was only because there'd been fewer of them in the first place.

"You've all heard of the famous battles of Marine Corps history, tracing our line back to the Eighteenth Century, to the founding of the United States of America. They're stenciled on the sides of our troop ships. Tripoli. Belleau Wood. Okinawa. Iwo Jima. Hue. Fallujah. Makung Harbor. Hermes. Barataria Bay. Well, from this day forward, ladies and gentlemen, Point Barber will be numbered among them." He shrugged. "Perhaps they'll call it the Battle of Deltaville, perhaps they'll use the Tahni name, Tahn-Khandara-Ankon. But you have lived through history here, my friends, my brothers and sisters. Some of you have covered yourselves in glory, others will not be remembered, but you were all part of it and no Marine from this day forward will ever forget this battle."

He sighed, a mighty wind from his deep chest, as theatrical and calculated as any other part of his image, a façade for our benefit, or perhaps history's.

"We have suffered terrible losses. Not just the losses that will matter to wives and husbands and fathers and mothers and sons and daughters back home, but the ones we will suffer here and now from the lack of leadership. Colonel Voss and her entire staff, Colonel Shepherd, Major Bray, Captain Covington. Men and women who were the backbone of the Corps, gone in a day. But I believe that each of you, the hardened iron come from the fire of this battle, will step up and take your place. The Corps needs leaders for the last push, for the invasion of Tahn-Skyyiah, and you will be those leaders."

Well, yeah, of course we would. What other choice did we have?

"We won't be able to move forward the final step in this war without reinforcements, and it will take weeks for them to arrive. So, we'll be bivouacking in Deltaville, here at the spaceport, but I want to assure all of you, you *will* be in on the invasion. You've all earned that. The replacements who come in to back us up will have the responsibility of keeping Point Barber pacified until the end of the war, not you."

I admit to sighing a bit with relief at that pronouncement, though the natural cynic in me wondered how hard he would work to keep that promise. Politicians and generals had ways of forgetting their promises when push came to shove.

"There will, of course, be a memorial for the dead once we have things secured enough. In the meantime, I will be sending out patrol schedules to each battalion. You'll each be responsible for detailing a company-sized element to patrol in conjunction with Force Recon and Fleet assault shuttles once per day until reinforcements arrive." His stare turned hard and stern. "We *will* take casualties during these patrols, so emphasize their importance and dangers to your Marines. We will also be going over company rosters and making adjustments to leadership and reorganizations of personnel as are needed until replacements arrive."

McCauley nodded to his staff puke and she called us to attention one more time so he could depart the plastic tent with the decorum to which he'd become accustomed. With the general's absence, Geiger turned to us, her company commanders.

"You know what I need," she told us. "Who you have, who's operational, what you need, on my 'link by chow, which is in two hours and forty minutes. The general wants a company, which might mean we have to combine platoons, so nobody get your nose out of joint if that happens, okay?"

Nods all around, though Cronje seemed determined not to respond to her.

"Alvarez, if you want, I can give your company tomorrow off from patrolling if you're looking for a good day for a memorial for Captain Covington. You guys arrange it, I'll bring the battalion around to your company area right before evening chow."

"Yes, ma'am."

I could feel Cronje's stare on me as Top and I headed for the exit.

"I swear to God, Top," I said to her, quiet enough not to be overheard, "I don't care if I get busted all the way back down to private, I'm going to kick the shit out of him so bad no auto-doc in the Commonwealth can put him back together."

"No, you won't," she told me, not a shred of doubt in her tone. "Because you're like him." I didn't have to ask who she meant by him. "Too responsible for your own damned good."

Shit. She was, I realized, probably right. When the hell had *that* happened?

[21]

"Captain Covington?" Top called.

There was no response.

"Captain Phillip Covington?"

Someone in the formation sobbed, but no NCO chewed them out.

"Captain Phillip J. Covington?"

His had been the last name read, though not the last one lacking a response. This was the final roll call, a ceremony older than the Commonwealth, maybe as old as the Marines, I wasn't sure. The helmet and the Gauss rifle propped up in a stand beside her were ceremonial—no one in Delta had worn them since Boot Camp—but they, too, were part of the ritual.

"Battalion!" Top barked. "Attention!"

And we all braced as neatly and sharply as we ever had for drill and ceremony, one final sign of respect. At some final roll calls, they had live buglers playing Taps, but this was a war zone, and if Fourth had ever had a real bugle, it would have been destroyed on the *Iwo Jima* anyway. The mournful notes came out of a portable speaker system set up by the engineers just for this ceremony. It would come down as soon as it was over, only

227

to be repurposed for yet another last roll call somewhere else. There would be a lot of them in the next few days. Each of our companies would have their own, but the whole battalion was only showing for this one.

The whole battalion minus one. Cronje hadn't come. I didn't think anyone minded, least of all Geiger. His XO, 1st Lt. Webster, had led the company into formation. I'd seen Vicky and Freddy, but hadn't had the chance to talk to either of them. I wasn't sure what I'd say to Freddy. I didn't know if he still blamed me for Port Harcourt or if he'd finally come to see who Cronje really was, and this didn't seem like an ideal time to find out.

At the final note of Taps, Top called the battalion to parade rest and she did something I'd never expected. She began to speak.

"Captain Phillip Covington and I," she said, her voice carried over the speakers to the depths of the cavernous tent, "served together for four years, nine months, twenty-seven days. In a day when most of us can expect to live two or three hundred years, if we're lucky, that doesn't seem so long. An eyeblink. A heartbeat. But in the military, it's an eternity. For some people, it's half a career. For us, it was the better part of this war. I knew him as a Marine better than anyone I've encountered in a very long life, better than some of the children I've borne. He was as dependable as the tide, a man who would do the right thing even when no one else saw it for what it was, a man who stuck by his principles even when it would cost his career. Because he didn't *care* about being a colonel, wouldn't hear of being a major.

"Captains fight wars, Top. That was what he would tell me. He would never let them promote him off the battlefield, out of combat, not because he loved it, though he might have, but because it was what he did best. He could see the flux of the battle, see who would break and who wouldn't, knew by instinct who to put where. It's a rare gift, and one tied, I think, to the bedrock of his conscience, to his instinctive knowledge of what was right. He could see it in others and valued it over all the ooh-rah bullshit and bravado. If you wanted to impress Phillip Covington as a Marine or as a person, you had to be willing to stand up for the right.

"When the time came...," she said, and her gruff, harsh voice finally broke. She didn't sob, and if there were any tears, they were hidden beneath the brim of her cover. "When the time came to make a choice between letting himself be saved or accomplishing the mission, Captain Covington made the only choice he could, the only one that fit with his unmovable conscience. He sacrificed himself not just to accomplish the objective but so his Marines wouldn't die trying to save him, because he valued their lives over his own."

She paused and sucked in a deep breath.

"The greatest memorial we could give such a man is to follow his example, and to lead by it. And the greatest honor we could give him now, at the end, is simply to say that this man, Phillip Covington, was a Marine."

We hadn't planned it, hadn't rehearsed it, but we said it in chorus as if we had.

"Ooh-rah!"

It was, I thought, the perfect eulogy, and she was the perfect person to give it. If Voss had lived, she would have insisted on giving it and while we all would still have honored the Skipper's memory, this was more fitting.

"Battalion, attention!"

I marched forward, ready to take over and say a few words of my own, but before I even had the chance to salute, Greg Cronje burst through the tent flap, his face red, his eyes wide. My first thought was that he'd brought a weapon and I made ready to either run or fight depending on what he did, but he was unarmed and when he lunged for Top, it was only to grab the mic on the stand beside her.

"I respected Phil Covington!" he insisted, his slurring words amplified across the tent. I could smell alcohol on him and I wondered where he'd gotten it. Any personal stash he might have had would have been destroyed with the *Iwo*, so he had to have bought it, or paid to have it made for him. "Honestly, I did! I would never have done anything to hurt him! It wasn't my fault. I had no choice but to...."

I'd heard enough. Maybe Top would have been right if the bastard had stayed away, had kept his head down and tried not to make waves, but to show up drunk for the Skipper's memorial.... I took a step toward him, full intent on turning him into hamburger.

But Top was closer. And I'll be damned if she wasn't faster, too. I didn't even see her knee rise up between Cronje's legs, but everyone heard the wheeze of breath leaving him as he doubled over. He didn't drop the mic then, miraculously, holding onto it as if by instinct. When the right cross smashed his nose, though, his fingers went slack and the microphone fell with a thump that came through the speakers, and the impact of the captain's back beside the mic came through as well despite his attempt to drown it out with a choked cry of pain.

There was no sound. Everyone had been at attention, and with the position came an inertial resistance to moving or speaking that lasted a few seconds into the event. And of course, there was the shock and disbelief, not that Top was capable of violence, but more that Cronje had dishonored the memorial. But the shock evaporated into outrage and concern, as embodied in the persons of Captain Geiger and Lt. Freddy Kodjoe rushing toward the front.

Top moved not a centimeter, hands at her sides, fists

clenching and unclenching, as if she were trying to decide whether Cronje deserved to be hit again.

"Did you fucking see that?" Cronje was whining, rolling to his side, blood gushing out of his smashed nose. "She struck a superior officer! I'm fucking filing charges!"

"Greg," Geiger growled, "you have exactly thirty seconds to get your worthless ass out of here or you're looking at a court-martial for drinking on duty. Don't make me repeat myself or we'll add assault and battery to the charges. As far as I'm concerned, you took a swing at First Sergeant Campbell and she defended herself."

Cronje squawked with outrage, wobbling slightly as he got to his feet. He cast a pleading glance at Freddy, who was standing off to the side, staring between the two captains.

"Freddy!" he said. "You saw what happened! You'll testify that she assaulted me, won't you?"

I searched Freddy's face and saw anger and disgust, though I wasn't sure just yet who it was aimed at. Freddy Kodjoe's lip curled in a scowl.

"I," he declared, "didn't see a Goddamned thing." He turned to go back to his platoon, but paused next to me, unable to meet my eyes. "I'm sorry, Cam. He wasn't worth it."

———

I wasn't surprised to be called into the Brigade Commander's office the next morning. If anything, I was surprised it took that long.

McCauley's office was the exception to the rules the rest of us were under because he was a general and they make their own rules. We were in tabernacles, the Hebrews wandering through the desert for forty years, while McCauley had one of the few surviving administration buildings at the spaceport, the doors repaired from where Force Recon troops had breached them, air conditioning already installed along with a collection of folding, plastic desks and wheeled office chairs, and a very expensive overhead holographic projector.

"Lt. Alvarez here for the general," I told the clerk in the front room of the office, walled off from the general's private offices with a curtain because the Tahni didn't have the same ideas about privacy that we did, apparently.

The clerk was a First Lieutenant, and I tried to imagine how I would feel going through the Academy, serving my time as a platoon leader...and then winding up filing reports and filtering appointments for a general. So, when the clerk scowled at me, I didn't take it personally.

"Let me check and see if he's available."

I stood at parade rest in front of the man's chest-high desk, savoring the smell of his hot coffee and wishing I'd had time to grab a cup to go before I'd been called here from the chow hall. I wasn't a huge fan of coffee before the Marines, but at this point, I would have taken an IV drip of the stuff. He murmured something into his 'link, then listened for a moment.

"Yes, sir," he said, then his eyes flickered upward to mine, meeting them as briefly as possible, as if he was disappointed at the answer he'd been given. "You can go in."

The divider was hard plastic, unfolding from one wall to another like an accordion, and the door was a part of it, just to give the office something more permanent than some flimsy curtain to push aside. I knocked, knowing it would be expected.

"Come."

I sucked in a breath, steeling myself for what was to come, and pushed the door open.

"Close it behind you," McCauley said, motioning to the door.

I shut it, then came to attention and saluted as sharply as I recalled how. It had been a while.

"Sir, Lt. Alvarez reports."

He returned the salute quickly, which was better than I'd hoped for. When senior officers were upset, sometimes they'd make a junior officer or enlisted man hold the salute for a long time while they decided whether or not to release them.

"At ease, Alvarez," he told me. "Have a seat."

I sat upright, not quite at attention but not relaxed even one little bit. I was sure the next thing out of his mouth would be an order to tell him what I'd seen at the memorial, and when it wasn't, I almost stumbled over my words, since everything I'd prepared was how to color the story to keep Top out of the brig.

"Alvarez," he said, fingers intertwined on the desk in front of him, expression unusually pensive, "you're getting bumped up to First Lieutenant. It's a little early, but not *that* early. You're going to be the permanent replacement for Phil Covington as Delta Company commander."

Oh, okay. That's *what this is about.*

I shifted mental gears and tried to think of something intelligent to say. "Thank you" didn't seem right because I was absolutely certain I didn't *want* the job.

"Yes, sir," I said, instead. "If I may, sir, how are we handling my company XO and my replacement as platoon leader?"

He regarded me evenly, a hint of approval in his eyes as if I'd asked the question he'd expected.

"You have the choice of Lieutenants Cano or Kovacs for your XO. There are a few platoons out there who lost enough people that we're folding them into other units and we're going to draw platoon leaders off that pool. You'll get two, one to replace you, one for your XO. I know you're entirely missing Second Platoon, I read the reports, but that will have to wait for the replacements to arrive from Inferno. You'll get a complete unit with a PL already in place before we ship out of here."

I nodded, trying to figure out why I was here. Captain Geiger could have told me all this herself, and I was sure he had to have gone over it with her. Brigade commanders didn't call lieutenants into their office just to discuss company business.

"Captain Geiger, by the way," he went on, "is now *Major* Geiger, and she is the permanent replacement for Colonel Voss." He waved a hand in a rolling motion. "And she'll be picking her XO from among her senior company commanders, and getting replacements for them, etc...."

He leaned back in his chair, regarding me with hooded eyes.

"*I'm* telling you this rather than her," he finally clarified, "because I wanted to let you know that Major Geiger, now that she is your battalion commander, is putting you in for a Silver Star for your actions at the spaceport." He shrugged. "After reviewing the recordings, I intend to approve it. I wanted you to hear it from me."

"Thank you, sir," I said, blowing a soft breath out through my teeth.

He raised an eyebrow, the corner of his mouth turning up.

"That will make, unless I've lost count, two silver stars and a bronze on your chest, Lieutenant, every one of them with a V for valor."

"I've been lucky enough," I said carefully, "to serve under some incredible leaders, sir, Captain Covington chief among them."

"And he will get his recognition as well, I assure you," McCauley told me, nodding as if he knew where I was going next. "But I wanted to talk to you about your future, Cameron."

Oh, boy. It's Cameron now.

"Where do you see yourself when this war ends, son?"

When the war ends? Shit, I had a problem even seeing the war ending, period.

"I thought I'd take my Resettlement Bonus, sir," I confessed. "Find a nice colony and set up a homestead there."

"And likely someone who joined the Marines to get out of the Trans-Angeles Underground would find that appealing," McCauley admitted. "For a while. But you're going to live a long time. Do you think you could settle for the life of a yeoman farmer for the next two or three centuries?"

"What did you have in mind, sir?" I asked, knowing he was going to get to it eventually and wanting to get it out of the way now instead of dragging it out.

"There seems to be a general belief," he told me, "that once this war is over and won, the military will be cut back to nothing. I am here to tell you, that is *not* the case. If we beat the Tahni at Tahn-Skyyiah, which I believe we will, the Fleet and the Marines will still be needed to enforce the peace." He shrugged. "And just because the Tahni are the only other intelligent life we've discovered so far doesn't mean they're the only ones in the galaxy. We'll still have a sizable military, and the problem in my estimation, will be a shortage of available officers." He pointed across the desk at me with a computer stylus. "With your record, son, you could be sitting in my chair in another ten years. You could be Commandant of the Marine Corps in twenty, if you're any good at schmoozing with politicians."

I rocked back just a centimeter, trying to imagine myself as a general. Hell, I was having trouble picturing myself as a company commander and I'd already *done* that. I had to admit, it was appealing—not the part about being a general, but the idea of a home, of something that would still be there for me after the war.

But isn't Brigantia a home? Isn't Vicky a home?

They were...but they weren't something I knew, at least not yet. I'd never been married, never lived with a girl for more than a few days. And I certainly had no idea how to be a fucking farmer. I knew how to be a Marine, and I knew I could learn to be a company commander or whatever came next, in that framework.

"You don't have to make up your mind *now*," McCauley told me. "Even if things go perfectly—and they never do—we'll be stationed here for weeks, possibly months. And God alone knows how long it will take to secure the Tahni home system. But I did want you to *start* thinking about it."

"Yes, sir," I told him, meaning it. "I will."

"Very good, Lieutenant." He made a dismissive gesture. "There are a lot of administrative duties that go with your new position, but I'm sure Major Geiger will go over those with you when you meet with her later this morning."

"Sir," I said, swallowing hard before I could force the words out, "there is one other thing. Captain Cronje, sir. I wonder if you've reviewed the recordings of his actions at the power plant."

McCauley's expression darkened, and I thought, perhaps, I had really stepped in the shit this time.

"I have," he said. "It was disturbing and shameful, but...." He tossed his head. "It's no longer something with which we need to concern ourselves."

That, I thought, was an odd phrasing.

"What do you mean, sir?"

He regarded me with eyes gone cold, and looking into them I decided maybe the man did have combat experience, after all.

"Captain Gregory Cronje," he told me, "walked to the edge of the perimeter fence at 0235 this morning, put the barrel of a service pistol into his mouth and pulled the trigger."

[22]

Aside from the general's digs, one of the first things the engi-neers set up in Deltaville was the Officers' Club. There has to be some deep, philosophical statement about the military in there somewhere, but since I was an officer now, I didn't try to find it, just went to have a drink.

It was the first night off I'd had in a week, every night where I wasn't leading the company on a combat patrol devoted to planning sessions the pacification of nearby cities. Deltaville wasn't the only city on this world, of course, though it was where the Tahni had shot their load and concentrated all their defenses. It was a difference in psychology, I suppose, putting all their eggs in one basket and chancing everything to one, huge battle rather than distributing them evenly and forcing us to root them out a bit at a time. It was tough to say which strategy would have killed more humans, but the one they'd chosen had left the other cities nearly defenseless, which had worked out pretty well for me, personally, because I hadn't looked forward to riding one COP to another. And the difference between a Forward Operating Base and a Combat Outpost is stark.

As things stood now, we were launching airmobile raids out of Deltaville, Force Recon troops mainly with Drop-Troopers on the outskirts for a rapid response force. The flight time was a bitch, but at least we could sleep in our own cots at the FOB most nights. I could live with it. The downside was, I hadn't had a chance to do more than wave hello to Vicky in six days, but we'd finally managed to get the same night off.

The Officers' Club had been a storage building for construction equipment, so it had plenty of room, though it was short on furniture. Some bright engineering crew had made a bar from a row of Tahni cargo containers covered by plastic doors salvaged from the wreckage. Barstools were actual Tahni chairs, and I guess there were advantages to going to war with another bipedal humanoid. The liquor was synthahol made in a food processing unit, the lowest common denominator of anything drinkable, but no one was complaining.

Vicky was waiting for me when I arrived, sitting at the bar, nursing a plastic cup with some sort of mixed drink and a forlorn expression.

"Hey," I said, leaning over to kiss her, not bothering to check who was watching. They could put the Article-15 right next to my silver star. One of my silver stars. I frowned at her expression. "Everything okay?"

"I love you, Cam," she told me, "but if you think I'm remotely okay, you're worse at understanding women now than you were when I first met you."

I shaped a silent whistle and sat down beside her, waving at the corporal tending bar.

"Whatever you have that's closest to tequila," I told him before I turned back to Vicky. "So, spill. What is it? You lose somebody on your last patrol?" I hadn't heard about any casualties in the Drop-Troopers the last few days, but sometimes the brass didn't want that kind of thing spread around.

"I haven't *been* on any patrols," she ground out, downing half of her drink in one gulp to punctuate the sentence.

"What?" My face screwed up in confusion. "But I saw the patrol roster. I know Alpha went out twice already."

"And Lt. Webster *conveniently* found administrative work that had to be done back here at the FOB both times, and assigned me to complete it." The bartender brought my drink and I paid for it with my 'link. "Another sonic screwdriver," Vicky told him, motioning with her empty cup.

"Webster is Alpha's XO?" I asked.

"Was," she corrected me. "Since Cronje blew his brains out, Webster is acting company commander." She shrugged. "He makes all the right noises about how Captain Cronje was troubled and made mistakes, but he still holds his suicide against you and, by extension, against me. He doesn't trust me and he's doing everything he can to undercut me."

"Shit," I sighed. "I'm sorry, Vicky. Maybe I could talk to Geiger. She was no fan of Cronje's. She could light a fire under Webster's ass."

She laughed softly, the sound touched with bitterness.

"And tell her what? That your girlfriend is whining about not being sent out on patrol? Even if she *did* say something to him, it would probably just make things worse. I have to just ride this out." She shrugged. "It probably won't last long after we pull out of here, whenever that is. When we're dropping on Tahni-Skyyiah, it's going to be all hands on deck. And if we survive that...." She knocked on the plastic of the bar top, pretending it was wood. "...then this will all be over." A faint smile tugged the edges of her frown up and she put her hand on top of mine, interlacing our fingers. "We can find that little, quiet colony world and figure out how we're going to spend the rest of our lives."

I nodded, then grabbed my cup and downed the tequila in a

single gulp, which is mostly what tequila is good for. The drink helped to hide the gulp. This wasn't, I decided, a good time to tell Vicky about my conversation with General McCauley.

"Until then," she went on, "I'll just keep my head down and do my job." She laughed. "Maybe I should ask for a transfer to your company."

"Oh, God," I moaned, setting the cup down, wishing it was glass so I could slam it with some authority. "Vicky, I was *just* starting to figure out how to be a damned platoon leader. I don't know what the hell I'm doing. I don't know why they put me in charge."

"You're a fucking liar," she accused, punching me in the chest. And it hurt. That woman knew how to punch. "You started out in our platoon as a damned private and every single time you've been promoted and given any responsibility, I always hear that same song and dance, that you don't know what you're doing." She snorted. "Yeah, right, you're so damned incompetent that you have a Bronze Star *and* a Silver Star...."

"Two Silver Stars," I corrected her, shrugging. I hadn't had a chance to tell her about that, either. "Geiger put me in for one for the spaceport, and General McCauley told me he's going to approve it."

"Jesus, give me strength," she pleaded, rolling her eyes. "*Two* Silver Stars, and you came up with the plan for probably the only covert op the brass ever let Drop-Troopers run in the whole war when you were a *squad leader*. So, Cameron Alvarez, I don't want to hear you tell me again how you don't know what you're doing, or how you won't be able to handle this. Bullshit. When they finally throw something at you that you can't handle, I want to be there to see it, because it hasn't happened yet."

"The Skipper was a legend, Vicky," I protested. "How the hell do you replace a legend?"

"Just look out for your people. Whether it's a fire team or a company or the whole damned brigade, look out for your people and accomplish the mission without wasting them. That's what the Skipper always did." She checked the time on her 'link and sighed. "Shit. I have to be up in six hours." A smile flickered across her face. "I think I might know a place where we could be alone for a while, if you want to get out of here."

Need stirred deep inside me and I suddenly remembered how long it had been since we had any time to ourselves. I grinned and grabbed her hand and we headed for the door. A pair of MP's was waiting for me there, their expressions grim.

"What's up, guys?" I asked them.

"Sorry to bother you, sir," the higher-ranking of the two, an E-5 told me. "Could, uh...could we step outside?"

"Sure," I said, shrugging incomprehension to Vicky.

The street outside the O-club was nearly deserted at this time of night, the glare from security spotlights at the FOB perimeter throwing odd shadows extending every direction from the surrounding buildings.

"Sir, this is kind of a weird situation, but we, um...we have one of your people outside." He sighed and shifted with obvious discomfort. "Look, sir, we ain't really got our shit together yet, you know that. They brought us in mostly to help control the locals, but we ain't got a brig or anything down here yet and I wouldn't want to be tossing any of our guys into it if we did. I mean, this was a tough fight, I understand that." He waved back across the street to where an all-terrain utility rover was parked. A single figure sat in the back of it, their face invisible from this angle. "I thought maybe you could deal with this however you wanted? I would've called your First Sergeant," he added, apologetic, "but the corporal said he thought you'd be in the O-club, so...."

"It's okay," I assured him. "I'll talk to him. Thank you,

Sergeant." I cast an apologetic look at Vicky. "Give me a few minutes?"

"Take your time," she said, putting a hand on my shoulder. "I'll be back at the bar."

The MP's held back and waited while I walked to their car and pulled the door open. Vince Delp was sitting in the back seat, looking miserable and smelling drunk. A nascent bruise was already beginning to swell on his right cheek and a fleck of blood stuck to his upper lip from a blow to the nose.

"Oh, for God's sake, Vince," I sighed, sliding in beside him. "You had to do this on my night off?"

"I'm sorry, sir," he said, head down, unable to meet my eyes.

"Was it a girl again?" I wondered. "Another loud-mouthed REMF or Fobbit?"

"Lieutenant," he said, his voice breaking just slightly, "I don't think it was really any of those things. It's just...." He trailed off and let his head rest against the back of the seat. "I keep seeing their faces, sir."

"Whose faces, Vince?" I thought I knew, but I had to ask. "Who do you see?"

"John...Corporal Muller, I mean."

I nodded. Muller had been Delp's team leader. He'd bought it this mission.

"And Mancuso before him," he went on. "And Benavidez, and Clarke and Sgt. Carson, and Gunny Hayes...." He stopped and in the splintered shadows and glare from the light outside the car, I thought I could see his shoulders shaking. His sob confirmed it. Delp bent over, face buried in his hands, and I put a hand on his shoulder, waiting.

"I'm okay when I'm out there," he explained once he could talk again. "When I'm in the suit. Nothing can touch me in the suit. It's like I'm immortal. But when I'm just around, just hanging in the barracks or the tent, when there's nothing to do but think, well...I just think. I think about them all. About how everyone I ever made friends with or played cards with or told stories about home with, they're all dead." He shrugged. "Not all. But you know what I mean, sir. It's like I don't *want* to get to know them anymore. Because the more I get to know them, the more I gotta think about them afterward. Do you understand what I'm saying, sir?"

"Oh, yeah," I assured him, sitting back. The inside of the car smelled like a drunk sweating synthahol out of every pore. "I know that better than anyone, Delp. Better than you. I've lost almost everyone who was ever important to me." Everyone but Vicky. "And that started long before this war."

"How do you do it then, sir?" he asked, pleading. "How do you keep them out of your head?"

I considered that, maybe for the first time, and I answered him honestly, as the answer came to me.

"They're never gone from your head, Vince. They never will be. But they don't have to haunt you. Every one of them took something from you and left something behind, and it wouldn't be right to forget them. But you keep making friends, keep letting people close, and the new memories help keep the old ones from taking over your head. You get what I'm saying?" He nodded.

"I think so, sir."

"And if you let new people close," I went on, "then maybe there'll be someone you care about there to tell you to stop when you try to do something this *fucking stupid* again." I put an edge to the last few words and his eyes widened. "Look, Delp, you're a hell of a Marine. I *need* you walking point. You save lives. You win battles. But I can't have this shit, not anymore. I'm the company commander, and I have dozens of Delps to look after. I can't be holding your hand anymore. So, here's the deal. We're going to be on Point Barber for at least a few more weeks. Since you get in trouble when you have time to think, I'm going to have a little talk with Top and Bang-Bang and I'm going to make sure you don't have *time* to think for the next few weeks. From the minute you finish breakfast to the minute your exhausted little head hits the pillow, you're going to be working, and not the kind of work where you'll have the mental energy to sit around brooding. This'll be the kind of work where you're so fucking tired, you'll dread reveille in the morning."

His eyes were wider now, like a cartoon character, and I felt a bit guilty but pushed it aside. That ship had sailed.

"You may think I'm being rough on you," I told him, "but I'm not. I swear to God and on my mother's grave, Delp, this is by far the most merciful of the options I have left open to me to deal with you. Unless you want to spend however long is left in this war in a cell, this is your best bet." He opened his mouth, but I held a hand up. "Don't bother thanking me, don't bother promising me you'll do better, because I've heard it all before. You're going to behave and do your job because Top and I and your platoon sergeant and whoever your platoon leader winds up being are not going to give you any other choice."

I jerked a thumb at the car door.

"Now, get out and get back to the tent and I want you to tell Bang-Bang *exactly* what I just told you. And when Top talks to him in the morning, he'd better recite back to me verbatim what I just told you. You got me?"

"Yes, sir."

I couldn't tell if he was grateful to me or just grateful to get out of the car, but he was grateful and then he was gone.

"You get it sorted out, sir?" the MP sergeant asked me when I slid out behind Delp.

"It's sorted."

One way or another.

I headed back to the bar to find Vicky and take my own advice.

245

[23]

I decided about twenty hours in that I didn't like the CSS *Hermes*. She had a smell to her, like the smell of new clothes fresh out of the fabricator, a sharp edge to every corner, and I just couldn't feel comfortable in her passageways. It was like no one had lived in her before, no stories had been told about her. I'd been sitting in my compartment since we'd entered Transition Space, working on the endless reports, documenting training, disciplinary action, simulator time, patrols we'd run in Deltaville, emerging only to eat or attend battalion and brigade meetings, otherwise stopping only to sleep. This was work that should have been done two days ago, though how I was supposed to do it *and* lead company-size patrols, I wasn't sure.

How the hell, I wondered, did anyone ever get any work done in this job?

My vision was starting to blur by the time I finished the last report and I whispered a prayer of thanks that no one else had knocked on my door looking for solutions to problems they should have solved themselves. I checked the time. It was 2330 ship's time, which was meaningless to my body since I was still on Deltaville time, and I was neither hungry nor tired. I tried

Vicky's 'link address and it politely told me that she was sleeping and not to bother her until morning unless it was an emergency.

Of course, I was one of the few people who could call her and say it *was* an emergency, but I wouldn't do that to her. I knew how rare and precious a good night's sleep was for a platoon leader, and it was becoming even rarer as a company commander. And I wasn't going to get it tonight, not unless I resorted to a pill. I tried to avoid that, because I'd seen some Marines who couldn't sleep without them at all after using them for years.

Instead, I pulled on my boots and my fatigue top and went for a walk.

It was, perhaps, a remnant of my enlisted days that I felt like an intruder entering the storage bays for the Vigilantes. They were off-limits to unauthorized personnel, and it took me a moment to realize I *was* authorized personnel now. If this was a Fleet cruiser, there would have been duty crews on shift work, pulling maintenance, but Marine troop ships did things differently. We were always headed planetside, and they did the best they could to get us ready for the day-night cycle we were heading toward, so there was a shipboard night and day, and at night, the lights were dimmed and the only people working were skeleton crews on the bridge, in engineering and damage control.

The storage bays seemed deserted; the suits relics left behind from some lost civilization like China's terracotta armies. I went to mine, first. It had been repaired a few days after the nominal end of the battle and I'd stripped and cleaned it five times for every patrol I'd taken it out on since, but I gave it a quick systems check again out of habit. Everything was nominal, and I knew it would be, but one more check never hurt. I pushed the chest plastron closed and let the palm of my hand linger there for a moment, like I imagined the old cavalry soldiers might have with their horse.

The Vigilante was, I thought perhaps with no small bit of prejudice, the finest weapons system ever fielded. I tried to imagine fighting this war without it and shuddered at the prospect. The battlefield was a nightmare of high-energy lasers, ionized gas and charged particles, and facing all that with nothing but the thin armor of a Force Recon Marine made my testicles want to crawl up into my stomach.

I left my suit and paced down the row of maintenance racks for the company Headquarters Platoon to the Boomers. To *my* Boomers. That was a kick in the ass. Their coil guns were long and awkward, forcing them to leave a drop-ship from the boarding ramp at a landing zone instead of jetting from a drop rack, but they were sledgehammers, specialized tools I had never had access to before. Besides the gun, their backpacks were larger than a standard Vigilante's, the hopper for the coil gun ammo bulging out on one side. I grabbed the lever on one side of the hopper and yanked it downward, admiring the angular, grooved lines of the tungsten darts.

"Impressive, aren't they?"

I very deliberately did *not* spin around like an idiot at the unexpected question, though my hand did tighten on the loading lever. I recognized Top's voice. I pushed the hopper shut and turned toward her. She was watching me, hands on her hips, an amused expression softening the hard lines of her face.

"They are. Did you come down here in the middle of the night just to get one more look at them before you went to sleep?" I smiled to take the edge off the words. It felt strange being able to talk to Top this easily. Even as a platoon leader, she'd intimidated the hell out of me. When had that changed?

"I came," she told me, not seeming to take offense, "because you've been buried under mounds of paperwork and I didn't want to interrupt."

"Paperwork?" I repeated, frowning in confusion.

"Sorry, old habit. Back when I was your age, the military still filled out all those reports on actual paper. It was a nightmare. We had warehouses full of that shit, too much to ever scan all of it into our computer systems, so most of it got tossed in the incinerator a century ago."

"That sounds horrific," I said. "It also sounds just like something the military would do. How did you find me here anyway?"

"I tracked your 'link." She nodded toward the device on my belt. "You can do the same to anyone in the company now, by the way, if the need arises."

"I knew that," I told her, "but I think I'd managed to make myself forget it, because I know how much I would have liked it when I was an enlisted Marine." I shuddered involuntarily. "So, what was it you didn't want to interrupt me about?"

"Many things," she said, being as cryptic as she'd always been, though at this point in my career, I found it less mysterious and fascinating and more annoying. She leaned against the bulk of one of the Boomer suits. "First of all, Private Vince Delp."

I moaned and covered my face with a hand.

"Don't tell me he's gotten into more trouble. I thought the extra work details were helping keep his nose clean."

"They have been," she said. "So far. He hasn't touched the booze since that one night on Point Barber, as far as I know."

I sagged with relief.

"Thank God. What is it, then?"

"It's a temporary solution, sir."

I blinked, realizing she'd called me 'sir.' It might have

happened before, but it hadn't struck me as significantly as it did in that moment.

"I get that," I told her. "He needs psych counselling, and I thought about ordering him to it, but...." I hesitated, wondering if I should admit it, then deciding she probably already knew. "I went to a head-shrinker myself, and I just know that if someone had ordered me to talk to her, I wouldn't have admitted a damned thing."

"Probably true. And keeping him busy might work through this next campaign." She shrugged. "And maybe this is the last campaign, but the kid is going to have to face this for the rest of his life."

"We all are," I muttered. "But yeah, I'm going to push through a medical recommendation for him afterward. I just didn't want to do it before the last push. I kept thinking how I would have felt if I'd gone through what he has and someone told me I couldn't be there for the last dust-up."

"What the hell do you mean 'if' you'd gone through what he has?" Top spluttered, half a laugh and half a snort of disbelief. "You've gone through twice as much as that kid. And it wouldn't matter if you hadn't. There's something my father used to tell me, Lt. Alvarez. Life, he would say, is a grindstone. Whether it grinds you down or polishes you up depends on what you're made of."

I shrugged, uncomfortable with the implications of that.

"Maybe so," I allowed, "but we don't get to choose what we're made of, do we? Delp has done the best he can for us when he's in the suit. I'm going to make sure he gets help the minute this whole thing is over."

"That's bad luck, you know," she reminded me. "Talking about the war like we've already won it."

"I know," I admitted. "But I've been thinking a lot about it lately. And if we don't, if I wind up dead...well, at least it'll be a surprise. But if this *is* the end of the war, I need to decide what I'm going to do after."

"Let me guess. General McCauley gave you his spiel about being Commandant of the Marine Corps."

I guess I must have looked shock, because she laughed, a remarkably burbling chuckle for someone I'd never thought of as particularly good-humored.

"Oh, yeah, he's pulled that one out of his ass before. Tried to use it on the Skipper once or twice until he gave up. The man sells the Corps like it's a multi-level marketing scheme."

Whatever that was. I didn't ask, figuring it was another one of those dated references to the old days.

"He's not wrong, though," she said, frowning as though she found the admission distasteful. "You're going out of this war with a shitload of fruit salad on your chest. You might not make Commandant of the fucking Marine Corps, but you could probably wear a star someday...if that's what you want. Is it?"

"A star?" I shook my head. "I don't know. The Skipper told me generals were mostly politicians and I never saw myself as a politician. But staying in the Marines...." I tilted my head to the side like I was trying to look at the question from another angle. "If you'd asked me a year ago, or even three months ago, I would have said no."

"And now you're not so sure. I thought you and Sandoval wanted to go live on a farm and make babies."

I didn't miss the mockery in the words, and I wondered if she would have had the same thoughts back when she was raising her own kids. Maybe a long life would make a cynic of all of us, in the end. Those who got the chance at one.

"And I still do want that." I raised my hands in surrender. "All right, I give up. Give me the fucking Tahni, Top, they're easier to understand. Was there anything else?"

"The new Second Platoon is doing well in the simulators.

Gunnery Sgt. Nichols seems competent and if her squad leaders are a little on the green side, they at least follow orders well enough. What do you think of Lt. Sarrat?"

"She's right out of OCS," I mused, "and was a corporal before that, so I won't be expecting too much when the real guns start shooting, but she's done okay in training." I shrugged. "What training we've had time for, anyway. And she managed to keep her Marines from shooting each other on that one patrol she pulled before we left Point Barber, so that's a plus. She's a bit by-the-numbers, but I think we can work with her. Maybe keep her paired with Cano's platoon when we're on the ground."

"Sanderson seems to be doing well with First Platoon. At least he'd seen combat before Point Barber."

"Honestly, I'm more worried about Third. I'm starting to think there's a reason Lt. Verlander lost his platoon in Deltaville and it wasn't just bad luck."

Top chuckled, eyeing me sidelong.

"You sure that isn't just the old Third Platoon leader being jealous of the man taking over his old outfit?"

I scowled at her accusation.

"Is it jealousy that made him run Third squad into an ambush in that last simulator run?" I countered. "Because to me, it looked a lot like an Academy ring-knocker who doesn't know their ass from a hole in the ground."

"You've got Gunny Morrel riding herd on him," she said with a shrug, sounding more philosophical about it than I was feeling. "I'll talk to Bang-Bang and make sure he knows he's going to have to keep a close watch. That's assuming he doesn't already know. You sound worried. What happened to Mr. The-war-is-over-I-have-to-start-planning?"

"Shit, Top, the war *is* over. The Tahni aren't going to give up as long as their Emperor is still alive, but there's no way they can win this and they know it. *We* know it. But that doesn't mean a lot of people aren't going to get themselves killed proving it."

———

I stared at the screen of the tablet, trying to organize my thoughts, trying to decide if I wanted to record this at all. I sucked in a breath and hit the button to start the video.

"Dak," I said, "I don't know when this is going to send. I'm on a troop ship heading for the Tahni home system. We won't be setting up any Instell ComSats until after we've secured the system and God only knows how long that'll take. But I didn't answer your last message and I wanted to do it now, just in case."

I didn't say in case of what. He knew, and despite what I'd told Top, I *did* sort of believe in luck.

"Congratulations on getting married. I'm glad you found someone. I've been thinking lately how hard it is to be happy, and how much harder it must be the longer you live. I've been ready to die since I was a little kid, but now that I'm ready to live, it's starting to scare me, and I'm getting worried I'm going to let it scare me away from being happy. I wonder if I'm scared of being happy with Vicky and I'm letting that make me want to stay in the Marines after the war. Or maybe I'm just scared of having to deal with the memories of what's happened to me without the framework and structure of the military. That might be it." I rubbed at my eyes. I was feeling tired now, and I had to get up in four hours. "There's a guy in my platoon who's already having that problem. He's a hard-charger when we're in battle, but he's falling apart the rest of the time. I think I'm afraid that's going to be me, that I'm going to drown myself in a bottle to stop the memories. I'm afraid I'm going to let Vicky down...that I'm going to let you and Maria down, too. You believed in me, not as a Marine, as a man. And I'm not nearly as worried about fucking up as a Marine as I am fucking up as a husband, or a father."

I smiled, tugging the corners of my mouth up against a ton of exhaustion and emotional inertia.

"I think I know what you'd say to that. You'd tell me I'm doing the same thing I always did, putting up a wall because I'm afraid of what's on the other side. That I just gotta go ahead and face the thing I'm afraid of. That's what...." I trailed off, my throat closing up as a memory stuck there. "That's what my mother would say, when I came to her at night, afraid to go to sleep in my room because it was dark. She'd take me into my room and show me every corner of it with the lights on, and she'd tell me there was nothing there with the lights off that wasn't there when they were on. She'd tell me what I was really afraid of was just the not knowing, and the only cure for not knowing was believing."

I laughed softly, shaking my head.

"It's funny, I talk to other guys and they can't remember shit from when they were that little. Little things here and there, a birthday or a trip to a park. But I remember every little bit of it. Maybe because I put so much effort into forgetting everything that came after." I opened my mouth, closed it again. "I think that's all I got right now. I might not send this. If I make it through. I might just come and tell you all this in person. So, if you get this, I just wanted to say thank you. I wouldn't have been able to do any of this without you and Maria. I owe you just about everything I am right now. I hope I don't let you down." I reached for the screen to stop the recording, but paused.

"One other thing. I signed over my military insurance and my colony-world stake to Vicky. I'd like to give her one other thing in case I don't make it. I'm gonna send her to you. She wants her own life away from Earth, some land to call her own, a chance to forget all this. I'd like you to help her with that. I'd like you to do for her what you did for me, give her a home. If you could do that, it'd mean a lot to me."

I touched the button and the recording ended. From there, it was a complicated series of menus to scroll through to set up an automatic send at the first opportunity and still give myself the option to cancel it.

There. I'd done what I could for Vicky if I didn't make it. I turned the light off and slumped back on my rack. Five days and a wake-up and we'd be there. For me, one way or another, this war was going to end.

[24]

I was drowning in data.

As a platoon leader, I'd been overwhelmed by the available tactical information available to me in battle, and had to relearn how to stay on top of it. We were still ten light-seconds out from Tahni-Skyyiah and I was already lost in the incredible flood of information the helmet's HUD was throwing at me.

I squinted and angled my head to the side and tried to focus on just one part of it and the best I could tell was that we were winning. Sort of.

The Fleet tactical channels were open to my probing and I tried listening to them, but the captains, helm officers, and tactical officers spoke their own language and I hadn't had the opportunity to learn it.

"I read four deltas at point oh-nine, pulling three gravities. Targeting with Alphas. Bravo Three, run interference for me."

"Copy that, *Trafalgar*, Bravo Three will pave the road."

And the visual accompaniment to that multimedia military poem was a starfield of blue icons heading inward toward the green and blue of a living planet, our path headed not through particles of red opposition but a cloud, a nebula of red stretched across the space between.

I *thought* I knew what the words meant, though I was mostly filling in the details through guesswork. Deltas might mean destroyers. Alphas, I thought, had to be Ship-Buster missiles and I thought the Bravos were the missile cutters. The *Trafalgar* was launching Ship-Busters at the destroyers, but the missiles were vulnerable to active and passive defenses and the Tahni would send their corvettes to try to destroy them *en route*, hopping in and out of Transition Space to take shots at them. The Attack Command missile cutters would run interference for the Ship-Busters, taking out corvettes and enemy anti-missile missiles and hoping like hell one of the damned things would make it through.

Fleet warfare was a game of patience, and thank God someone else was in charge of it because I didn't have any. I wanted to scream, already tired of the three-gravity boost crushing me into the cushioning inside my suit, ready to be off this ship, thinking about the last troop ship I'd been on, about the way it had come apart around us. And the only distraction I had was Major Geiger asking for status reports every ten minutes, as if somehow Delta Company's status had changed while we were sitting in our drop racks.

Oh, and the Frag-O's. If I'd thought Frag-O's were bad when I'd been a squad leader and one filtered down through the platoon a couple times before a launch....

"Alvarez," Geiger's voice crackled in my earphones for the twentieth time since we'd loaded in the drop-ships. I'd counted. "We have a fragmentary order coming through from Brigade. Change to Situation: Weather. Current orbital probe drones indicate a possible tropical storm forming in the gulf outside Tahn-Khandranda." Jeez, that was a tongue-twister. Every other Tahni planet and city, we used our own designators, but the command insisted on using the Tahni language names for this world and its cities, just to show us how momentous it all was. As if we couldn't figure that out for ourselves. "The approach pattern for the drop-ships has been adjusted to the northwest to compensate. The targeted drop zone remains the same, but be aware if there's an early abort, you'll be three kilometers farther northwest of the target."

"Copy that, ma'am," I told her as the same data scrolled down the lower left portion of my helmet's HUD. Then I noticed something. "Ma'am, that's going to put our early abort smack in the middle of Assault Squadron Four's air support targeting pattern."

"Shit," she spat. "Goddamnit, wait one."

I rolled my eyes, grateful she couldn't see the exasperation on my face. The suits were nice and private. I couldn't imagine working on the bridge of a Fleet cruiser, where everyone could see every disgusted expression I made. Years in the Vigilante had, I was sure, made me a shitty poker player.

"Sir? Are you busy?" That was Sarrat, right on cue. I'd learned she was absolutely dependable. I could count on her to come to me with something she should have been able to figure out on her own at least once an hour. Unless we were in combat, and then it would be three times an hour.

"Of course not, Lieutenant," I told her. "It's Marine policy that all company commanders be left strictly to their own devices during combat so they can be available to their platoon leaders at all times."

I thought, for a second, that she was going to actually buy that one, but when she spoke again, I could hear the embarrassment in her voice. Too bad. It would have been funnier if she'd bought it.

"Oh, um, sorry, sir. But I just got the new Frag-O and...."

"And you wanted to let me know that our early abort path

runs right through the fire support targeting plan?" I anticipated, my estimation of her tactical intelligence going up a notch. "Good catch, but Battalion knows and they're working on it."

"Oh, no, sir, I hadn't noticed that." Of course not. "I just had, well, maybe this is a stupid question...."

"There are no stupid questions, Sarrat, only stupid people who ask questions. Go ahead."

"It's just that the new Frag-O says that there's a tropical storm coming in over the gulf outside the Tahni capital city, sir. And the Tahni are already going to be using a shitload of ECM jamming, right, sir? So, I was wondering how the assault shuttles are going to target at all? Because they won't be able to use IFF transponders and if there's a huge storm, they won't have visual."

Damn. That *was* a good question.

"The answer is, I don't know, Sarrat. And while that is, indeed, a troubling question, it's not one that they're going to give us an answer to, because that's Fleet's problem. If we don't have air support, well, neither will they. And to be honest with you, that's about the way it's been in every battle I've seen since this war started, not counting the patrols we ran against insurgents after a planet was occupied."

Which was the *only* combat Sarrat had seen, so I understood her concern. She was used to being able to call in a shuttle for a gun run whenever there was entrenched opposition.

"Lt. Alvarez?" Oh good, that was Lt. Verlander. I was sure his question would be much more intelligent.

"Yes, Verlander?"

"I was looking at that Frag-O and if they shift our emergency drop zone, we're gonna be right in the path of the fire-support targeting zone, sir!"

Breathe. Count to ten. Keep your voice down.

"Thank you, Lieutenant. I'll pass that along to Battalion and see what they have to say about it."

"Okay, Alvarez," Geiger said, exasperation in his tone, "Frag-O number four. Execution, Tasks to Combat Support, Fire Support. Assault Squadron Four's fire support targeting plan has been shifted southeast in the case of emergency drop. I should have noticed that, damn it."

"Ma'am," I told her, "you're probably ten times as busy as I am and I'm barely keeping my head above water."

"We're all learning on the job," she sighed. "You wanna know the big picture? They told me, for all the good it's doing me."

"Hit me, ma'am." We'd all received a situation briefing on the trip from Point Barber, but it had been damned hard to get detailed intelligence reports out of the Tahni home system and I had a bet with Cano on how close the enemy strength estimates would be to reality.

"It's not as bad as Point Barber," she said, "but there was no way it could be. We knew they threw almost everything they had into that system. There's maybe half the destroyers on station here, and only a quarter the number of corvettes, at least that we've detected so far, but they make up for that with nearly three times the static defense platforms. We could basically walk on the anti-ship missiles coming in from the defense platforms, and I've been advised to expect a couple of micro-Transitions to get us past them."

"Micro-Transitions?" I repeated. "On a fucking *troop transport?*"

"That's what they said," she told me. "They didn't say we'd like it."

There was a reason the Attack Command missile cutters had been so successful for the Fleet in this war: they were small enough to pull off multiple micro-Transitions in a battle without ripping themselves to pieces. I couldn't have explained the physics of it with a gun to my head, but for some reason, the more mass a ship pulled, the more energy it required to enter Transition Space and the more stress on its physical structure it endured during the Transition. Trying to jump in and out of T-space within the space of a couple seconds could damage the molecular structure of a ship as big as a troop transport.

It doesn't matter if we lose a transport. This is the last stop.

The realization was cold in the pit of my stomach. We were burning our ships behind us like Cortes. Well, maybe not quite as dramatic as that, but it was a sign we weren't saving anything for the trip home.

In the corner of my HUD dedicated to the tactical feed from the *Hermes*, something disappeared in a halo of white, a new nebula in the darkness and I changed my mind. Maybe it wasn't so much determination to win as a fear that going anything less than balls-out was suicide.

"We have multiple Alphas inbound," one of the bridge officers announced, as calm as if he were telling his coworkers lunch would be chicken today. "Deploying ECM's and targeting with laser batteries."

"Can we shake them?" That was the transport's captain. I'd never seen her, but I recognized her voice from the announcements she made over the speakers periodically.

"Probability is pretty low, ma'am. Bravos are heading our way to try to take them out, but they're too close."

"Secure for micro-Transition one light-second ninety degrees from galactic north. Ten seconds."

An alarm began whooping, a distant, mournful sound that barely made it through the drop-ship's fuselage, though thankfully not in my earphones.

"All personnel, secure for micro-Transition. All emergency

barriers up, all damage control teams to independent air sources."

"Shit," I moaned, then switched to the company net and tried to imitate the calm of the ship's tactical officer. "Hold on. We'll be fine, but it's not going to be fun."

It wasn't. The feeling reminded me of when I was ten and got my ass kicked by a couple of teenage boys who decided I had looked at them wrong. I ached all over and couldn't understand why. Marines were cursing in one ear and Fleet crews were cursing in another and something was flashing yellow with the warning that there was an atmosphere leak in the Marine quarters. Which was no big deal since none of us were occupying them at the moment. Hell, most of us didn't even have any personal effects on the ship because we'd lost them all on the *Iwo*. The *Hermes* wasn't a home, it was just a ride.

"We're clear." The tactical officer was equanimous, as if it hadn't mattered to him either way. "The Alphas aborted. Bravo Squadron Three falling in for escort."

I was breathing hard and I had to bring it under control before I could address the company again. Thrust pushed me into the back of my suit, a steady two gravities, not exactly comfortable but not painful.

"We're good," I told them, perhaps trying to reassure myself. "Everyone okay?"

A chorus of "ooh-rah" came from the officers, who probably hadn't had time to even check their platoons but didn't want to admit any of them had puked inside their suits.

"Status report, Delta?" Geiger asked almost before the echo from my platoon leaders had died.

"We're good, ma'am." *No, we have fifty percent casualties and all our suits are down.* What did she expect me to say?

"Revised ETA to our separation point is fifteen mikes. Pass it down to your Marines and run final checks."

"Yes, ma'am." Fifteen minutes sounded like forever. I passed it on to the platoon leaders, the words tumbling out on automatic, barely registering in my own ears. Except Kovacs. I made sure to get him on the line because he was my XO and would be in charge of the other two platoons until we touched ground.

"Francis," I told him, "separation in fifteen mikes. You remember the link-up plan, right?"

"Yeah, I got it," he insisted. "If we drop too far separated for visual identification, I take my section of the company to the open square just to the west of that funky Washington Monument-looking building on the east end of the city and wait for you there until 1700 local time. If enemy activity forces me off that area, the backup rally point is the industrial parking lot behind the fusion reactor complex."

Well, he mostly had it.

"The Washington Monument-looking building is the Civil Government Central Planning Headquarters," I told him, "but close enough. And if we don't link up by 1700, you're to..." I trailed off, waiting for him to finish it.

"I take First and Second Platoons and go link up with Battalion in the public square outside the Imperial Palace," he said, sounding exasperated I was making him go over it again.

"Right. Go ahead and start the final checks on your bird."

I had checks of my own to make, redundant but also required, because if anything *did* go wrong and I had neglected to make the final checks, only one Marine would pay the price. One of my training NCO's at Officers' Candidate School had told me officers were human shit-collectors. In the military, shit rolled downhill and if it wound up hitting the NCO's who did all the *real* work, why then, the Marines would fall apart in a day. That's why they had to have officers like me, to catch the shit before it could hit the NCO's and take all the blame when things went wrong.

I hadn't been an officer all that long, but I still hadn't had a single experience that would have disproven the theory.

I devoted one ear to the preparations of my platoon leaders, spying on their inter-platoon nets, double-checking their double-checks, another to listening to the tactical feed from the ship. I couldn't keep track of the threats and I wasn't sure they could either. As we approached Tahn-Skyyiah, they were piled too thick and the cruisers running interference for us were bulling through them, counting on their shields and their weapons to get them through the gauntlet. I winced with every missile that struck, every railgun round that glanced off their deflectors, dreading, waiting, *expecting* one of them to explode into a supernova. Once, I'd thought of the big ships as invulnerable, wished I could be on one of them instead of the vulnerable troop ships. I'd had that illusion shattered at Point Barber.

"You doing okay, sir?"

The question took me by surprise. Of all the questions, all the demands for status reports, no one had asked me that. It was Top. She wasn't on my drop-ship, of course. She and the Headquarters platoon had to go down separately because the Boomers couldn't drop. They'd land in an LZ secured by assault shuttles and get off near the edge of the city, then make their way in and try to link up with us.

"I want to be off this fucking ship, Top," I told her, thinking it would be useful to be completely honest with someone. "I feel like I'm sitting in a target range while everyone comes up and takes a shot at me."

"The enemy always has a say, sir," she reminded me.

"I'm talking about our own side. How are the Marines doing? I hear all the rah-rah bullshit, but how are they *really* doing?"

"Just like you, ready to get off this ship, ready to shoot at something."

"Separation in one minute."

The announcement caught me by surprise. Had it already been fifteen minutes?

"You get that, Alvarez?" Geiger asked and my eyes bugged out from keeping my jaws clenched. I tried to remind myself this was her first time, too.

"Yes, ma'am. Passing it along."

I said something inane and banal, the sort of thing I'd always found so redundant when I was enlisted, reiterating the announcement that they'd already heard. I was still talking when the drop-ship's crew chief interrupted me to repeat the same thing, except it was happening in ten seconds.

"Good luck, Delta," I said. "See you on the ground."

The two-gravity thrust had been good practice, because now the real punishment began. Six gees, I guessed from the tunnel vision and the way the sounds in my helmet earphones faded away into the background. I didn't try to follow the external cameras because I couldn't have focused on them if I'd wanted to.

"Well, you got your wish." I don't know how Top managed to talk under the pressure, but there were a lot of things about Top I didn't know. Like how she knew just how to wring the last second of connection we'd have to the troop transport's comms before the drop-ships were out of range. "We're off the fucking ship."

She always got the last word.

[25]

I missed the flood of data. It had been overwhelming, but at least it had been something to grab onto, a measure of control. In the drop-ship, there was nothing. I was separated from half my company, and couldn't keep track of their bird even if I could have overcome the punishing boost long enough to concentrate on the feed from the sensor suite. This close to the planet, the ECM jamming was thick enough to slice for sandwich meat, and the drop-ship's laser line-of-sight comms were being dedicated to the assault shuttles running interference for us. I couldn't even gather the breath to talk to the people in my own bird, and if there was any upside to the isolation and the crushing acceleration, it was that I didn't have to listen to Major Geiger's constant demands for status reports.

I think I must have greyed out. My eyes snapped open to a hypnic jerk, but this one wasn't waking up from a dream, it was regaining consciousness after having the blood pushed away from my brain for too long. The boost had cut off abruptly and I sucked in a huge breath, trying to take advantage of the moment of weightlessness to get air and blood flowing, and almost didn't register the flashing warning that we were about to experience a violent maneuver.

It was my favorite, a barrel roll at high gees, not just for the way it threw my stomach into a blender but for the knowledge of *why* we were doing it. A Tahni corvette, a dual-environment fighter, or orbital platform was trying to focus a weapons laser on us from long distance and the drop-ship pilots had thrown us into a roll to keep the enemy from hitting the same spot on the fuselage long enough to burn through. And if us passengers in the back didn't like it, well, we'd like breaking apart and floating helplessly in high orbit even less.

"When are we gonna drop?" Cano asked, sounding as if he was desperately trying to keep his stomach contents down.

He could look at the damned tactical readout just as easily as I could, I grumbled silently. Then I realized I hadn't looked at it in minutes. I assumed it was minutes. It felt like hours, but I'd done this enough times to realize that meant it had actually been minutes.

I couldn't make sense of the optical cameras because everything in the picture was spinning crazily and so was I, and every time I tried to force the image to hold still, I felt as if I was going to pass out. I concentrated on the altitude reading instead, at least trying to get an idea if we'd entered the atmosphere.

"Holy shit," I whispered.

We weren't just in the atmosphere, we were at 3,000 meters and I hadn't even noticed the transition from the plasma drives to the turbojets. And then the roll ceased, the boost from the rear cut back to almost nothing and the belly jets roared their defiance of gravity.

Every organ in my body dropped into my lower intestines and tried to push their way out, and I was certain I heard something in the superstructure of the drop-ship crack and all I could do was hope it wasn't something they needed to stay in the air.

The vibration from the belly jets firing rattled my teeth in my skull as they pulled our nose up, bringing us to a near stop and letting a pair of assault shuttles shoot past us, their exhausts an angry red, shock diamonds stretched out behind them.

Proton cannons struck out with the fury of an ancient, angry god, splitting the sky apart, their thunderclaps audible even kilometers away through the fuselage of our drop-ship. I couldn't see the enemy fighters the assault shuttles were targeting, couldn't pick the incandescent fury of their deaths from the rest of the endless chain of explosions in the air, but the shuttles banked away, their job done.

Ours was about to begin. I recognized the terrain beneath us, the incredible scope of the capital city of Tahn-Khandranda. It was nowhere near as large as Trans-Angeles, was home to less than a quarter of the population of that hive of humanity, and yet I found it terrifying; huge and intimidating in a way I had never thought of Trans-Angeles. I suppose it was the concept of taking on a whole planet that hit me in that one instant. We'd fought the Tahni on colonies they'd settled, worlds they'd conquered, outposts they'd set up against the howling wilderness, but this was their home. It was like landing in Capital City and trying to conquer all of Earth. It was impossible, ludicrous, and yet here we were.

Monoliths and twisted spires and steppe pyramids were arrayed in ways that made no sense to my human eyes, yet still displayed a pattern, something deep beneath the surface, designed by an inhuman imagination. And at the center of it all were the brilliant white spheres of the temples. The Three Temples of the Faith was what the intelligence briefing had called them, the foundation of the Tahni belief system, wrapped up in some complicated process of incarnation and reincarnation, where their god, their Spiritual Emperor, inhabited the mortal body of their physical Emperor. The ceremony was solemn and respectful and, if the briefing was to be believed, ended in the suicide of the old Emperor to allow the new civil, military and spiritual leader of the Imperium to become the sole possessor of the spirit of the deity. Their belief was, as long as the temples stood and their Emperor inhabited the palace, the Tahni Imperium could never fall.

We were here to test the prophecies, I supposed.

"Drop warning!" the crew chief bellowed into the PA speakers. "Drop warning! Drop in sixty seconds!" She sounded as if she'd be happy to see us go, probably so they could fly off somewhere to comparative safety and wait out the last battle of the war.

Fleet or Marines, Drop-Trooper or Force Recon, no one wanted to be the last one killed in the war.

"You're leading us off, Third," I reminded them, particularly Verlander. Maybe Top had it right, maybe it bothered me that some marginally-competent Academy grad who'd gotten his last platoon killed was in charge of *my* platoon. "We don't expect there to be a huge concentration of High Guard in the city. Intelligence says they sent most of their battalions to Point Barber. But there'll be a shitload of Shock-troopers, and even if they're smaller than us, you get enough of them together, they can bring you down. Don't get decisively engaged. We can't fight a whole city. We have to remember our objective."

"Yes, sir," Bang-Bang said. "Ooh-rah!"

He said it respectfully, as if I'd just delivered the best speech of my life, but I knew him well enough now to know he was telling me to shut up, that I was droning on with rah-rah bullshit. I shut up.

"Drop! Drop! Drop!"

I echoed the words without thinking, from instincts honed during thousands of hours of practice, and they echoed through the platoon leaders to the platoon sergeants to squad leaders, and for what was probably the last time, we dropped.

The fact we were able to make it to the ground without dying was a miracle not from God but from the hallowed halls of Fleet Intelligence. And the fact that Fleet Intelligence had planned *anything* that actually worked might just have been a miracle from God, come to think of it.

The city had massive air defenses, just as anyone would have expected from the capital of the homeworld of a militaristic empire, but the one weakness Fleet Intelligence had determined was the centralization you'd expect from a city of this size. Unlike their colonies, where things were spread out and power systems were localized, Tahn-Khandranda's air defenses were all powered by a massive fusion reactor at the edge of the city's industrial zone, or as much as the place could be said to *have* an industrialized zone.

And the fucking Fleet Intelligence boys had taken it down before we even set boots on the ground. *How* was being kept deliberately vague, and we'd been told not to ask, which of course, had everyone guessing. The rumor I'd heard was that it was some sort of top-secret special operations unit, something that had been around for years but no one had ever officially acknowledged its existence. That sounded like a load of barracks-room bullshit to me, but I couldn't come up with a better explanation, so I decided I'd raise a toast to the super-commandoes the first chance I got.

I'd almost forgotten what it felt like to not be shot at during a drop, and I kept swiveling my head from side to side, checking the sensors, waiting for someone to call out the contact, but no one did. I touched down on the pavement a hundred meters back of Private Vince Delp, able to watch Third Platoon spread out in a textbook wedge formation by squads. Verlander, I reflected, hadn't yet had the chance to fuck up all the good work I'd done.

The only thing that had gone wrong so far was that Kovacs and the other half of Delta Company was nowhere to be seen. They *should* have dropped right next to us, but that was always the plan and it almost never happened. We'd hook up with them at the rally point. I hoped.

There was a difference to the streets of Tahn-Khandranda from the other Tahni worlds I'd seen, and it wasn't just the sheer number of them here, or the age. There seemed to be a care taken with the construction of this city, right down to the sweeping curve of the low walls separating the paved roads from the grass and well-tended shrubs of what looked like a cross between a green belt and a city park. It was all smooth and neat and *established*, lacking the raw, rough-hewn nature of their colonies.

Which made the armored personnel carriers all the more jarring when they pulled out from an intersection, flattened and angular and rolling on rounded, caster-style wheels, heavy KE guns spitting tantalum darts and thousands of meters per second. Orders swelled in my throat, trying to bust their way out with an instinct to take charge of the platoon, to micro-manage right down to the squad level, but I pushed the words down and let my people do their jobs.

Verlander might have shouted something, but no one needed his orders any more than they needed mine.

"Contact, front!" Sgt. Medina snapped. "Enemy vehicles! Delp, Calhoun, take them out!"

And even his orders were redundant, because Delp was a walking ball of nerve and instincts, and if he wasn't quite as good as Henckel had been, he was close enough for government work. He was in the air before the lead vehicle had completed its turn onto the main road, firing a blast from his plasma gun down through the roof of the APC just fore of the KE turret. A spear of plasma that could burn a hole through the chest of a High Guard peeled the lighter armor atop the vehicle like a can opener and turned the crew compartment into a blast furnace.

He should have waited for Calhoun to take out the other APC. It would have been the sound tactical decision, even though it would have meant waiting an extra second, giving the enemy another chance to take a shot at us. Delp went another way, went the way I might have gone if it had been me. He gave his jets another burst and landed on top of the second vehicle, grabbing the emitter of the heavy KE gun with his suit's articulated left hand and yanking backward. The Vigilante ripped the weapon off its gimbal mount, leaving power cables torn and sparking, sending tantalum darts scattering over the roof of the APC.

Delp tossed the electromagnetic weapon to the pavement, then aimed his grenade launcher into the gap he'd left in the roof and fired a burst through it. Dust and smoke billowed out through the firing ports in the APC and it began to drift aimlessly across the road. Delp jumped down and sauntered away from the thing, and if a Vigilante's face could have had a smug expression, it would have.

"Stop showing off, Delp," Bang-Bang told him, sounding unimpressed.

"Enough distractions," I said, not waiting for Verlander to get his shit together. "Move out, Delta. We have a deadline and we ain't gonna be the company that was late to the Imperial Palace."

———

Civilians. There were so many damned civilians here.

On their colonies, the farther out from Tahn-Skyyiah we'd

been, the quicker the civilians had gotten their asses to shelters, stayed out of the way. It wasn't that way here. They stood in the streets or on rooftops and watched us as we lumbered by, some of them simply staring with dark, sullen eyes, others throwing rocks or pieces of concrete, none even coming close. Males, all of them, old men and adolescents, except for a few prepubescent girls still young enough to live with their male relatives. The females moved to their own enclaves when they hit puberty, and we were going to do our damnedest to steer clear of them, according to command guidance.

It was morning here. It took me a second to remember. The primary star was concealed behind the ever-present overcast, and my optics showed me everything in bright daylight no matter what the current mood of the day, but it meant these people should have had plenty of warning to get to shelter. Yet here they were, acting as if this was a parade.

"Want me to launch a few grenades into the middle of the street?" Delp wondered from up front. "Get them back inside?"

"Not unless they start shooting at us with something big enough to cause trouble," I declared. He might not have been talking to me, but I was the one who was going to be held responsible for that decision and I was damned well going to be the one who made it. "Don't get decisively engaged."

Nightmare images of Port Harcourt and Confluence flashed across my HUD like the suit's threat computer was displaying them for me, of civilians killing us, us killing them, of them swarming us and leaving us no choice. But I first had a sense that trouble was coming when the civilians started to fade back into their houses, the oldest first, then the younger males. A few still watched, but crouched from behind cover, waiting for the show. I was about to warn Verlander when Delp warned me, first.

"Something's coming." He sounded damn calm about it. "Aircraft inbound, one o'clock, nap-of-the-earth."

The civilians had called ahead a warning. I'd known they would, and nothing short of slaughtering them all would have stopped it. The dual-environment fighter was a fragile thing, lacking much in the way of armor, just an SCRamjet aircraft that could make orbit, barely. It lacked the heavy armament and thick armor of an assault shuttle and counted mostly on numbers to overwhelm opposing aerospacecraft.

But it could sure kill the shit out of us.

"Scatter!" I ordered. "Take cover behind the buildings!"

I waited until the last, ignoring Billy Cano's pleading to move, making sure no one froze and stood in the middle of the street. I'd seen it happen back in the Underground, a bunch of young kids trying to work a heist at the train station and someone had called the Transit Authority Police. The TAP's had barged down the center aisle of the station, shouldering the crowds aside with their big, armored bulk and the threat of their sonic stunners and someone had yelled for us all to run. And we all had, except this one kid, a thirteen-year-old everyone called Ginger because of his red hair. He'd frozen in place and let them come and bowl him over and put him in restraints, and that was the last we'd ever seen of Ginger.

We apparently lacked any Gingers in this half of the company, since everyone got the hell out of the way, and I found myself the last one still standing in the street, watching the fighter line up to make its run down the residential street.

Unless that means I'm *the Ginger.*

"Sir, for fuck's sake!" Bang-Bang yelled at me and I finally gave in and loped forward and to the right, ducking into a gap between buildings.

I didn't retreat all the way back, partially because the alley was littered with trash and debris, depressingly like any human alleyway I'd encountered, but also because I needed to see. That was the part about being a leader that fit in with my personality, the need to know, the need to see for myself. It would have been easy to bury my head and wait until someone called the all-clear, but I couldn't bring myself to do it. I didn't want to die from a threat I didn't see coming.

I could, theoretically, have used a camera drone, but there wasn't enough time and the ECM jamming crackling in the air would make it impossible for me to do anything but line-of-sight, anyway. So I stuck my head out around the corner of the building, my shoulder pauldron scraping stucco off the surface, and watched the missiles cut loose from the fighter's hard-points.

I had to guess the Tahni didn't get too many briefings from their battalion staff about avoiding collateral damage, because this asshole put those missiles directly into the first floor of the line of rowhouses across the street from me, only a hundred meters away. Now I ducked, barely in time. Heat washed over me, prickling my skin even through the armor, and I crouched low, knowing what was coming next. The concussion didn't knock me over, but only because the buildings took the brunt of it. And the civilians inside.

The wave swept outward in an expanding circle of destruction, buildings collapsing where it touched them, their façades engulfed in short-lived gouts of flame where dust burned away before the fire-resistant material beneath it extinguished it. The ground conducted the rumbling vibration into my suit and through it into my bones and I knew the building I hid behind was about to collapse, maybe forward into the street, maybe sideways right on top of me, but I stayed behind its cover until I caught a glimpse out of the corner of my optical camera's view of the fighter banking and ascending, pulling out of its run.

Was he going to come back for Battle Damage Assessment and maybe a second strike, or was he too busy with other targets? We couldn't sit around here with our thumbs up our ass, so I'd have to hope he was too busy. I left the alley.

The row housing hadn't been anything fancy, maybe the equivalent of the Surface Dwellers in Trans-Angeles, not the poorest, working taxpayers. They had shops on the lower floors of those houses, I recalled from the briefings. Fabricators of the Tahni sort, metal workers, craft shops. They lived above them with their children, sometimes with their older male relatives, six or seven individuals to a house. On a block like this, there'd be maybe four or five hundred Tahni civilians.

Nothing was left. Not one building was intact. A few were still standing, their supports teetering precariously, but the interiors were piles of rubbish, smoking, sometimes burning. There were bodies inside, but I couldn't see them for the haze and didn't want to.

"Cano, Verlander, I need a casualty report."

It sounded like someone else's voice, someone who hadn't just been in the middle of an enemy airstrike, someone who wasn't engulfed in roiling black smoke. Debris littered the street, some of it still burning, crunching under my feet as I wobbled slightly on the uneven surface. But there were things I had to know, and things they had to tell me, and they had to stay calm to do it. I had to be their example on how to stay calm when everything's going to shit.

Nothing. Someone coughed on an open circuit, which was psychological since none of the dust, smoke or particulate cloud was going to make it through our airtight armor.

"I said, casualty report!" I snapped. "Cano, Verlander, did we lose anyone? Any damage?"

I could read the IFF. They were all lit up and flashing red, but it meant nothing once I read down in the small print of the report. Their signals were being partially blocked by the haze and smoke and probably by a few hundred kilos of debris in some cases.

"Working on it, sir!" Cano told me. There was anger in his voice, maybe at me for rushing him, but that was okay. It was better for him to be angry at me than afraid. Anger could focus the mind if you kept it under control.

"Third has no...," Verlander began, then spluttered and tried again. "I mean, sir, we don't have any KIA. I've got a couple people buried under this housing unit, but Gunny Morrel is trying to get them out."

The motion caught my eye, barely visible on optics, a hazy red and yellow on thermal, fifty meters down from me and twenty meters into the rubble. The row houses were built as narrow as an Underground Housing Block apartment in Trans-Angeles but three times as deep. Three Vigilantes were digging into the rubble, tossing aside meter-wide sections of concrete to try to free the battlesuits buried beneath it. I wanted to run over and help, but I wasn't a strong back anymore and if Bang-Bang needed more strong backs, he'd ask for them.

A chunk of concrete smacked into a pile of debris near the street and scattered it. Beneath was a body. A very small one. My world shifted, the ground turning at an angle, and I threw out an arm to balance myself and stumbled a step.

"You okay, sir?" Cano asked. By the tone of his voice, it wasn't the first time.

"Yeah," I said, squeezing my eyes shut for a moment, but unable to erase the sight of the dead child.

I didn't kill them. It wasn't me. They killed their own people. Yeah, and I just ordered my Marines to take cover behind civilian homes, knowing the Tahni didn't give a shit about the lives of their civilians.

"Fourth is good to go, sir," Cano told me. "Couple guys get

shook up, might need some maintenance work later, but nothing that'll keep them from completing the mission."

"Lt. Verlander," I said, "are we close to having those Marines dug out?"

I could have looked for myself, but I wasn't going to. I didn't want to see what else they might dig up.

"Yeah. I mean, yes, sir." He sounded distracted, paying too much attention to the job in front of him and not to his situation. A sergeant could get away with that, but not a platoon leader. "We're up, we're good to go."

Delp broke in, his voice wavering, so shaken he broadcast it on the general net instead of a private one.

"Holy God, sir…all those people…." His armor was still smoking, like condensation on a cold morning as he stared into the wreckage, looking at something I didn't want to see.

"That's what they get for narcing on us," Verlander snapped, no remorse at all in his voice. "Morons."

"Lieutenant," I told him quietly and privately, "shut up and move out."

[26]

"Goddamn, Cam, it's good to see you," Francis Kovacs said, sounding as if he was about to collapse with relief. "I didn't know how long we'd be able to stay here."

For once, I didn't blame Kovacs for being overdramatic. The rally point was a public square, or as close to one as a Tahni city came, an open courtyard a kilometer on a side, with strips of pavement alternating with long, straight stretches of what passed for grass, and vaguely phallic marble...statuary? Or whatever they were. For all I knew, they could have been the Tahni equivalent of road signs. A low wall that might have been decorative enclosed the concrete dick-statues, two meters tall and twice as thick at the base as it was at the top.

That was how the square *had* been when we'd seen the few stealth drone shots the Scout Service had managed to get. Now, it was scarred and burned, charred black in great swathes of destruction, and painted in blood. It was impossible to tell how many enemy troops had died in the square because what was left of them was in pieces. At my best guess, there had been well over a hundred. Their armored personnel carriers sat half-melted, still smoking at the eastern edge of the square, where the main road ran into it, eight of them, the Tahni equivalent of a company.

Behind us, a monolith a hundred meters at the base and narrowing to a pyramid capstone two hundred meters above us loomed over the carnage like a gravestone, probably the tallest free-standing building I'd seen.

"How long have you been here, Francis?" I asked him, staring out at the devastation.

"Ten minutes," he said, breathing the words out like a prayer. "Ten fucking minutes."

"Casualties?" I hadn't noticed any on the IFF display, but I asked anyway.

"Some suit damage, but nothing that would affect function. No injuries. Their weapons," he said, pointing out at the dead Shock-Troopers with his plasma gun, "can't penetrate our armor unless we sit around and let like four of them shoot at the same spot at once. But the crazy bastards just kept coming anyway...."

"Have you seen any other allied forces?" I interrupted. He sounded like he was going to drift on me and I needed him focused.

"Just them," he said, gesturing overhead.

The overflights of the assault shuttles were nearly constant now, their missiles and proton blasts heading mostly downward, which told me the Tahni fighters had been taken down. I flinched as a lightning bolt shot out of the sky and touched something off to our west, a massive fireball rising above the skyline of the city.

"And more of that, too," Kovacs added. "Lots of that."

We'd seen it too on the way in. The Fleet was taking advantage of the lack of outgoing defense laser fire to pound the city, taking out concentrations of enemy with proton blasts from orbit, which was akin to swatting a fly with a sledgehammer.

"But I tell you what, boss, there's more of them coming." He waved at the dead Tahni. "Every time we send a drone camera up, we can see them moving. I ain't seen any High Guard yet, just Shock-Troopers, but they're everywhere, thousands of them."

"We need to get to the palace," I said, "and hope Top is already there." I turned until I saw Delp's IFF signal. He was at the east end of the square, crouched down in the cover of the burning APC's, watching outward. It was so easy to see past the armor, to picture the man inside it down on one knee, holding a rifle, to see the tremble in his hand and the tic in his cheek like I'd seen him in the back of the MP vehicle back on Point Barber. Best not to let anyone sit around stewing for too long.

"North, Verlander," I instructed. "Just another three or four klicks along the main road."

I dropped in behind Third Platoon and adjusted my pace to theirs, a slogging, cautious shuffle, an itching in the middle of my back screaming at me that we were moving too slowly. I wanted to run on the hop, to bounce off the sloping faces of the buildings lining the broad, paved road, to get us there in five minutes instead of fifteen. But it wasn't just me, wasn't even a squad or a platoon. Leading a full company meant adjusting to the pace that the least competent leader was capable of keeping up without losing his grasp of the situation. It wouldn't help us to run faster into an ambush. But it sure would have felt better.

Every building we passed felt like a sniper hide and I began to wonder why more of them weren't. The Tahni hadn't seemed shy about using their civilians for cover on colony worlds, and certainly hadn't seemed reluctant about blowing them up if they got in the way. I wondered if the difference here was merely a matter of the same sort of differences I'd noticed between city-dwellers on Earth and citizens of the colonies, the lack of initiative and self-sufficiency, the reliance on the government that urbanites everywhere seemed to share.

They called the cops on us and the cops wound up burning down their neighborhood.

That was the old Outsider talking, the Trans-Angeles street kid who resented authority. Now, I *was* authority.

A signal crackled in my earphones, staticky and weak at first, then getting stronger as if the drone relay passing it on had just made its way overhead.

"Delta One Actual, do you read? This is Zero Four Actual. Over."

I grimaced. This was the old good news-bad news joke. The good news was, we had comms again, which meant I could call in and direct fire support and coordinate with the rest of the brigade. The bad news was, now Geiger could micromanage me again. I thought about pretending I didn't receive the transmission, but then sighed and keyed my microphone, trying to remember our official comms call signs. None of us used that shit when we were talking via line-of-sight because it was incredibly unlikely the enemy could intercept it and, more importantly, what would they do with it if they did? It's not like they could send kill teams to find our families or access our military records and blackmail us. Most things the military does are done because they've always been done that way.

"Zero Four Actual, this is Delta One Actual. I have linked up with Delta One Bravo and Two Bravo and we are inbound to Objective One, ETA ten mikes, over."

"Copy that, Delta. Zero Four Hotel is at Objective Two with Alpha and Charlie." Which was a military base three kilometers from the palace, Objective One. "Enemy jamming still exists, but drone relays are in place at all major objectives. Foxtrot elements are in place at Objective One and waiting on you before proceeding. What is your status? Over."

"No casualties," I reported. "Still have not linked up with Delta Hotel elements. All others are combat-effective."

"Keep me updated, Delta. Zero Four Hotel, out."

Oh, yeah, I'll keep you updated. But since comms were working...

"Delta Hotel Actual, this is Delta One Actual. How do you copy? Over."

It was still a long-shot. The drones might not cover the whole city and I had no idea where Top and Headquarters Platoon was. I heard nothing but the scrape-bang of my feet pounding into the pavement for a long moment before I tried again. Second time was the charm.

"Delta One Actual, this is Delta Hotel Actual. I copy five by five, over."

Top sounded as if she were out for a family picnic instead of leading a light platoon through the enemy capital in the biggest invasion in human history.

"We are inbound to Objective One," I told her. "What is your status? Over."

"What's taking you so long?" she asked, the hint of a grin in the words. "We've been here for three mikes. It's dead as a church social here, but I have a feeling the Gomers are waiting for us to move on the objective before they come out to play. Over."

"Tell them to hold the party till we get there. The Gomers promised Delta the first dance. Out."

Now I knew what the starships had been targeting with those proton blasts.

The Tahni Imperial Palace was nearly a kilometer on a side, its base an octagonal wall twenty meters tall, with a half-dome structure rising from the base, the opposite side of the curving dome a sharp, downward angle etched with arcane designs no human had been able to decipher. It was widely recognized as the grandest, most ornate single-purpose building ever constructed, the wording tortured into a shape that excluded the mega-cities on Earth so academics and popular journals could have a catchy headline.

It didn't seem so grand anymore. There had been, I remembered from the briefing, anti-aircraft turrets and ground defense bunkers all around the perimeter wall, and the cruisers had left not a one of them intact. Sections of the wall dozens of meters long had collapsed into charred cinders, the main entrances to the palace buried under tons of rubble. The half-dome had spider-web cracks running up the curve of it from the damage to its supports and huge sections of the top had fallen inward. It didn't seem as if anything inside could have survived, but I knew that the Emperor's living quarters and the military command center were deep underground.

We'd been within sight of the palace for nearly ten minutes, and it had taken every second of that to reach the rendezvous point. Top was there waiting for us, the Boomers set up in a defensive perimeter, using the corpses of dozens of armored personnel carriers destroyed in the orbital bombardment as cover. The Force Recon element was there as well, sensibly behind cover, but there weren't as many as I'd thought there'd be. A company at most, counting all the scattered elements, though maybe there were more around the other side of the palace.

Top wasn't behind cover at the moment, standing beside a Force Recon officer who my IFF display told me was a Lt. Medupe and a man in some sort of weird camouflage suit. It didn't look like armor, exactly, but it shifted colors when he moved, as if it were actively trying to fit into the background. He was tall and jacked like one of the bare-knuckle fighters from the illegal fight clubs in the Underground and wasn't wearing any sort of helmet, which seemed like a damned reckless thing to do in a war zone. His tightly-curled black hair was cut short but not buzzed like a Marine's and there was something...I don't know, *regal* about his bearing, the sort of thing generals tried to imitate unsuccessfully.

He was carrying something that looked like a cross between an issue Gauss rifle and the plasma gun attached to my suits, something that looked impossibly heavy for a human being to carry without the benefit of a battlesuit.

And he had no IFF signal whatsoever.

He was a spook, and I had the immediate flash of insight that he was one of those mythical Fleet Intelligence commando types who'd taken out the fusion reactor.

"Sir," Top told me, "Lt. Medupe here is the CO of the Force Recon element that's going into the palace. And this other fella here...well, God only knows who he is and neither one's about to tell me."

"My people," the tall man said, "will be taking Lt. Medupe's Marines inside the palace through different ingress points. We can handle anything inside, but we need you and your Drop-Troopers to prevent enemy reinforcements from entering behind us."

"Are there any?" I asked him, using my external speakers. "Reinforcements coming, I mean?"

I hadn't seen any, and Geiger hadn't mentioned them, but if this guy was a spook, he might know more about it than us average grunts. His lips thinned out and I had the impression that this was as close to a smile as he ever gave anyone.

"The cruisers have been taking out any concentrations of troops in the open," he told me, "but there's an underground bunker at the military base north of here. Your Alpha Company has been keeping an eye on it, but they've been hunkered down up till now. Our intelligence estimates that, once we enter the palace itself, they're going to push outward and come for us."

"Why not just take out the bunker from orbit?" I asked him.

"Because the collateral damage would kill somewhere on the order of five thousand civilians." He shrugged. "It's not my call. We're heading in. The mission is to find and capture or kill the Emperor, which will, effectively, end this war. We show him or his corpse to his generals and political and religious leaders, this thing is over. We won't have comms once we're inside, so you're our last line of defense." He inclined his head toward me. "Don't let us down."

"Right," I said, then added, "sir. I guess. I mean, I have no idea what your rank is."

That half-smile again.

"I'm Major M'Voba. Do your job here, Lt. Alvarez, and you'll never hear my name again."

He turned and left us there, and the Force Recon straight-legs followed him.

"Don't seem fair, sir," I said privately to Top, watching them go, "that we fought all the way here and all we get to do is watch them fire the last shots."

"Oh, don't be worrying about that, sir," she said, laughing softly, without humor. "I have this feeling we're all gonna have an excellent opportunity to get shot."

[27]

"Zero Four Actual, this is Delta One Actual," I called, feeling like I was back at Armor School. "How copy? Over."

Nothing moved in the city around us, not so much as a stray bit of debris carried on the wind. No civilians flocked to the palace to save their beloved Emperor, apparently convinced their version of God would prevail. Delp was out farthest, which seemed natural, a good two hundred meters from the ruined remains of the front entrance way. Stone columns had collapsed into the center of the broad passage, some sort of performance-art commentary on the fate of the Tahni Imperium.

"This is Zero Four Actual," Geiger responded on my third try. The damn drone relays kept getting blocked by clouds of smoke drifting from parts of the city that were on fire. "What's your status, Delta? Over."

"We're dug in like a tick on a dog, Zero Four," I said, using a phrase I remembered from Scotty. Gunnery Sgt. Scott Hayes had been a farmboy on Hermes and was full of more down-homey bullshit sayings than I'd heard on the dumbest parodies of colony-dwellers on the ViR-net back in Trans-Angeles. I

289

missed hearing them, sometimes. I missed Scotty all the time. "Heavy assets deployed high and low." By which I meant I'd stationed a couple of Boomers on top of intact sections of the palace's support wall, tucked into the niches between the wall and the half-dome. "Intelligence sources tell me you should expect a significant breakout attempt from Objective Two. Over."

"Haven't heard that one, Delta," Geiger said, uncomfortably close to a blithe dismissal. "We're called in air support for a push on the bunker entrance, but we've been put on hold. Will let you know when we're clear to proceed. Over."

"Copy," I said, trying not to grind my teeth as I said it. Vicky's company was with Geiger. "Do you need me to split out a platoon to reinforce your position? The threat will likely come from there and I think we can handle anything here with three platoons and the Boomers. Over."

"Negative, Delta, we can handle it. Hold your position. Over."

"Copy, Zero Four. Out."

I made sure I'd logged off the command net before I swore. But I swore loud, maybe loud enough to be heard by someone standing beside my armor. Like Top. The two of us were side by side up on the parapets next to one of the Boomers, looking out over what we could see of the city from here.

"Problem?" Top asked me.

"Don't know yet," I admitted. "I guess that depends on who's right about how many troops are in that bunker."

"Major Geiger is...."

Whatever Top thought of Major Geiger, it was lost in the distant explosion. There's a sequence to an explosion, and you can see it all in order if you're far enough away that it doesn't all seem to hit you at once. First, there's the flash. It's moving at the speed of light, so of course it comes before anything else, and in this case, it shone through the intervening buildings like the primary star glinting off glass and reflective metal, not the second sun of a nuclear device, but a *big* conventional blast.

"What the fuck?" Delp asked on an open net.

As if in answer, the shockwave came next. It wasn't huge, wasn't enough to bring down buildings, just a hot wind passing through along with the crack-rumble of the sound, something gut deep, vibrating up through the ground, sending a cloud of dust and debris floating upward in its wake. By the gap between the flash and the shockwave, I knew exactly how far away the blast had been. Three kilometers.

Three kilometers in that direction was the military base.

"Zero Four!" I yelled into the mic. "Zero Four, what's your status? Do you copy? Over!"

A black cloud was rising into the sky, huge and ominous, the sort of cloud I would have expected from an orbital strike. I repeated my call, waiting, hoping someone would answer.

"Even if they're able," Top pointed out, "the debris cloud is going to block the line-of-sight link to the drone relays."

How the fuck, I wondered, was she so calm?

"What are we gonna do, Cam?" Kovacs asked me. He was a quarter the way around the other side of the palace, across the square, guarding the open hatchway the Intelligence spooks had used to enter on that side. It had been a concealed emergency exit, but no one had tried to use it. Yet.

It was a damned good question.

"That's Alpha," Cano said from down below my position, off to the right, tucked in behind the burned-out APC's. "We have to go help them."

Cano knew who was in Alpha, knew what Vicky and I were to each other. And I thought, after all this time, that Billy Cano was finally my friend.

"We got our orders," Verlander insisted. "We're supposed to stay here and keep the enemy out."

"Keep them out?" Cano repeated, disbelieving. "They're gonna be coming from that fucking military base, Verlander!"

They were both right. Lt. Sarrat said nothing, too new to her rank, her position, and this company to feel comfortable voicing an opinion, I supposed. Not that it would have mattered. This was my decision.

It struck me between the eyes, freezing time in a blinding revelation, and I just knew. This wasn't just a command decision; it was a personal one. It would define who I was and what I did from this point on, and I had seconds to make it. Like every decision I'd had to make in my life.

"Francis," I said to Kovacs, my XO, the words pouring out without conscious thought, "I'm leaving you here with Cano and Fourth, and Top and the Boomers. Sarrat, Verlander, Sanderson, we're going to relieve Battalion."

I took a step off the parapet and gave my suit a burst of jump-jets to deposit me safely on the ground below.

"Follow me, Marines."

———

Three kilometers. It didn't sound like much, not in battlesuits that could run at thirty klicks an hour, could fly faster than that for short hops. But it stretched out like one of those endless hallways in a nightmare, where you can never quite reach the end. Dust and smoke swallowed me up after a kilometer and not even the IFF signals from the friendlies behind me could penetrate, much less from the ones ahead. Thermal was nearly useless since everything seemed to be on fire, and the only sensors that told me a damned thing were the sonic detectors.

My biological ears couldn't make out much more than the

loping crash of my own footfalls, but the suit's computer systems were able to absorb everything; the sounds, their echoes, the interval of the echoes, pinpoint the direction they came from and assign it a likely source, then project that source on my Heads-Up Display in very lifelike computer animation.

What it showed me was a big, fucking hole. I didn't need to guess what the explosion had been, I could see it, sort of. The military base wasn't the usual thing we'd seen on so many Tahni worlds, not a collection of pragmatically-designed boxes at the edge of town, surrounded by empty space, maybe bordering on a spaceport that doubled as a landing field for fighters and cargo shuttles. No, this was something old, something pre-spaceflight maybe, a complex, steppe-pyramid type structure right at the center of the city, at the terminus of a broad road that came right through the heart of the place all the way from the spaceport.

The pyramid was gone now, smashed into powder by a railgun projectile from orbit along with buildings a couple hundred meters on either side of it, and that still hadn't been enough to take out the underground bunker beneath it. Or, apparently to set off the shaped charges under the street. There had to have been dozens of kilos of the stuff, enough to blow a hole outward, to collapse the broad thoroughfare into the passage below for nearly two hundred meters from the wreckage of the ziggurat. Enough to take nearly a company of Vigilantes down into the hole with it.

And streaming out of that gigantic hole in the street were High Guard battlesuits. Dozens of them, maybe two companies of them. They had to be the last of the things in the city because the Fleet had pounded every collection of enemy forces they'd seen and the Tahni had no defense against it, no deflectors, no anti-ship lasers, nothing. Their orbital platforms had been destroyed before our drop-ships had even made atmosphere. This was their last full measure, the final stone they had to throw, and they were throwing it at me. And I couldn't call in air support without killing our own people.

"Launch full complement of missiles, then volley fire and peel off on the hop!"

I didn't have any expectation that the transmission would get through, even with laser line-of-sight, through the clouds of smoke and particulate haze, but Third was behind me, and even if they couldn't hear me, they'd be able to detect what I was doing and imitate it. At least I hoped Delp would, since I didn't have that much faith in Verlander.

I targeted four Tahni at random and launched my missiles one after the other, as fast as they could load, each of them kicking free with enough of a jolt to make me miss a step. When the last one had kicked free, I fired my plasma gun at the closest of the High Guard troopers, the first one out of the hole, then hit the jets.

I wasn't sure how sophisticated the sonic sensors were in the High Guard suits, so I didn't know if they'd detected me before, but they sure as hell saw me now. Electron beams cut through the smoke like lightning in a midsummer storm on Inferno, seeking me out, and I couldn't quite clench my jaws against a scream as one of the beams of high-energy particles brushed against the armor over my right thigh. It didn't penetrate, though flashing yellow warned me it had sublimated away a surface layer nearly a centimeter thick, but the heat transfer left a second-degree burn on my leg.

I would have died in the next few seconds, unable to dodge that many of the energy blasts, if it hadn't been for Third Platoon...if it hadn't been for Delp. They heard my order, or understood it, at least, and a rain of missiles flashed out of the sky into the mass of High Guard troopers. Chains of explosions crackled back and forth across the clusters of enemy suits, knocking some out of the air as they tried to jump, slamming others into the ground with the force of their detonation.

We could, conceivably, have taken out half of them in one stroke if there'd been the time or any method to make sure we each targeted a different enemy trooper. Unfortunately, that wasn't what happened. Everyone hit the front lines because they were the closest, and ninety-seven plasma blasts and somewhere north of 375 missiles all went into the same two dozen High Guard suits. It killed the shit out of them, of course, and bought us seconds, and I worked with what I had.

I didn't see it so much as I sensed it, a combination of the instinctive feedback from the interface jacks and the winnowing down of the wave of data in my HUD to something understandable that only came from years in a suit. There wasn't time for a complicated strategy, wasn't time for more than the most basic of orders, the simplest of tactics.

"Wheel left and volley fire, then across their lines on the hop!"

The last word left my mouth just as my suit touched down on the shattered pavement, only meters from the gaping holes leading downward. I described an arc to my left, trying to keep the enemy suits targeting us constantly turning, trying to bring the weapons mounted along their right arms around in time to take another shot at us, trying to make it impossible for them to get a target lock with their missiles.

My capacitors had recharged and I fired my plasma gun again. I cut the arc short and fed power to the jump-jets, cutting across the enemy's line of travel. The lot of them had tried to stop, tried to spread out to face us, but that was easier said than done with a reinforced company, well over a hundred suits all rushing in the same direction, trying to overwhelm Geiger and Vicky and the rest of the Vigilantes before they could recover from the explosion. Electron emitters that had been trying to swing across bodies to the left suddenly had to try to track me upward, overhead, back the other direction, and before they could, the rest of my Marines were wheeling and firing and flying.

It was another tactic that, had it continued to be successful, would have wiped the Tahni force out. It couldn't, of course, and I knew that. Because the Tahni, for all their failings, weren't stupid, and their High Guard was the best of them. It took them precious seconds and cost them precious lives, but they finally began to lager. It wasn't a formation I'd seen in actual combat before, because the battles I'd fought in with Tahni High Guard had been more dynamic, more individual. The suits were designed for their mobility and versatility and most of the time, neither side wanted to waste those capabilities by grouping them all in one, big mass and trying to organize a defense.

But there was a time for it, and a tactic, and we learned it as well as they did. The lager. It went back to a day when settlers in wagons had to defend themselves against more mobile bands of warriors, and their best defense was to circle the wagons and form a ring, making sure they had a 360-degree field of fire. I saw it coming, saw the first of the electron beamers begin to hit us. IFF signals winked out, each stripping off bloody flesh from my soul, but the cold, calculating veteran instincts operated my brain like I operated the suit, and gave orders independent of the spiritual and emotional pain running through my gut.

"First and Second, wheel left and volley fire. Third, follow me into the hole."

Another risk, a damned big one. The Tahni were still flowing out of the hole in the pavement, up from a ramp leading into the bunker, revealed by the shaped charge, and it was very possible there were more of them in there, more High Guard troops still rushing to join the fight. Taking a platoon inside might get us all killed. But standing out in the open with three platoons and trading broadsides with the better part of two companies of enemy would *definitely* get us all killed. I had to get some of the troops to cover, be able to draw enemy fire away from the others.

I was first into the hole as I'd been first to charge into the enemy because when I'd made the decision to disobey direct orders and throw away everything I'd worked for these last five years to save Vicky, I'd also decided that if I was going to do it, I was going to run point on it. If there were enemy in that hole, they were going to kill me first and maybe give the others more time to deal with it.

There were enemy in that hole. But they weren't High Guard. Shock-Troops were swarming up behind their battle-suited big brothers, dozens of them, God alone knew how many because they were still coming up a ramp through a tunnel down into the bunker complex. I blasted the front ranks with a shot from my plasma gun and a good five or six went down with the one round, huge chunks of their bodies simply vaporized, the attenuated globe of ionized hydrogen scorching through the armor of another row behind them.

"Third, lay down suppressive fire on the battlesuits." I squeezed the words out, flinching as four separate KE guns opened up on me, the tantalum darts ricocheting off my chest plastron, my helmet, leaving craters in the armor where it hit. I couldn't stand there and take it—the rounds would penetrate eventually.

I waded into them, swinging my arms like a mad titan scattering normal humans from him in a Greek myth. Impacts travelled up through the armor, jolting me through the padding, spears of pain coming from wrenched muscles and joints. Shock-Trooper powered exoskeletons were an improvement over regular infantry, but nowhere near the power of a battlesuit. I outweighed each of them three or four times over and each blow from my isotope-reactor-powered byomer muscles smashed helmets, crushed chests, sent the ones it didn't kill scattering, with no time to coordinate their fire to take me down.

Still, there were too many, and I would have been overwhelmed eventually, a full-grown man taken down by an army of toddlers, had it not been for a second Vigilante suit stepping up beside me, firing their plasma gun to clear out another six or seven, giving me the time to charge up for another shot. The last star-bright ball of plasma seemed to convince the ones who were left that they weren't going to get past us. They retreated back into the bunker and whether they tried to escape to fight another day or just committed ritual suicide was all the same to me.

"You're a company commander, you idiot!" Vicky told me, smacking my suit on the shoulder with her articulated left hand. "What the hell are you doing out front?"

"Everything wrong," I admitted, smiling at the fact she was still alive. "If you have anyone who can fight, follow me."

The skirmish against the Shock-Troops had taken seconds, yet the tides of this battle seemed to change with each heartbeat. Without the suit's display, it would all have been a blur of light, a wash of heat and a clamor of impossible noise, rending metal and evaporating concrete, and I would have been lost, just another target fighting blind. *With* the display and without the experience I had, I would have been in the same position as Sarrat, barely able to keep myself alive with no chance of leading a squad, much less a platoon.

But I knew things and I couldn't have told anyone exactly how. I didn't remember seeing them, surely didn't have the time to read them, but I knew. Third Platoon was laying down volley fire by squad from the cover of the shallow end of the ragged hole in the street, ducking down into a niche just over two meters deep, while First and Second had circled around to the opposite end of the scrum. The lager wasn't going to work, and the Tahni were losing troops faster than we were, and while they had more to lose, just killing us wasn't their aim—their intent was to defend the palace, which meant they had to kill us *and* live through it.

This was the test of a leader. If the Tahni were poorly led, if they had a Cronje in charge, they'd double-down, charge the hole, try to mix with Third Platoon and what was left of Alpha and Battalion HQ to keep First and Second from shooting at them. It would buy time, help them attrit our numbers, but it wouldn't accomplish their mission. A *good* leader, a Covington, would break contact under fire, hit the jets and try to put buildings between them and us, then circle back around to the palace. Which would work just fine for us, too, since I'd left the Boomers there.

These poor bastards were poorly led and charging straight into us, which also meant we were all likely going to die. Fucking Cronje was still haunting me from beyond the grave.

"Hit the jets!" I ordered, reflexes and instincts still pulling my strings like a marionette. "Delta, Alpha, all Zero Four elements, hit the jets! Get out of the hole and clear the area!"

I'd heard the static in my headphones just a moment before I gave the order, the distant echo of a preternaturally calm voice, the tone of a combat pilot in an assault shuttle.

"This is Assault Four-One. I read your IFF as Delta, Fourth of the One-Eight-Seven. Do you need air support? Over."

Oh, fuck yes, we need it!

"Assault Four-One, this is Delta One Actual. Airstrike at my transponder coordinates, danger close, now! Over."

"Delta One Actual, I confirm, airstrike at your current coordinates, danger close. Assault Four-One out."

Vigilantes were pouring out of the hole, burning away on jump-jets, all of them following my orders despite the fact that I was only technically in command of two platoons of them, and I held back, firing in support, trying to keep the Tahni pinned down just a few seconds longer, keep them firing at me.

It worked. The electron beams converged on my position and it would have been suicide to hit the jets, so I ducked down instead, waves of heat washing over me, through the armor, singeing my exposed skin. The assault shuttle was coming. I could see its IFF signal in my helmet display. It would be firing in just seconds and I would still be here because there was nowhere left to go.

And I was okay with it.

I'd read a short story once, at the Skipper's behest, called *Occurrence at Owl Creek Bridge*. It was about a spy who was caught by the other side and was about to be hanged off the side of a bridge. The rope breaks and he takes off running, having all sorts of progressively weirder experiences until at the end, you find out the whole thing was a hallucination he had in the seconds before the rope strangled him to death.

I felt as if my life these last five years had been just that sort of hallucination, that I'd actually chosen the Fridge, gone into punitive hibernation, and this was all a dream I was having in stasis, too good to be real. It was a dream where I had friends and family and a father figure who welcomed me, and a lover who wanted to make a life with me, and above all, a *home*.

And now the dream was going to end, and I wasn't sad or angry, because all dreams end.

Then I wasn't alone, and it wasn't a dream. There were three Vigilantes beside me, laying down suppressive fire. Delp was beside me, standing straight, firing his plasma gun into the incoming horde of High Guard suits, ignoring the electron beams ripping up dirt and pavement and rock all around him, ignoring the charred, smoking groove through his left shoulder pauldron that had to have hurt like a son of a bitch. On my other side was Vicky, pulling me up by my left arm, and behind them was...Top? What was she doing here?

And it wasn't just them. Even the three of them couldn't have held the High Guard off long enough to get me out. Coil gun rounds were slicing giant wedges through the lines of Tahni battlesuits, fired from almost a klick away, and I realized that Top had brought the Boomers with her.

The scream of turbojets penetrated the din from way too close overhead.

"Dammit, Cam!" Vicky yelled. "Jump!"

And I did.

Something smashed me in the face and the world ended in brilliant light.

———

Except it didn't. Not for me.

I couldn't hear, I couldn't see anything but bright flashes of color, couldn't move. But I knew I was alive. I don't know how I knew. I was a Catholic, sort of, and I guessed somewhere deep down, I still believed in an afterlife. So, I don't know why I was so sure that I was alive rather than a spirit about to leave my battered body behind and ascend into Heaven, but I was.

Maybe it was the idea that I didn't believe a spirit would be feeling this much pain.

I waited for the armor to tell me what was wrong, what was broken, what was burned, but it said nothing, showed me nothing. I sucked in a breath, held it, tried to get my heart rate and respiration under control. Hyperventilating wouldn't accomplish anything. I felt around for the emergency release and yanked it downward, freeing the catches of the chest plastron, sending it swinging outward. A convection-oven heat sucked the breath from my lungs and I nearly passed out, sagging against the interior padding for a few seconds before I could manage to gather up enough strength to pull myself out.

The suit was on its side, resting on the left shoulder, and most of the heat was coming from the exterior metal. It had been scorched black, none of the markings and stencils visible anymore, and it looked as if the joints at the elbows and knees were partially melted. I jumped out with ginger, hesitant motions, trying not to touch the outside of the suit, cringing with pain despite my best efforts as just being within centimeters of the hot metal made blisters rise on my hands.

I cursed and just jumped out, trying to get clear, landing hard on my shoulder and side because I didn't want to try to catch myself with my burned hands. They weren't the only thing burned. My combat fatigues weren't melted away, but that was more a testament to their construction than my condition. Black scorch marks ran from my thighs down to my ankles and I could feel the dampness beneath my clothes where blisters had risen and burst and the only reason I wasn't in unspeakable agony was the pain-killers the armor had dosed me with before it had lost power.

The pain was a dull ache, just below the point of tolerable, but I ignored it. I had more important things to worry about. My Vigilante had come to rest in the lee of a collapsed building, and the haze blowing across at street level made it difficult to tell anything else for a good ten seconds. Then a hot breeze washed away the smoke and I saw the hell the airstrike had left behind.

I was a good five or six hundred meters from where I'd started the jump, and I couldn't have sworn as to how much of that was my jump-jets flying me there and how much was me being carried by the blast. The ragged hole in the road hadn't been enlarged all that much by the missiles from the assault shuttle, but the rubble had been shifted and where there had once been chunks of broken cement, now there were bits of burning metal and the scattered corpses of High Guard battle-suits. Dozens of them, pieces of dozens more, littered the square, along with similar but slightly different shapes that had to be Vigilantes.

How many of us had died before the strike? How many during?

Where was Vicky?

A battered, scarred Vigilante came down on a whining roar of jump-jets, touching down with a metal-on-concrete impact that shook the ground beneath my feet even a dozen meters away.

"Alvarez," Top's voice was loud and distorted over external speakers probably damaged in the fighting. "You okay?"

I hissed out the breath I'd been holding, disappointed that it wasn't Vicky and immediately guilty for being disappointed.

"I have been better," I admitted. I hesitated, knowing what I wanted to ask, what I needed to ask, but asking the question I was *supposed* to ask first. "Casualties?"

"A lot. Six dead, mostly from Second Platoon." Which made sense. They had the least combat experience. I should have left them behind at the palace, in hindsight, but I hadn't known if the force at the palace would need to be able to fight off the enemy and I trusted Cano and his platoon more. "I think we have about a dozen seriously wounded, but I haven't gotten a full count. Cano already called in Search and Rescue. Major Geiger and Alpha...I don't know. Lot of wounded, lot of dead in the explosion. Gonna take a while to sort through it."

I blurted it out, unable to keep the words inside anymore.

"Lt. Sandoval and Private Delp were with me. Did you see where...."

"They're over here."

I didn't like the way she said that.

Her Vigilante walked at a slow pace, short, shuffling steps, yet I still had to jog to keep up with her and every impact of my boot soles on the uneven, rock-strewn ground sent lances of pain stabbing upward through my legs. It wasn't far, maybe fifty meters further down the street, where they were stretched out one beside the other, their suits as scorched as mine and Top's, and I couldn't tell one from the other.

"Are...," I stuttered, unable to finish the sentence. "Are they...?"

"Their suits are offline," she said. "I called an SAR bird in and it's SOP to not open the suits until they arrive...."

She trailed off and a burst of static was the mic's interpretation of her sigh.

"Fuck it."

She went down on one knee beside the closest of them, grabbing at a particular spot on the suit's left shoulder with the claws of her Vigilante's left hand and twisting. The chest plastron fell open and I gagged at the scent of burning flesh. The burn-through must have been in the backside of the suit since I hadn't seen a hole through the Vigilante's chest. I could see the one through Vince Delp, though. His face was, miraculously, untouched, but there wasn't much left between his shoulders and his sternum.

His eyes were closed and he seemed, for once, at peace.

"Goddammit, Vince," I whispered. We could've gotten him help. He could have lived a normal life. He could have been happy.

"He was a good Marine," Top said, the words akin to a prayer for the dead. Her feet shuffled and the massive suit of armor turned toward me, looking down like a parent at a child. "Are you sure you want to see...?"

I swallowed hard and nodded.

She moved toward Vicky's suit, bent over, then hesitated.

"What?" I asked her.

"I just got a transmission from the palace," she told me. "The Emperor is dead. They've captured the Tahni military leadership and they're going to bring them in to witness the body." There was something in the words, some bitter amusement that I wouldn't have been able to understand without living her life. "The war's over."

I didn't respond. It meant nothing to me. My war had ended minutes ago.

Top reached down, grabbing the catch on Vicky's left shoulder, and twisting it. The chest plate fell open and the helmet swung backward and I didn't want to look at what was inside, but I had to.

The utility rover pinged and ticked and clacked plaintively behind me, the metal cooling rapidly from the long drive out from the spaceport on the brisk, autumn morning. Brigantia never got *that* cold, but I zipped my light jacket up just the same, too used to the intemperate climes of Inferno these last three months.

Two months on Tahn-Skyyiah helping to set up the peace-keeping operations, another month at Port Harcourt putting down a nascent insurgency, then finally three interminably long, miserable summer months of outprocessing and waiting for transport on Inferno.

There hadn't been any thought of staying in, not after what had happened in Tahn-Khandranda. All General McCauley's talk of sitting in his chair and being Commandant of the Marine Corps had blown away on a hot, bitter wind. The Corps might have been my home, but it was a home with too many bad memories, and every time I opened my eyes in the morning, I'd be facing them. Besides, I'd made that call the second I'd disobeyed orders to try to save Vicky. That I'd accomplished the mission was beside the point, though no one else seemed to understand that.

Certainly, McCauley hadn't. He'd offered to put me in for a Commonwealth Medal of Valor, the highest military award, for my part in the battle if I stayed in. Since Major Geiger had died in the explosion, there wouldn't have been anyone to gainsay it, even if she would have. She probably wouldn't have cared. Yeah, I'd disobeyed her, but Geiger wasn't close enough to colonel to think she was God. I'd heard they'd promoted her posthumously, though.

I shook off the memories and considered the house. I hadn't seen it the first time I'd been here. The opportunity hadn't come up, what with the Tahni and the battle and all. When I thought of Dak's home, my mind always pictured the camouflaged trailer towed into the high-desert draw to hide it from the enemy. Of course, that had been an expedience. Dak Shepherd was one of the founders of the colony, the man who'd named its capital city, Gennich. His house was large and, if not opulent, at least comfortable.

Three stories tall, constructed of local wood and brick, cradled in the nook of century-old oak trees, it looked like something I could have seen in history videos from the Nineteenth Century on Earth. A barn loomed behind it, pragmatic sheet metal, and a garage beside that with an autoharvester peeking out the open doors, a flatbed cargo truck parked beside it. In the dirt driveway beside the house was a utility rover not too different from the one I'd rented and driven here.

No one was outside, which I thought odd. Surely on a place this size, he'd have hired workers. But I didn't know shit about farming so maybe this was the wrong time of year and there would be nothing for them to do.

The steps to the front porch squeaked under my weight, the sanded plank flooring giving just slightly beneath the soles of my boots. They were military boots, though I'd had basic, utilitarian outdoor clothes fabricated before I'd left Inferno. I had a good-sized stake in my credit account, but I didn't own much besides these clothes. My whole life was in the passenger's seat of that rental car.

I knocked on the door.

Footsteps echoed inside, slow and deliberate. Dak opened the door. He hadn't changed a bit from when I'd last seen him in the medical center in Gennich after Maria died, not even down to his style of clothing.

No, maybe there was a difference. Just a bit of softness around the eyes, whether from the pain or perhaps because of the presence of the woman standing in the living room behind him. She was very attractive in a rough, homespun sort of way, just the kind of woman who I could have pictured Dak winding up with.

"Cam," he said and pulled me into a hug.

It was brief, a quick grip and a pat on the back, but I hadn't expected it. Dak hadn't struck me as the hugging type.

"How was your trip?"

"Long," I said. "I guess I got spoiled by military transports that took you right where you were going instead of making half a dozen stops along the way to drop off cargo and passengers."

"It's very nice to meet you, Cam," the woman said, shaking my hand, her grip warm, dry and solid. "I'm Hannah. I've heard a lot about you."

"You've come such a long way," Dak said, frowning. "Are you sure you can only stay a few days?"

"The transport pulls out of orbit in a week," I said, shrugging. "And while I really appreciate the offer to make a life here, I think it's time for something new. Something not the Marine Corps and not from my past. Time to make some new memories."

I heard the footsteps coming up onto the porch behind me and grinned.

"Speaking of new memories, Dak, Hannah, there's someone I'd like you to meet."

There was still something crooked in Vicky's smile, something that went beyond the physical. She'd never seen herself as I had when we'd pulled her from her suit, third-degree burns over half of her body. She'd been unconscious and the medics from the SAR bird had kept her that way until they were able to get her into an auto-doc. But just the knowledge of what had happened to her seemed to have affected her nearly as much as it had me.

"I'm Vicky Sandoval," she said. "It's wonderful to meet the both of you."

"And you, my dear," Dak assured her, smiling broadly as he took her hand. "From everything I've heard, you've managed to turn Cameron into a happy man, and God knows, there were times I never thought that was possible."

"Well, come on in!" Hannah said, waving toward a couch.

"It's been years, boy!" Dak said. "For God's sake, tell us everything that's happened to you!"

I shared a look with Vicky and laughed softly, gripping her hand tightly in mine.

"That," I said, "could take quite a while."

CONTACT FRONT
KINETIC STRIKE
DANGER CLOSE
DIRECT FIRE
HOME FRONT

If you enjoyed Drop Trooper, you will love Wholesale Slaughter!

Start a new adventure today!

Thank you for reading *Direct Fire,* book four in Drop Trooper.

We hope you enjoyed it as much as we enjoyed bringing it to you. We just wanted to take a moment to encourage you to review the book on Amazon and Goodreads. Every review helps further the author's reach and, ultimately, helps them continue writing fantastic books for us all to enjoy.

If you liked this book, check out the rest of our catalogue at www.aethonbooks.com. To sign up to receive a FREE collection from some of our best authors as well as updates regarding all new releases, visit www.aethonbooks.com/sign-up.

JOIN THE STREET TEAM! Get advanced copies of all our books, plus other free stuff and help us put out hit after hit.

SEARCH ON FACEBOOK:
AETHON STREET TEAM

RICK PARTLOW is that rarest of species, a native Floridian. Born in Tampa, he attended Florida Southern College and graduated with a degree in History and a commission in the US Army as an Infantry officer.

His lifelong love of science fiction began with Have Space Suit---Will Travel and the other Heinlein juveniles and traveled through Clifford Simak, Asimov, Clarke and on to William Gibson, Walter Jon Williams and Peter F Hamilton. And somewhere, submerged in the worlds of others, Rick began to create his own worlds.

He has written a ton of books in many different series, and his short stories have been included in seven different anthologies.

He currently lives in central Florida with his wife, two children and a willful mutt of a dog. Besides writing and reading science fiction and fantasy, he enjoys outdoor photography, hiking and camping.

www.rickpartlow.com